Love Boat

By Helen Kaulbach

Love Boat

Copyright © 2017 Helen Kaulbach

ISBN: 978-0-9952355-1-9

Author: Helen Kaulbach

e-mail: kaulbach45@gmail.com

For Dougie, my love and favorite traveling companion,
who loves cruising almost as much as I do.

And for all the great friends we've cruised with
over the years, as well as the new friends we've met
shipboard along the way.

Many thanks to my editor and proofreader, Kristal Kaulbach,
who probably enjoys correcting her mother's mistakes.

PROLOGUE

Susan Jeffrey waited impatiently to disembark from the Trans Global Airbus at LAX, Los Angeles International Airport. The air-conditioning in the terminal building momentarily surprised her. Then she smiled in appreciation, February in L.A. was quite different from February in Buffalo. During the five-hour flight from Buffalo she'd had some hard thinking to do, and the warm spring weather in California had not even infringed on those thoughts.

A hand crept up in an unconscious gesture to smooth her fine blonde hair. Usually, at this time of day, it was a flyaway mess, "Like a birch broom with the fits" as her Swedish grandmother used to say. Today, however, it was pulled back in a neat chignon with not a hair out of place, thanks to a few minutes spent in the aircraft's tiny restroom just before landing.

She went down the escalator to the arrivals area and waited, again impatiently, in front of the baggage carousel. Most of the people waiting were couples, obviously on vacation, and obviously from up north by the look of their heavy clothing. She noted most of the businessmen on the flight carried a small bag that fitted in the overhead bin plus a briefcase or computer bag. She knew that, to a person traveling on business, waiting for checked luggage was another delay to be avoided if possible.

One businessman, she noticed, had not been smart enough to hand-carry his bags. He was standing at the back of the crowd on the other side of the carousel, scanning the arrivals lounge as if looking for someone. *He probably has a limo waiting and is trying to find the driver*, she thought as her eyes took in the expensively tailored suit.

She caught him appraising her. Her heart lurched, and, for a moment, she wondered if this was the man she had come here to meet. He fit the description with his dark hair and eyes.

Then she dismissed the thought. Adam's flight wasn't due for another hour, and he most certainly wouldn't be wearing a suit. He'd specifically asked her if the cruise they were taking was casual, because he seldom wore a suit at work. She'd suggested that he bring at least one suit as a jacket and tie were required some nights in the dining room.

Thinking of Adam brought a shiver of apprehension. She wondered if she should forget the whole thing and catch the next flight home. She couldn't believe she'd actually agreed to do it. Sane and sensible Susan Jeffrey was out of her mind.

She was going on a ten-day cruise with a man and sharing a cabin with him

. . .and about an hour from now she was meeting him for the first time.

CHAPTER 1

Three years earlier

It was Buffalo's first winter storm, that first Friday in December. It snowed during the night, and, although only a couple of inches fell by morning, it slowed the rush-hour traffic to a crawl. Susan Jeffrey inched along Interstate 90 in her small silver hatchback, grateful for the front-wheel drive and winter tires that kept her on the snow-covered highway with hardly a skid.

On days like this she regretted not living closer to the city. She loved her little bungalow on Grand Island, an island in the Niagara River about three and a half miles above the famous Falls, and on a good day she could get to work in just over 20 minutes, but Buffalo winters seemed to get worse every year. She sighed and tried to turn her thoughts to something else. She knew that, come summer, she wouldn't trade her house and garden on the island for anything.

The wind-driven snow blowing across I-90 caused whiteouts that reduced the visibility to almost zero. Only the ghostly red tail lights of other cars looming out of the blizzard told her she was still on the highway. Hunched over the steering wheel trying to see the center line, she pushed her fine blonde hair back out of her eyes, wishing she had taken the time to braid it or tie it back. She passed several accidents and dozens of cars either stalled or off the road. There were tow trucks every couple of hundred yards, and one accident had two police cars and an ambulance in attendance. The young policeman in the bright-colored slicker directing traffic around the accident looked as if he were freezing.

What a miserable job, thought Susan. *I hate driving in this stuff, but at least I'm inside and warm.*

Leaving I-90 for the downtown streets made the driving a little easier. The streets had been sanded, and, although they were wet and slushy, they were not slippery. It was a relief to pull into the parking garage under the Harbor Square Shopping Mall. She was half an hour late and would probably be running late all day, but at least she'd arrived safely.

Susan sprinted up the service stairs and let herself in the back door. She hung up her coat and took off her boots, then stopped for a moment to look around the small travel agency office. She'd started the business two years earlier after working for another travel agency for several years and was immensely proud of her success. The office was tastefully decorated in burgundy and gray, and 10-inch-high silver and black letters spelling out "Harbor Square Travel" bisected the glass wall and doors leading into the mall. In smaller script letters underneath was the slogan, "Please Go Away". She smiled to herself at the double meaning and at the way it always brought a smile the face of a customer who saw it for the first time. One of her theories about business was that a customer who walked through the door of her agency with a smile on his or her face was comfortable being there and much more likely to do business.

Only one of the four desks was occupied. Terri O'Neill, her only full-time employee, a couple of years older than Susan's 27 years, had been with her since day one. The other two desks belonged to the two part-timers, Odel Alexander and Nancy Baker. Odel was a black mother of five in her forties with the sunniest disposition of anyone Susan ever met. She claimed Susan was her lifeline and that working in the travel agency on Saturdays and two afternoons a week was the only thing that kept her sane. Nancy was a travel student at Niagara Community College who worked Saturdays and the two evenings a week that the office was open. She loved the travel industry so much that she'd recently gotten a small tattoo of an airplane on her upper arm.

Terri was on the phone when Susan came in. She waggled her fingers and went on talking. Terri lived in a small apartment right in the city and took the Metro to work, so regardless of the weather she usually made it to work on time.

"Hi," she said when she hung up the phone. "Clifton said the Interstate was a horrendous snarl this morning."

Clifton Skye was a weather reporter on the rock station that Terri kept her radio tuned to most of the day. She also followed him on Facebook, so got updates on the weather several times a day. He'd come into the agency one day to

8

pick up an airline ticket to New York City. Terri sold him the ticket and promptly developed a crush on him. From then on she referred to him by his first name. Any discussion of weather or road conditions was usually preceded by "Clifton says..." or "Clifton said yesterday..."

Susan thought Clifton Skye was a bit of an egotist, starting with his name. Skye was too perfect a name for a weatherman.

"Clifton was right this morning," she conceded. "A few more mornings like that and I'll put my life savings in General Motors and Chrysler stock. Just replacing what got smashed this morning could be a real boost to the economy."

She sat down at the computer and started her first job of the day, answering e-mails. It wasn't her favorite job but it had to be done.

When Susan opened her travel agency in the Harbor Square Mall in downtown Buffalo two years earlier, she drew up a marketing strategy for attracting corporate clients. She knew that, located in a mall, she would get a lot of drop-in traffic for vacation travel, but to be a financial success she needed the regular income from business travel. Part of her strategy was personal service to business clients. They could easily have booked their own flights online, but she promised to save them time and money by getting them the best routings at the best price while still keeping their individual Frequent Flyer Miles accounts in mind. So far, she'd kept that promise and had a very satisfied clientele.

Most of the electronic tickets could be faxed or e-mailed, but one of her clients was an elderly gentleman, the vice-president of a shoe-manufacturing company who was going to the Orient on business. Mr. Wu hated computers and faxes and although he knew he needed them for his business, refused to have anything to do with them himself. He insisted on an actual ticket with everything printed on it that he could check himself.

Susan scanned the booking information to see if it could wait until Monday, but no luck. Mr. Wu was catching a commuter airline to New York that night and from there connecting with a flight to Hong Kong.

Regardless of the weather, his ticket would have to be delivered today.

After a couple of interruptions, to answer the phone and to find some cruise brochures for an elderly couple, Susan had almost finished her ticketing when Terri said in a low voice, "Oh, oh, here comes Bouncing Betsy."

She looked up to see Betsy Braddock, still several stores away along the mall, coming toward them with her characteristic bouncy walk. The woman had been coming into the agency almost every day for the past two weeks, riffling through the brochures, picking one or two and walking out again. After she had done this several times, Susan walked up to her one day and asked if there was anything she could help her find. The woman looked flustered and said she belonged to a club, and this year the members decided to vacation together. It was her job as club secretary to find a place to go that would suit everybody. So far, no place she had chosen was acceptable to everyone, so that was why she was still picking up brochures.

After she left Terri grumbled that the club probably consisted of four ladies who played bridge together, each of whom really wanted to go to Las Vegas but none of whom would admit it to any of the others. Susan agreed with her and added that they would probably end up taking a Greyhound to Toronto and staying at a budget hotel on the subway line within easy reach of a bingo hall and a shopping mall.

Another day when Susan tried to get the woman to list all the places that had been eliminated in hopes of finding something compatible, she finally managed to get her name. Terri immediately named her Bouncing Betsy, and Susan had to agree it was apt. Mrs. Braddock bounced. She bounced as she walked, she twitched her hips in such a way that the hem of her skirt bounced, her ample bosom bounced, and even her hair bounced on her shoulders like a puppet on a string.

"I swear," said Terri, "If she walks out with one more brochure, I'm going to start charging her for them." This time Bouncing Betsy surprised them. She bounced into the office and without even looking at the brochures went straight to Susan's desk and sat in the customer's chair.

Glancing at the nameplate on the desk, she said, "Miss Jeffrey, I know I've been a nuisance to you these past few weeks, but our square dance club finally decided where we want to go for our vacation. It took a lot of discussion, but we've agreed on Hawaii."

"I'm sure you'll love it there." Susan smiled. "So you're a dancer. I should have known, the way you bounce when you walk."

"I do?" asked Betsy. "Bounce when I walk, I mean." She laughed. "I guess maybe I do. It must be all those hours of dancing and practicing how to make those ruffles and crinolines flip."

Susan knew instantly she was going to like this woman, and not just because of the business she was bringing her. That was substantial. Betsy Braddock was booking a flight to Hawaii for 28 people. She was the best client to walk through that door in ages.

"Do you have any preference for a hotel?" asked Susan. "Do you want to be on the beach, or would you prefer a smaller hotel?"

"I think we'd like the beach," answered Betsy. "I've always heard that Waikiki is where the action is, and I don't want to miss any of it. Actually, one of our group members has been to Hawaii before and recommended the Honolulu Bay Hotel."

"I think that's a good choice," agreed Susan. "The Honolulu Bay is highly rated in the travel agents directory, and it's in the medium price category. Also, I've stayed at its sister hotel, the San Francisco Bay Hotel, and was impressed by the way they run it."

"There's one problem though," said Betsy. "My husband Bill is in a wheelchair. The airlines are excellent about preboarding and stowing his folding chair if they're informed beforehand. But we have to make absolutely certain the hotel is wheelchair accessible."

Susan was mortified when she blurted out the first thing that came to her mind. "A square dancer? In a wheelchair?"

Betsy's laughter pealed out. "Oh my, that's funny. Bill

will love it. He's our caller, you know, and he can do that as well from a wheelchair as he could on his feet."

Susan turned pink with embarrassment, and then she laughed too. "I'll e-mail the hotel right away and check out the wheelchair accessibility. But I probably won't hear back until late this afternoon as there's a six-hour time difference." She glanced at her watch and saw it was just a few minutes after noon. "It's only six a.m. there now."

Betsy stood up, beaming. "I'm so thankful I finally got this trip organization started. Give me a call when you have everything confirmed."

While Susan was talking to Betsy Braddock, Terri went out for a walk around the mall. She came back with two hot, delicious-smelling containers of soup from the deli in the Food Court.

Sitting at their desks eating soup and crackers, the two friends chatted about their plans for the upcoming weekend. Susan usually worked on Saturday with the two part-timers Odel and Nancy and took Monday off, while Terri was off Saturday and worked Monday. The next time the two would see each other would be Tuesday morning.

"Richard is having a party tomorrow night," said Susan. She bit into a cracker with more force than was necessary, scattering crumbs across her desk. She frowned as she brushed them off into a wastebasket. "With his flexible schedule, I don't understand why he can't have a party some other night besides Saturday. I'm usually so pooped when I leave here on Saturday night that all I want is a hot bath and then bed...alone."

"But to Mr. Richard Penrod, the Perfect," said Terri wryly, "Saturday night is party night and there's no changing his mind."

Susan smiled to herself. Richard Penrod, the Third, a devilishly handsome airline pilot, and Susan's boyfriend for the past two years, was not one of Terri's favorite people.

Her soup finished, Susan got up from her desk and stretched. "I hate the thought of going out again but Mr. Wu's tickets have to be delivered today."

Terri looked up from her desk. "Clifton says the snow has turned to rain, so the roads shouldn't be as slippery."

"Thank Clifton for me," muttered Susan, as she put on her coat and boots. "But tell him I'd be more appreciative if he'd stop it completely and bring out the sun."

The wind-driven rain lashed the car as she drove along Highway 33 toward the Greater Buffalo International Airport. As she got farther from the downtown area the air got colder, and the rain turned to freezing rain. It started to coat the windows and the car's flat surfaces with a pebbly, shiny veneer. The wipers kept the windshield clear so she was able to see, but she couldn't help wondering what the icy stuff was doing to the road surface. She was coming up to the industrial complex where the tickets were to be delivered. Tentatively touching the brakes, she was relieved when they held and slowed the car.

Her relief was short-lived. At the foot of the off-ramp the road made a sharp left turn. Braking the car caused it to slew sharply to one side. She quickly took her foot from the brake, and the car straightened out, but it was approaching the turn far too fast. In a panic, she started pumping the brakes like she'd been taught in her winter-driving classes. The car spun around and started sliding sideways and Susan knew she was in the grip of that most hated of all winter driving conditions, black ice.

Helplessly she watched as the bottom of the hill rushed toward her. She knew the car would roll over if it hit the gravel shoulder of the road while still traveling sideways, so at the last moment she hit the brakes hard and turned the wheel at the same time. The car started into a slow spin and, luckily, was pointed straight ahead when it hit the soft shoulder.

Susan was still standing hard on the brakes when the car left the icy road and the sudden stop on the gravel slammed her against the steering wheel, knocking the wind out of her.

Gingerly she lifted her head and looked around, grateful the car was still upright and she didn't appear to be hurt. Also grateful that the airbags hadn't deployed.

"Damn you, Clifton Skye," she said. "You said it warmed up and the roads weren't slippery. I wish you were here right now instead of in your nice warm broadcast booth."

Susan tried for the next ten minutes to get her car back on the road, but it was no use. The front wheels were over the edge of the road in the ditch and one of the back wheels was in the air, not even touching the ground.

Realizing the futility of trying to move it herself, she considered what to do next.

Mr. Wu's office was only about two blocks away. She could walk there and call a tow truck. The rain was still lashing the windows and gusts of wind rocked the small car. The prospect of walking even two blocks in that was daunting, but anything was better than staying in the car. The next vehicle to come down the ramp could skid the same way and end up smashing into her.

She stuffed the tickets into her shoulder bag, grabbed her gloves, tied her scarf around her hair and sat for a minute to psyche herself up before opening the door.

It was even worse than she imagined. The wind-driven sleet stung her cheeks and eyelids. Before she had gone a dozen yards, wetness seeped through her leather boots, chilling her feet. The nylon shell on her down-filled coat was no match for the pelting rain. Within minutes the inside of the coat was damp, and, by the time she reached the office building she was soaked to the skin and chilled to the bone.

The manufacturer's secretary was shocked to see her. "But I thought Mr. Wu called you earlier to tell you he was leaving early and to send the tickets by courier to his home?"

Susan sighed in exasperation. Slapping the tickets on the desk, she said, "It's obvious I didn't get the message in time. And as I have no idea when I'll get back to the office, you'd better look after the courier yourself." She turned and stalked out the door, knowing she'd been rude and probably lost a customer, but too miserable to care.

Going down in the elevator, she shivered from the chill of her wet clothes. Tears of frustration sprang to her eyes as she realized she still had to find a cab and call a tow truck.

14

She pulled her phone out of her coat pocket, grateful that she still had it and it was working.

For the first time that day, luck was with her. Just as she was leaving the elevator a cab pulled up in front of the building to drop off a passenger. She broke into a run and was able to catch it before it left.

When Susan arrived back at the office, Terri was on the phone again but stopped talking abruptly in mid-sentence when she took in her boss' disheveled appearance. While Terri hastily finished her call, Susan stripped off her outer clothes and boots. Terri took one look at Susan's wet clothes, went in the back room, and reappeared with her gym bag.

Taking out a fleece-lined track suit and pair of heavy socks, she thrust them at her saying, "I was going to the fitness club after work, but I think you need these more than I do. What in the world happened?"

A few minutes later, changed into Terri's dry clothes and feeling warm for the first time since she'd stepped out of her car, Susan related her story. By the time she finished, the towing company was on the phone asking what she wanted done with her car. After making arrangements to have it brought to the parking garage in the mall, she finally turned to the work on her desk.

Betsy Braddock's file was still on top. Glancing at the clock, she saw it was almost five. That meant it was eleven a.m. in Hawaii. The sun would be shining, the surf would be rolling in on the beaches, but most of all it would be warm. What she wouldn't give to feel the warm Hawaiian sun right now. She wondered if the staff of the Honolulu Bay Hotel realized how lucky they were.

Sighing, she pulled her keyboard closer and began to key in Betsy Braddock's reservation request.

Adam Joffrey watched from behind the reception desk of the Honolulu Bay Hotel as his staff checked out a group of guests who had been there for a convention. The group had arrived a week earlier, pale skinned, with serious faces,

15

dressed in business clothes or coordinated city casuals. Most of them were alone or in groups of two or three.

Now, they were a noisy, raucous group, joking with one another, breaking out of the line-up to greet newcomers and good-naturedly worming their way back into the line. The faces that had been pale a week ago were tanned or showing the first signs of peeling from too much sun. The frown lines were gone. So were all the typical signs of stress. Gone, too, were the carefully casual clothes in dark colors. The lobby was an assemblage of riotous hues. Brightly flowered Hawaiian shirts fought with even brighter muumuus to catch the eye. They were, in Hawaiian jargon, "hanging loose".

Adam wondered what weather awaited them back on the mainland. Whatever it was, they were ill-equipped to handle it unless they'd been smart enough to pack warmer clothes in the bulging carry-on bags that were strewn about.

Adam smiled to himself. This was what he liked best about his job as manager of the Honolulu Bay Hotel. He liked to think of his hotel and his island as a filtering system. They filtered out the stresses and strains of the working world.

A planeload of pale, uptight individuals arrived here straight from the pressures of big-city life on the mainland. From the first soft "Aloha" greeting and the traditional lei welcome, they were pampered, fed, baked in the hot Hawaiian sun, tossed in the warm surf, stretched out to dry on the beach, and exhorted to "hang loose." All the stresses and problems were winnowed out leaving them tanned and relaxed. A week or two weeks later he sent them back to their real life with tensions eased, mellowed and in a state of tranquility, leaving them better able to cope with life back home.

He personally thought a week in Hawaii was better than a series of sessions on a psychiatrist's couch and far better than a tranquilizer. The convention group checking out certainly proved his point. He was proud of his island and proud of his hotel.

It was funny how he thought of this as his island when he had been here only three years. That he thought of the Honolulu Bay as his hotel was not so strange. It was one of the Bay Hotels, a chain of hotels owned by his family. His father was chairman of the board of the corporation and manager of the San Francisco Bay Hotel. Adam was a shareholder in the corporation. Like his brother and sister, he'd worked his way up in the business, at some point in his career doing every job there was to do in a hotel.

Three years ago the Bay Hotels bought this hotel on Kalakaua Ave from a Japanese conglomerate. It was renamed The Honolulu Bay Hotel, and Adam was appointed manager. Under the previous owners it had been targeted at a very upscale market, had a low occupancy rate, and was steadily losing money.

The Board gave him three years to pull the hotel out of the red and start making a profit. With a lot of hard work, he did it in less than two.

He started by completely renovating the hotel, breaking up most of the multi-room suites into regular hotel rooms. Then he'd gone after the group and convention business, pricing the rooms competitively and hitting an almost one hundred percent occupancy rate in peak periods. The combination of moderate room rates, excellent service and its location right on Waikiki Beach and Kalakaua Avenue virtually guaranteed its continued success.

The checkout was progressing smoothly and some of the conventioneers wandered outside for a last bit of sun before boarding their bus for the airport.

Adam was on his way back to his office when he noticed the flashing light on the computer screen on the reservations desk. He looked around for Penny, the reservations clerk, and saw her at the counter helping a guest with a safety deposit box. One of Adam's rules for his staff was, that if they weren't busy and someone else was, they were to help out if at all possible. That went for everyone on staff, even the manager.

Without even thinking about it, Adam sat down at the computer and opened the reservations e-mail. It was a travel agency in Buffalo, New York, wanting to book 14 rooms for a square dance group and enquiring about wheelchair accessibility.

He started to key in a reply when he realized that they would probably have more questions and, not wanting to lose this booking because of lack of information, decided to call them instead. Checking the phone number in the signature line of the e-mail, he picked up the phone.

"Harbor Square Travel," said a lilting voice.

"Good morning. This is Adam at the Honolulu Bay Hotel."

"And a good morning to you too," said the voice. "Although it's afternoon where I am and not a very good one at that. It's been snowing all day, and now it's freezing rain."

Adam smiled. "In that case, I'll say `aloha.' That's an all-purpose Hawaiian greeting suitable for any occasion. Are you Susan? The agent who's booking the 14 rooms for a group? I just picked up your e-mail."

"That was me," she said cheerfully. "I have a booking for a group of square dancers for two weeks starting February 15th. 28 persons, 14 rooms required. Before I confirm I need to know about your wheelchair accessibility."

"Wheelchair accessibility? For square dancers!" Adam was fascinated by the low husky laugh on the other end of the line. He wondered how he could make her laugh again.

"I know. I asked the same question when I first heard. Apparently the man in the wheelchair is their caller, the one who calls the steps and tells the dancers what to do."

"To answer your question, yes, we do have facilities for wheelchairs." Adam explained the wheelchair accessibility in the hotel's rooms and restaurants.

"Just a minute," he said. "I'll check the computer for availability." He pulled the computer keyboard toward him and punched in a code, then studied the screen. Picking up the phone again, he said, "Susan, it looks like I can do it for you. I have a handicapped room empty on the 9th floor for that date. I also have ten regular rooms available on that floor and, with a little juggling, I'm sure I can free up three more."

"May I have an option on those 14 rooms for one week?" asked Susan. "I should be able to confirm by fax with deposits by then."

"Done. It's already booked into the computer."

"Thank you for your help, uh... Adam, is it?"

"It's Adam." Adam looked up and shook his head as Penny came back to her desk and asked if he needed any help.

"Thank you, Adam." Susan's husky voice came over the phone. "I'm sure the square dance group will have a marvelous time in Hawaii in February."

Adam hesitated a moment, then a smile stole over his face as he looked out the window at the blue sky and the sun sparkling on the ocean. "It's been nice talking to you, Susan, way out there in snowy Buffalo."

"So far it's mainly freezing rain, but unfortunately, in Buffalo, in winter, snow is inevitable." Susan sighed. "And freezing rain is bad enough when you have to drive home in it."

Adam chuckled. "If it gets too bad for you, around about February, you can always come to Hawaii. I could probably spring loose another room for you."

"I only wish," muttered Susan as she hung up.

Adam was smiling as he got up and went back to his office. Sometimes he missed the personal touch. E-mailing just wasn't the same.

Half an hour later, Adam still stood looking out the window at the skimpily-clad midday crowds on Kalakaua Ave. The intriguing, sexy voice of Susan-in-snowy-Buffalo intruded on his thoughts. Then he did something entirely uncharacteristic; something he would never have thought about only an hour ago. He googled Harbor Square Travel on his computer and got Susan's e-mail address.

Subject: Square Dancing
Hi Susan. Do you think your Square Dancers would be interested in performing while they're here? We have a free show every Wednesday afternoon in the hotel. We get local talent, usually from the schools, to perform, and quite often some of our guests participate as well. Then we serve dessert and cold drinks afterwards so the guests and performers can mingle and get to know one another. Square dancing is

something our Hawaiians might like to see. If you think they'd like to do it, I'll clear it with our entertainment director, Keoki, and get him to put it on the list.
Adam
Honolulu Bay Hotel

He'd no sooner sent it when he had second thoughts. She was probably only 19 years old and two months out of travel school. She was also an ocean and a continent and six time zones away. If he started fantasizing about every sexy voice he heard on the phone, it was a good thing he wasn't still on the reservations desk.

Sitting at his desk, he saw Liana Becker's name on his calendar. Instead of mooning about a woman half a world away he'd better start thinking about the one he was seeing there that night. He was taking Liana to a dance at the yacht club, and she would expect him to bring flowers. He wondered what she would wear, and then remembered that Liana was enough of a Hawaiian traditionalist that she would prefer a fresh flower lei to a corsage with even the most formal dress.

He picked up the phone and called the hotel florist to order a white orchid lei.

"Just leave it in the cooler for me," he said. "I'll pick it up on the way out this evening."

Adam and Liana had been an occasional twosome for the past several months. At one time Adam would have liked to progress to a more serious relationship, but the longer he knew Liana, the more he realized she wasn't ready to settle down.

The dance that night at the yacht club was in honor of a club member who won the prestigious Southern Cross Cup, one of the sailing world's highest honors.

Michael Dodd, a native of Australia, was, like Adam, an adopted Hawaiian. He was a wealthy playboy who liked to sail and, fortunately for him, had enough money to allow him to do it full time. He carried the colors of the Diamond Head Yacht Club in the grueling trans-Pacific sailing race and won first place. Tonight they were welcoming him home.

Adam had never met Michael Dodd, but Liana had. She'd met him in Australia during a surfing championship and dated him briefly when he first moved to Hawaii. Adam supposed that he should feel some jealousy at the thought of taking Liana to a dance where she would see an old flame; especially an old flame who was a returning hero. He couldn't scare up a shred of jealousy, and it gave him a reason to wonder just how important Liana was to him these days.

He put Liana from his mind and turned to the pile of paperwork on his desk. Regardless of his love life, or lack of it, he had work to do. He still had a hotel to run.

When Adam arrived at Liana's house that evening he took the orchid lei from its plastic bag on the car seat and put it around his own neck. Her mother answered the door wearing a long gown modeled on a traditional Hawaiian style and also wearing a lei. Noelani Becker was a striking woman, tall like her daughter, but with a regal bearing inherited from her Hawaiian ancestors that Adam suspected Liana would never have.

"Good evening, Noelani." Adam dropped a kiss on her cheek as he stepped into the entryway. "You look lovely tonight. I swear if you get any younger looking I'll have to start coming around to see you instead of Liana."

Noelani laughed. "You're good for my ego, Adam. Liana's not ready yet. Why don't you come out on the patio and watch the sunset with me?" Adam followed her through the house and out the patio door. They sat in chairs under a canopy of plumeria and hibiscus and watched the sun set across the golf course and the Pacific Ocean in the distance.

"This is my favorite time of day," said Noelani softly. "The hustle and bustle of the day is over and the problems of the evening haven't yet begun. It's an oasis of time. It's a time just to sit and enjoy the important things in life," she smiled at Adam, "like sunsets."

Adam was silent. It was a comment that didn't require an answer, but it did require some thought. He wondered what her "problems of the evening" were, or if it was just a figure of speech.

Adam was still searching for something to say to Noelani when Liana appeared on the patio. One look at her and anything he might have said was forgotten.

She was stunning. Her hair, which she usually wore pinned on top of her head or caught in a braid, flowed in loose waves down her back. A white orchid was pinned over her ear. Her dress, what there was of it, was also white with tiny pink flowers. The top was cut very low and barely held with two tiny straps, leaving her shoulders and arms bare. The skirt was ruffled, very short and very full, and showed off Liana's legs to perfection. On her feet were white shoes, the toes almost hidden by pink satin roses. Since she usually sported casual Hawaiian wear regardless of the occasion, Adam guessed that tonight she'd dressed for Michael Dodd, not for Adam Joffrey.

He glanced at Noelani who stared at Liana in shock. She opened her mouth to say something but changed her mind.

Adam got to his feet and started across the patio, meeting Liana halfway. He took the orchid lei from his own neck and placed it around Liana's, giving her the ritual kiss as he did so. He couldn't help noticing her lips were cold.

"You're beautiful tonight, my dear," he said. "Well worth the wait. Shall we go?"

When they entered the Yacht Club, the guest of honor was in the center of a group of well wishers. When he saw Liana his eyes widened and he waved from across the room. He pushed his way through the crowd and, completely ignoring Adam and Noelani, lifted Liana in a bear hug and whirled her around. As a flushed Liana was set back on her feet, Adam noted the orchid lei, lying crushed and broken against the white dress. When Liana finally introduced them, Michael Dodd barely glanced in Adam's direction before returning his attention again to Liana and dragging her off to meet someone.

Adam shrugged at the slight, made a mental comment on the man's manners, and after escorting Noelani to their table, went in search of the bar.

Liana came back to him when dinner was announced but barely spoke to him all through the meal. Her attention was obviously elsewhere. Michael spoke for half an hour after the dinner, telling about the race and the problems they encountered. Adam thought he dwelled a little much on the dangers involved but then pushed the thought aside as uncharitable.

Shortly after the speeches were finished and the band started playing, Liana disappeared. Adam sat there for another hour, slowly sipping his drink and making small talk with an embarrassed Noelani. He was outwardly calm, but anger simmered beneath the surface. He didn't like being made a fool of.

A shout went up near the doors leading out to the terrace. Adam heard Michael Dodd's name called and went to see what was going on. The terrace steps led down to the dock area, and, just as Adam pushed his way through the crowd, he saw a sloop pull out of its mooring, sails still unfurling. Adam recognized it as the small boat that Dodd kept at the yacht club for his personal use when he wasn't racing.

Adam stepped down off the terrace thinking that now Michael Dodd had gone, he should find Liana and take her home. Someone bumped against him and, stepping quickly to one side, he tripped against something on the top step. He reached down and picked up a pair of shoes, white with pink satin roses on the toes. Obviously, their owner had hastily discarded them as she ran down the steps to the dock. Under the shoes, petals already turning brown, lay the broken remains of the orchid lei.

I guess you can't wear high heels on a boat anyway, thought Adam as he watched the sloop, under full sail, disappear around the headland.

Susan arrived at Richard's house shortly after six o'clock. Knowing Richard expected her to go early and eat a light supper with him before the party; she went directly from work carrying a change of clothes in a tote bag.

Richard met her at the door with a wide smile on his handsome face and drew her into the house. Stopping only long enough to plant a quick kiss on her forehead, he disappeared around the corner into the den calling out as he went, "I'm just setting up the bar. I'll have a drink for you in a minute."

"No drink for me just yet," she said. "Give me about 15 minutes. I'd like to shower and change first."

The whirlpool tub in Richard's top-floor bathroom was inviting, and she looked longingly at it thinking how good it would feel after the stresses of the past two days. However, patience was not one of Richard's virtues, and she knew he was waiting for her downstairs, so she opted for the shower.

True to her word, fifteen minutes later she was back downstairs clad in a pair of straight-legged silk pants and a long glittery top that fell to the top of her thighs. Her straight blond hair was caught up in a French twist and held with a sequined bow.

It was not one of Susan's better nights.

It was also not one of Richard's better parties.

As each guest came in the door, Richard handed him or her a Tequila Sunrise and, reaching for one of his own, proposed a toast to "Sun, Sea, Sand, Surf and Sex, but definitely not Snow." At first one of Richard's drinks lasted for several guests, but eventually he was drinking on a "one for you and one for me" basis, with every person who came in.

Clearly, drinking at that rate, he wouldn't last long, and he didn't. Shortly before midnight his friend Walt found him asleep on the bedroom floor.

Susan started serving the food, thinking that if she got the group fed they might think about going home. She'd had more than enough party for one night.

Before leaving she went upstairs to check on Richard and, finding him still sound asleep on the floor, put a pillow under his head and covered him with a blanket.

Carefully locking the door behind her, she drove home in the chill predawn. The road was as empty as her heart. All her life she had been a responsible, conscientious, person. She knew that, for her to be happy, the man she married would have to have those same qualities. She had hoped it would be Richard. After all who could be more responsible or conscientious than an airline pilot who literally held peoples' lives in his hands every day? Tonight she had seen another side of Richard, an uncaring and irresponsible side. He'd willfully got drunk and left her to act as host and entertain his guests.

His behavior tonight was reprehensible, and she wasn't sure she could ever forgive him for it.

CHAPTER 2

Adam looked up from the mound of paperwork on his desk as a soft knock sounded on his partially opened door. Penny, the reservations clerk, pushed the door open a bit more and popped her head into the office.

"I just got a deposit this morning on that booking you did for 14 rooms for Harbor Square Travel in Buffalo," she said. "I pulled a printout of the booking with a confirmation number. Shall I just send it, or do you want to add something? I don't know what you discussed other than what was in the computer."

"They're a square dance group," answered Adam, "and I arranged with Keoki for them to perform at a Wednesday afternoon show. You could add a note to the effect that the arrangements have been made for the performance."

"Square dancing!" exclaimed Penny, her eyes lighting up. "I've never seen square dancing. I'll have to watch them myself"

Adam smiled at her enthusiasm. Penny was an expert hula dancer and occasionally danced at the Wednesday shows when they were short of performers.

"So, shall I take care of this?" asked Penny, waving the letter.

"Yes, please," said Adam absently. Then as Penny turned to leave, he stopped her. "On second thought, Penny, before you seal the envelope drop it back here. I may add a personal note anyway."

When Adam returned from an early dinner in the dining room, he saw the envelope addressed to Harbor Square Travel sitting on his desk. He picked it up intending simply to seal it and mail it when the name on the envelope caught his attention. He thought at first that Penny had made a mistake and put his name on it, but a closer look told him that the letter was addressed to Susan Jeffrey.

Suddenly he smiled, took out the single sheet with the booking confirmation on it, and wrote across the bottom:

Dear Susan-in-snowy-Buffalo-Jeffrey
In 18th century literature the o and e were often used interchangeably. Do you think we might have a common ancestor?
Yours
Adam-in-sunny-Hawaii-Joffrey

He looked at the note, feeling quite pleased with himself. Then on impulse he reached for a packet of Hawaii Visitors Bureau information and flipped through it until he found what he wanted, a sheet of colorful stickers. He peeled off one and stuck it next to his note. The sticker read, "I Love Hawaii" with the word "love" replaced by a heart held by a voluptuous hula dancer.

Sealing the envelope, he tossed it in his "out" basket and left the office humming to himself.

When Susan opened the mail a few days later the note and the colorful sticker brought back memories of the sexy voice on the phone that snowy Friday. She'd had so many problems that day she'd almost forgotten about him.

The next morning there had been an e-mail asking if the dancers would like to perform during their stay. She'd forwarded it to Betsy Braddock to answer and thought that was the end of it.

Now, with the memory of that afternoon fading, the cheerful reservations clerk at the Honolulu Bay Hotel crept back into her mind. She peeled the sticker off the letter and stuck it to her phone where she could see it as she talked. She photocopied the letter, put the copy into Betsy Braddock's file, and put the original in a file labeled "personal stuff."

She and Adam had exchanged only first names when she made the reservation two weeks earlier. She wondered if the conversation would have been different if they realized their last names were so much alike. Probably not. She sighed.

Flirting with a Hawaiian reservations clerk, even if he did have a sexy voice, was really not her thing.

Christmas was only two weeks away and Susan remembered she had yet to finish her shopping. She flipped open the notebook she always carried in her handbag and checked her shopping list. At the top of the list were her sister Trish and Trish's husband Ted, and their two sons Timmy and Tommy, aged four and seven. Next came Terri and the two part-timers, Nancy and Odel. Then Jacey of course, her best friend who ran the florist shop in the mall, and Mrs. Treadwell, her elderly next-door neighbor who looked after Brutus, her cat, whenever Susan was traveling.

She frowned over the last name on the list. She wasn't sure where she and Richard stood right now. She hadn't seen him since the ill-fated party two weeks ago and had talked to him only once. He had been embarrassed and apologetic when she lashed out at him for his neglect of his hosting duties, but gave her no real explanation for his behavior. He told her he was on an overseas schedule for the next few weeks and wouldn't be around much. She hadn't heard from him since.

Leaving Terri alone in the office she started walking through the mall looking for Christmas gift ideas. In front of a store called "Sophisticated Playthings" she saw two teenage boys playing with remote-controlled cars. The rugged-looking little cars climbed over obstacles and even over the boys' feet. Thinking her nephews might like something like that, she went into the store only to recoil in shock when she looked at the price tag. Those little cars were three hundred dollars each! "Sophisticated playthings indeed," she muttered to herself. "Too sophisticated for my budget."

She wandered into a few other stores, not really seeing anything that interested her. Then her eye was caught by the display in the window of a lingerie store. A pale pink teddy with cocoa brown lace hung against the back wall of the display window. It was cut low in the front and high at the sides and held up by tiny wisps of straps over the shoulders.

She tried to imagine herself wearing it for Richard, but somehow the image didn't ring true. Unbidden, a different image came into her mind. She could see herself in the pink teddy on a balcony overlooking a sunny beach in Hawaii. She could almost hear a husky voice saying "Susan-in-sunny-Hawaii."

She shook her head as she came back to reality. What he had actually said was "Susan-in-snowy-Buffalo," and she couldn't imagine wearing that pink confection in a Buffalo winter. Then she remembered that Jacey, happily engaged to a handsome veterinarian, was getting married in the spring. The pink teddy would make a perfect shower gift. Ten minutes later she came out of the store carrying her purchase. Checking her watch she realized she'd been away long enough and headed back to the agency so Terri could go to lunch.

A week later, on Sunday afternoon, just a few days before Christmas, Susan was at home wrapping Christmas gifts when a knock came at the door. She opened it to find Richard standing there, wearing a sheepskin-lined leather bomber jacket and a wide grin. She faltered for a moment and left him standing there while his grin faded before finally stepping back and motioning him inside.

"I wasn't really expecting you, Richard," she said, as she put the finishing touches on the gift she was wrapping when she'd heard the knock. "How were your overseas flights? Any problems?"

"No. No problems." He paced around her small living room like a caged tiger. "You know the old joke about long-haul flights into unfamiliar airports. `Hours of sheer boredom ending in minutes of sheer terror.'" He smiled wryly, and then abruptly sat down on the sofa. "Susan, can we talk?"

"Sure," she said, as she put the finished Christmas gift on the dining room table. "Would you like a drink?"

He shook his head. "Can't," he said. "I'm flying tonight."

"Can you stay for dinner?"

He shook his head again. "The flight leaves at eight. I'll grab a bite in the crew lounge before boarding."

"Where are you flying tonight?"

"Europe. One stop on the way, and two stops on the way back day after tomorrow. Actually that's one of the things I wanted to talk to you about. The other is this." He pulled a

29

small flat box from his jacket pocket and grinned at her again. "Your Christmas present. I won't be here over Christmas, so I thought I'd bring it today."

He caught a stricken look on her face and misinterpreted it.

"I'm sorry, Babe," he said. "I know you expected us to spend Christmas together, but several of us single guys volunteered to take most of the long-hauls over Christmas so the ones with small children could spend more time with their families during the holidays."

"I think it's great, what you're doing for the married guys, although I'm sorry you won't be here over Christmas. But," she gave an embarrassed laugh, "the problem is, that I haven't finished my shopping yet, and I don't have anything for you."

"No problem, love. Since I won't be here, do your shopping in the after-Christmas sales, get me something nice and save yourself pots of money."

Susan burst out laughing, knowing that Richard had probably never shopped at a sale in his life.

She took the small flat box and tore at the wrapping, relieved that it was the wrong size and shape for a ring box. She didn't want that complication right now.

Inside was an exquisitely fashioned gold and diamond bracelet.

"Oh, Richard, it's beautiful," she said. "But I can't take it. It's far too much."

"I want you to have it. And it's not too much, if it's cost you're thinking of. You know how inexpensive jewelry is in some of the countries we fly into, and Customs never checks the crews. We just walk through."

Susan felt a bit uncomfortable with that statement but it was possible that the bracelet was within his legal declaration limit, so she pushed aside her misgivings.

"Thank you, Richard. I love it. I'll wear it Christmas Day and think of you." She reached over and kissed his cheek. "Are you sure I can't get you something before you go, some coffee perhaps."

"No thanks, love. I have a few things to do before I head out to the airport." He stared over her shoulder out the window. "I probably won't see you now until mid-January."

"January! You're not flying all that time, surely?"

"No, of course not. But my last flight before New Years is a layover in Zurich, so I decided to take some vacation time while I'm there and get in some skiing." He got abruptly to his feet, pulled her up in a bear hug, and kissed her soundly. He looked down at her and smiled warmly. "'Bye, love, and take care. I'm gonna miss you over Christmas." Then he was gone, leaving a bemused Susan staring out the window as he got into his car and drove off.

She went slowly back to her gift wrapping and said out loud to Brutus, her long-haired ginger cat who was curled up on a dining room chair, "He could at least have asked me to go skiing with him." Brutus blinked back at her and closed his eyes. "You're right, I wouldn't have gone anyway." She knew she wouldn't take extra time off over the holidays, because that would leave her staff working extra hours. "But the least he could have done was ask."

As she wrapped the rest of her gifts and fussed over fancy bows on each one, she thought about her relationship with Richard.

She had met him two years ago at a Christmas party organized by his airline for their locally-based staff. They also invited certain Buffalo area travel agents who had been responsible for booking volume business with them the past year.

Susan went to the party alone, and she and Richard danced together most of the evening. When she left, he asked for her phone number, and she gave him her business card, thinking she wouldn't hear from him again. With his good looks and obvious charm as well as the glamour of his job, she figured he didn't lack for feminine companionship.

To her surprise, he called her several weeks later when she had all but forgotten him. Apologizing for his long delay in calling her, he explained that he had spent Christmas with his sister in Texas then had been flying almost constantly since.

He asked her out to dinner that evening. They fell comfortably into a relationship that had lasted for two years.

Susan frowned as she put the finishing touches on the gifts and took them into her spare bedroom. She and Richard had a lot of fun together, but recently something was missing. At twenty-seven, she felt it was time to make a commitment and settle down, but did she want to settle down with Richard? He gave no indication of making their relationship permanent, and she wasn't sure he wanted to.

The next question, she mused, as she wandered back into the living room where the fingers of twilight were starting to encroach on the day, was, did she love Richard?

She supposed she did love him. It wasn't a question she asked herself before. She just assumed what she felt for him was love.

Did she, however, love him enough to marry him?

Was he happily-ever-after material, or simply as-long-as-it-lasts? She didn't know, and she wondered if Richard did. He never spoke about love or commitment or even the future, any further away than next month.

Maybe when he got back in January she would ask him. It was time she knew where she stood.

Suddenly there were so many questions she wanted to ask him. The frustrating thing was that it would be several weeks before she could ask him any of them.

Susan decided to close the agency at noon on Christmas Eve. Once the "closed" sign was up and the lights were dimmed, she and Terri shared a half-bottle of white wine as they exchanged gifts.

Susan was still buoyed by the Christmas spirit when she left the office and locked it up for the long weekend. It was only later as she ate a lonely supper and settled down to watch TV with all its upbeat holiday programming, that the reality hit her that she was sitting there alone while the rest of the city celebrated.

For the first time in years, her pillow was wet with tears that night.

Susan spent Christmas Day with Trish and her family. Even though she spent Christmas with them every year since the death of their parents, this year was somehow different. For the first time Susan felt like an outsider. She saw the obvious love between Trish and Ted, the meaningful looks as they exchanged gifts, the pats and hugs as they passed each other during the day. She wanted some of that love for herself. Somewhere there must be a man who would love her like Ted loved Trish. Somehow she didn't think it would be Richard Penrod the Third.

After dinner a sleepy Tommy demanded that his Auntie Sue read him a story. Curled up on the sofa with the small warm body cuddled against her own, she felt such a pang of yearning that tears clouded her eyes, and she could hardly see to read. Being an "auntie" was nice, but somehow, sometime, she really wanted a child of her own.

The last day of January, Susan phoned Betsy Braddock and told her that the group's airline tickets were ready for pickup.

"Great! I'll see you tomorrow."

Susan left the office a few minutes early that evening, before the other stores in the mall were closed. She wanted to buy a birthday card for Trish's oldest son, Timmy, who would turn eight that weekend.

In the Greetings & Gifts store she found the card she wanted and was just about to pay for it when a display of souvenirs near the counter caught her eye. One particular item, by itself near the back, made her smile delightedly. It was a plastic paperweight, the kind that snowed on the landscape inside when you turned it over. Around the bottom edge, printed in gold letters, was "Souvenir of Buffalo, N.Y.." But what attracted Susan was the object inside the plastic dome, a scruffy-looking, dark brown, plastic buffalo with staring blue eyes. The most tacky souvenir possible and the perfect gag gift for a Hawaiian reservations clerk whose sexy voice saying `Susan-in-snowy-Buffalo' she could still hear more than two months later.

Before she could change her mind, Susan picked up the snow globe and turned toward the cashier. On an impulse, as she was paying for her purchases, she asked the clerk to gift wrap it for her. The clerk looked at the plastic snow globe and back at Susan with an incredulous look on her face. She looked about to say something, but prudence prevailed, and she wrapped it without a word.

Betsy Braddock bounced into Susan's office the next day with a smile that lit up the room.

"I'm just so excited about this trip. I can't believe it's only two weeks away." She plopped down in the chair in front of Susan's desk and opened her handbag. "Before I forget, I have something for you. We're performing next Saturday night at the Buffalo Convention Center, as part of the entertainment at a trade show, the Hobby and Leisure Show. I have two passes for you, if you and a friend would like to take in the show and also see us perform. We're doing two shows, at six-thirty and eight-thirty."

Susan was touched. Occasionally her clients did little favors for her, but more often it went the other way. "Thank you, Betsy. I'd love to go. Ever since I met you, I've wanted to see your group dance. I think Richard will be home this weekend, and maybe he'll go with me."

"That's great!" bounced Betsy enthusiastically. "I'll introduce you to the dancers between the shows. They're all dying to meet you, especially the men. I've given them glowing reports on you."

"Thanks for warning me," said Susan wryly. "Now I'll have to get my hair done before I go." They both laughed.

Susan went to a locked filing drawer and took out a stack of tickets in colorful plastic airline folders. The top one was Betsy's, so she picked it up and put the rest aside. Taking out the ticket and the itinerary printout, she explained it to Betsy.

"Whew! You've done a lot of work for us. I really appreciate this, Susan."

"That's what I'm here for," said Susan, smiling. "The other ticket folders have essentially the same information, but I have another information sheet here just for you, since you're the leader of this group."

"Not really leader," she laughed. "Just the one who got talked into doing the work."

"Do you remember I asked you about performing in the hotel's Wednesday afternoon free concerts?"

Betsy nodded. "And I answered that e-mail you forwarded to me. I said we'd be happy to show our stuff."

"Well, the arrangements have been made, and the person to contact is the entertainment director, Keoki. I've put his name here." She indicated a smaller sheet of paper tucked into the ticket folder. "I've also attached my card with the agency address and phone number. If you have any problems, don't hesitate to call me, and," she grinned, "if you're having a marvelous time, send me a postcard."

"I sure will," Betsy enthused. "I really appreciate this, Susan."

"There's..er..ah. one other thing." Susan was suddenly embarrassed. "There's a favor you can do for me in Hawaii, if you don't mind." She reached into her desk drawer and pulled out the small gift-wrapped package. "This is a small gift for Adam, the reservations clerk at the Honolulu Bay Hotel who looked after booking your rooms. He's probably just a young kid, new in the business, but he was so helpful that I'd like to say thank-you. I've written his name, Adam Joffrey, on the back of my business card and taped it to the box. If you can find room in your luggage I'd appreciate it if you'd deliver it to him. You'll probably find him working at the front desk of the hotel."

Betsy's laughter pealed out, making her shoulders and hair bounce again. "Of course I can find room. I always travel half empty so I'll have lots of room to bring back my purchases. I'm a compulsive shopper, you know."

It was one of the worst Februarys on record. Blizzards howled across the lake and dumped several feet of snow on Buffalo in back-to-back storms. Channel 4 television, long known for its live coverage of fires, ran footage of serious accidents, multi-vehicle collisions, and even two instances of bodies found in abandoned cars. All Buffalo wondered if this winter would ever end.

When she was in the office, Susan spent most of her time on the phone. At least half the flights she booked were canceled, which meant rebooking a second or even a third time.

The square dance group's flight was delayed when a snowstorm unexpectedly turned to sleet, coating everything with ice. Betsy called from the airport, worried about their reservations on the other end, but was assured that the booking was confirmed and guaranteed and their rooms would be waiting for them regardless of their arrival time. They finally left several hours late.

Adam Joffrey crossed her mind only once. One day when she was snowbound at home she got out her cross-country skis and went to the store for bread and milk. As she crossed a field of unbroken snow, the sun came out. The sun on the snow was dazzling, and, for a moment, it reminded her of a white sand beach on a Caribbean island. Her mind drifted momentarily to a Hawaiian beach, and she wondered if hotel staff ever walked along the beach, or was that something only tourists did?

On Monday morning, the day after she returned from Hawaii, Betsy Braddock called.

"Susan, we had a marvelous time! Hawaii was great, the beach was superb, the hotel was everything you said it was, and I can't wait to give you all the details. As soon as I get out from under this pile of work and shake off the jet lag I'm taking you to lunch and telling you all about it, especially that yummy Adam Joffrey. Susan, you were holding out on me. You didn't tell me he was so handsome."

Late that afternoon, her friend Jacey came into the travel agency carrying a box covered with green florist paper and accused her of the same thing.

"Susan, you've been holding out on me." She set the box on Susan's desk and carefully lifted out an exquisite crystal rose bowl. Floating in an inch of water in the bowl was a single bright red hibiscus blossom.

As Susan stared open-mouthed at the delicate bowl and flower, Jacey dropped a small white card on the desk. A smile tugged as she picked up the card, somehow knowing before she even opened it who it was from. The short doggerel verse made her burst out laughing as she handed the card to Jacey, remembering as she did so that Jacey must have already seen it.

Look at me
And fantasy
That you will be
On Waikiki.

A.J.

"I repeat. You've been holding out on me. Who is that man with the sexy, bedroom voice who would think of a romantic gesture like this?" Jacey demanded.

"How do you know what he sounds like? Didn't he order this through FTD or whatever?"

"No, he did not order this through FTD or whatever. He called me direct and was very specific about what he wanted, even to the red hibiscus. Pink or yellow simply wouldn't do. He wanted one the color of a Hawaiian sunset. Now how's that for romantic, I ask you?"

Susan took the bowl and flower home with her that evening, putting it back in the box and covering it with a woolen scarf to protect it from the sub-freezing weather. She put it on her kitchen table while she ate dinner and tried to imagine white sand, rolling surf, and a red sunset, but, outside her window the howling wind of yet another winter storm taxed her creative imagination.

Before she went to bed she sat down at her home computer and sent a note of thanks to Adam Joffrey.

It was Thursday before Betsy Braddock came to take Susan to lunch. They went to The Steering Place, a steak house across the street from the mall, that served superb hamburgers at lunch.

"I think I'll have the Teriyaki Burger," said Betsy. "I learned to love teriyaki in Hawaii, and I still haven't resigned myself to being back."

"I'll have the same," said Susan with an amused smile. "Since I'm obviously going to hear all about Hawaii, I might as well get in the spirit of things."

Betsy laughed. "I had such a marvelous time that I'm sure I'm going to be a bore for all my friends for the next few weeks. Except, of course, for the ones who went with me. And they'll bore *me* because I won't be able to get a word in edgewise."

The waitress came, and they ordered their burgers with a small salad on the side. As soon as she left Betsy started to talk.

"The person I really must tell you about is Adam Joffrey. Lord, that man is handsome! The second day we were there, I went to the front desk with the box you'd given me and asked for him. The receptionist told me he had gone to San Francisco on business and would be gone about ten days."

"The Bay Hotels' head office is in San Francisco," cut in Susan. "He must have gone there for a training seminar or something."

"I never did find out why he had gone," answered Betsy. "I considered leaving your gift with someone at the hotel desk, but they were so busy I thought it might get lost. I knew I would still be there when he got back, so I left a message that I would like to see him before I checked out."

"I hope I didn't put you to a lot of trouble with this," said Susan anxiously.

"No, of course not. In fact, I put the box in a drawer and forgot about it until Saturday night, the night before we were to leave. I had just finished dressing for dinner when a knock sounded at the door. I opened the door, and there was this devastatingly handsome man, so tall I had to look way up at him, wearing a white dinner jacket. I thought he had the wrong room until he said, `I'm Adam Joffrey, Mrs. Braddock. I understand you were asking for me.'" Betsy arched her eyebrows at Susan. "You could have knocked me over with a feather. I thought you said he was a young kid. That man was no kid! Anyway, I got your gift and gave it to him. He looked at your name on the card and turned to leave. He was halfway out the door when he turned and said, `I'm sorry to be so rude, Mrs. Braddock. Thank you for bringing me this.' Then he stood there for a minute as if trying to make up his mind to say something else, and finally he asked, with sort of an embarrassed look on his face, `What's she like?'"

Susan gasped. "He didn't!"

"He sure did."

"And what did you say."

"I don't think I did you any favors. I wasn't expecting that question, and I sort of stumbled over the answer. I finally said you had straight blond hair, were sort of tall, sort of thin, and real smart."

Susan burst out laughing. "Even if he was interested, he wouldn't be after that description. Actually, I don't even know why I asked about him. I only talked to him once on the phone and got a scrawled note on the bottom of a confirmation letter." She didn't mention the flower that arrived the next day or the silly poem with it.

Their burgers arrived, and neither said anything for a few minutes. When she finished, Susan picked up her coffee and blew on the surface to cool it, then said absently, as if there had been no break in the conversation, "Other than tall, and `devastatingly handsome', what's he like?"

Betsy must have been on the same wavelength, because she answered just as casually. "He has black wavy hair and dark brown eyes. I don't think he's Hawaiian because he's not as deeply tanned as someone who has lived in Hawaii all his life. And he most definitely is not a kid. I'd say he's in his early-to-mid-thirties."

"That old?" asked Susan musingly. "And still a reservations clerk? I would have thought at that age he would be at least an assistant manager."

"Well," said Betsy. "I really have no idea what he does at the hotel. As I told you, he got back from San Francisco only the night before we left. Maybe he's just started in the business, or maybe he's not serious about his career, just a playboy using his job to meet a lot of women."

"Anything's possible," said Susan, as if she didn't want to believe it. "And he did flirt with me on the phone. Anyway, I think we've talked that subject to death. Tell me about the shopping in Waikiki."

Betsy didn't need to be asked twice and for the next half-hour regaled Susan with stories of clothes shopping, bargains in shell jewelery, and the sightseeing trips they had taken in.

"But do you know what the highlight of the trip was? Something we enjoyed more than anything else?" Betsy giggled and went on, not really expecting Susan to answer. "One night Bill and I went out on our own, and we went to a strip club. We felt so risqué. That was something we'd never do at home because we'd be afraid we'd run into someone we knew. And it was really funny, because two of the couples in our group were also there. They ignored us and pretended they didn't know us, and we did the same to them. And none of us mentioned it to the others the next day. Wasn't that childish of us?" She laughed again, her shoulders bouncing in a way that had become familiar to Susan. "But so much fun."

Adam sat in his office staring at his desktop. It was a solid, no-nonsense desk that he had chosen himself, heavy oak with brass drawer pulls and a large enough work surface for even a confirmed workaholic. The only things on the desktop were a multi-line telephone and a pottery jar full of pencils, and, of course, the computer. The e-mail from *susan@harborsquaretravel.com* had been in his inbox when he turned on the computer a few minutes ago and he had, so far, resisted opening it.

He swung around in his chair and glanced at the credenza against the wall behind his desk. On it were gifts from members of his family and things that were important to him; the trappings of a wealthy man from a wealthy family. The desk clock from his father, picked up at the famous Brughan watch factory in Geneva, on one of his many trips there. The 14K gold pen in the Steuben crystal penholder, a gift from his mother; and from his sister, the day he graduated from college, an antique glass paperweight, signed by the artist. He shuddered to think what she'd paid for that little bauble.

Then there were a couple of sports trophies that he was proud of, as well as a civic citation that embarrassed him a little. Next to that was a perfect shell he'd found while snorkeling off Maui. Finally his eyes rested on the newest acquisition, a plastic snow-filled paperweight with a tiny buffalo in the center. To the casual observer, out of place, yet important to him because it had been chosen, with a lot of thought, by a young girl who really had no reason to give him a gift. Thoughtfully, he picked it up and turned it over, making it snow on the plastic buffalo.

It had been over three months, yet he could still hear her lilting sexy voice as well as if he had just finished speaking to her. He thought when he ordered the bowl with the hibiscus delivered to her that would be the end of it. Now there was this e-mail, and somehow, he suspected if he opened it he would be turning a corner in his life. It was silly because it was probably just a thank-you note for the crystal bowl.

He decided before he opened it that he would read it, delete it and forget it. He clicked on the message and opened it. He read the message all the way through, glanced at the signature on the bottom with her home address, and clicked on "reply".

CHAPTER 3

Later they would argue about what started it all. Was it her thank-you note, or was it when he decided to answer? Was it fated from the moment he picked up the reservations message the day Penny was busy?

Who can guess on what tiny hinges hang the wings of fate.

Dear Susan;
...Whispering Wood Lane. What a marvelous address! It conjures up pictures in my mind of rustling leaves, oak, linden, and birch, and, of course, aspen, the loudest whisperers of all. I imagine them whispering to you when you arrive home at night, welcoming you home. It's been years since I've seen trees like those. I love the name of your street. Somehow Kalakaua Ave. doesn't have the same ring...
Adam

The e-mail was in her inbox when she arrived home. She hadn't really expected to hear from him. She'd sent the thank-you note because the crystal bowl was obviously expensive, unlike the paperweight she had sent him. It was a gift that didn't deserve to be ignored, or so she told herself.

She glanced at the bowl where it sat on her kitchen table. She'd kept it there as a centerpiece; every few days picking up another fresh flower for it, always red ones. Right now it had a red carnation.

She ignored the computer while she took off her coat and boots and made a pot of tea. She started to reheat some leftover chicken stew for her dinner, relishing the anticipation. When the tea was ready she sat at the computer with her cup and finally opened the message.

On her way to work the next morning, Susan noticed the trees lining the streets on Grand Island. She had never really looked at them before. Now she could hardly wait for them to be in leaf so she could see what kind of trees they were.

April was very busy at the agency. Business travel was up, and people were beginning to book their summer vacations. Richard's airline was in the slow "shoulder" season, between winter holidays to the south and summer vacation travel, so she saw him several times in the first two weeks in April.

It was a couple of weeks before she got around to answering Adam's e-mail. Whether or not to answer it was never an issue.

Dear Adam;

Your imaginative description of my trees is off by a season. The trees on my street are not whispering but stark and silent. From a distance they are bare of leaves and dead looking, but up close the buds are swelling and starting to turn green.

My tulips and daffodils are up, only green so far, no flowers. The pussywillow in my backyard is full of furry buds, and the rhubarb leaves are starting to unfurl.

What can I say except -- Hurrah, it's spring!

Winter in Buffalo is so awful that spring is doubly welcome.

I disagree with you on the name Kalakaua Ave. To me it has a special ring. It brings to mind white sand beaches, pounding surf, and outrigger canoes. And what about the whispering palm trees...?

Susan

Adam carefully saved Susan's e-mail into his private correspondence, the file that was password-protected and no one else had access to. He stood at the window and looked out on Kalakaua Ave, smiling to himself at Susan's description. Kalakaua might have sand beaches and pounding surf at its other end near Diamond Head, but here in front of his hotel, at that hour of the morning, it was crowded with tour buses and tourists.

Her sand, surf, and outrigger canoes were there all right, but on the beach side of the hotel away from the street. He knew if he were to walk through the lobby and out onto the terrace overlooking the beach it would be like walking into another world. He would see the crescent that was Waikiki Beach curving toward the sentinel of Diamond Head. Soft waves would be breaking on the sand and he would hear the excited voices of children bouncing in the waves. Farther out from shore, near a sandbar-covered reef, larger waves would be breaking, and the first surfers of the day would be riding the crests.

No matter how often he saw it he was fascinated by it. Waikiki could never be commonplace. For a moment, as he stood there, he wished he could share it with her.

Dear Susan;

You really do live on an island!

When I first saw Grand Island on your return address, I thought it might be just a suburb of Buffalo with a fanciful name. I've seen places called Maple Heights with not a maple tree in sight and not a hill higher than the lowest garage roof. But Grand Island is really an island.

Last week I looked up the Buffalo area on Google Earth *and found your island.*

I still have your business card, and I see by the zip code that your office is right in downtown. Grand Island looks quite a way outside the city. Don't you find it rather a long drive every day, especially in winter...?

Adam

She didn't know why the knowledge that he still had her business card made such a difference, but it did. He didn't say he had it on file, or that it was in the hotel reservations information. What he said was that *he* still had it.

He had taken the time and effort to look up a map and find Grand Island.

Dear Adam;

No, it's not a particularly long drive to work. Buffalo is not a large city. It's rather compact. I can drive to work in about 20 minutes on a good day. On a bad day in winter, of course, it's a different story. But I wouldn't trade my little house

44

on Grand Island for a fancy condo in the city. Living here in the summer is worth any inconvenience the winter may bring.

Where do you live? Near the hotel, or do you have a long commute...?
Susan

Susan's question about where he lived surprised Adam. He supposed anyone connected with the travel industry would know that the manager always lived in the hotel.

Dear Susan;
...and in answer to your question, I live in the hotel, as do most of the senior staff. I have a suite with a view of Kalakaua Ave, the same view I have from my office window. The ocean-view rooms are, of course, reserved for paying guests....
Adam

Susan wondered how senior a staff position was a reservations clerk. She would have thought it a very junior position and, in fact, had trouble connecting the breezy young man who flirted with her on the phone with the mature sophisticated man described by Betsy Braddock.

She didn't have time to think about it at length. July was a very busy month, and the printout of Adam's e-mail sat on her kitchen table, propped against the crystal bowl, for about two weeks. She still kept a fresh flower in the bowl, having gone through the tulips in her front yard, then the geraniums, until now, when the bowl held one perfect red rose.

Dear Adam;
By the time you read this tomorrow morning, I will be halfway across the Atlantic on my way to jolly olde London. I've agreed to escort a group on a Mystery Murder Tour to England. That, my friend, is why I haven't written you for a long time.
I have been involved in promotion and public appearances, in cooperation with a local radio station, to advertise this trip. It's something I haven't done before.

You see, the radio station is involved in a fund-raising campaign for a CAT scanner for the Erie Memorial Hospital, so they organized this Mystery Murder week. The money comes from three different sources. The station donates the air time to promote the tour; I get publicity for the agency on every ad spot, and donate what the advertising would cost me; and a portion of the cost received from the participants for the tour is earmarked for the fund. Everyone involved benefits.

I'm really looking forward to the trip. I haven't been back to England myself since I went with my parents while still in my teens.
Susan

Adam, when he finished reading the message, glanced at the time and put in a call to Harbor Square Travel in Buffalo. He got Nancy, who was in the office by herself and was busy with a customer. Playing on the girl's inexperience, in less than a minute, and without identifying himself, he had Susan's itinerary in London.

He then sent a long e-mail to his friend, the manager of the London Bay Hotel.

Her last evening in London, Susan came back to her room to change for their groups' farewell dinner and the show afterward.

On the night table beside her bed was a Royal Doulton china cup and saucer with a rosebud pattern. Tucked into the cup was a corsage made of three miniature red roses, each one perfect and no more than an inch in diameter. On the saucer was a card. Thinking it was from one of the passengers in their group, she smiled as she picked it up.

Stunned, she read it twice to be sure it said what she thought it said.

Wear this tonight to dinner and the show.
The Mousetrap is one of my favorite plays.
Adam

Her eyes widened as she stared out the window, seeing, not the dingy row housing of downtown London, but a bright, new hotel on a sunny beach and a tall young man leaning over a balcony smiling at her. Goosebumps danced across her shoulders as she looked swiftly around the room, half expecting to see Adam sitting there. Except she wouldn't recognize him if she did.

She smiled ruefully as she sniffed the roses. Her friend Adam was an enigma. He was sensitive enough to send her a china teacup that she could keep and a corsage to wear tonight, and smart enough to find out exactly where she was going tonight and order the gift even though he was on the other side of the world.

Nothing could have pleased her more than the Royal Doulton teacup because she usually read Adam's e-mails while relaxing with a cup of tea. She wondered how he knew that. She couldn't remember ever telling him.

Thinking of the two gifts he had given her, the china teacup with the red roses, and the crystal bowl with the red hibiscus, she marveled at how appropriate they both were. It was as if he had put a lot of thought into choosing the perfect gift just for her, and he didn't even know her.

She gasped as she looked at the clock and realized she had only a few minutes to dress and meet the others down in the hotel lobby. She pulled out the soft ivory shirtwaist dress with the narrow red belt she had intended to wear tonight and pinned the red corsage to it. It went so well that for a moment she wondered if Adam had been able to look into her closet as well as her appointment book.

Smiling at herself in the mirror, she decided to pretend, just for tonight, that Adam was the special man in her life. It might also, she hoped, serve to discourage Kirk Stevens.

Kirk was the station DJ who was the celebrity escort on the Murder Mystery Tour. He and Susan were billed as co-hosts, but it quickly became apparent that Kirk was always around when there were speeches to be made or compliments to be accepted, but never around when there was work to be done.

He made it plain, right from the beginning, that bedding Susan would add the perfect sweetener to his trip. He was so open about it and so zealous in his pursuit that some of the tour members began laying bets on whether or not he would succeed.

Susan simply wasn't interested. He was nice enough but not really her type.

She swept across the lobby to the agreed-upon meeting place, her smile lighting up her face like a beacon. Kirk Stevens smiled back, thinking the smile was for him until he noticed the corsage on her shoulder. His smile abruptly shut itself off.

"You have a secret admirer?" he growled.

"Not really a secret," she said with a smile. "It's from a very special man back in the States. He ordered it for my last night here. I found it in my room this evening along with a very thoughtful note." She didn't mention the state was not New York, but was instead out in the middle of the Pacific Ocean. Neither did she mention she had never even met the man.

One thing was true, however, he was a very special man.

Susan had been looking forward to seeing Agatha Christie's The Mousetrap, London's longest-running play. She might as well have stayed back at the hotel for all the sense it made to her.

Her mind skittered back and forth between Adam and Richard. She knew she was comparing them from an unfair vantage point. She'd known Richard for almost three years, knew his weak points as well as his strong ones. She had only been corresponding by e-mail with Adam for six months, had only spoken to him once, and knew about him only what he chose to tell her. Except that wasn't exactly true. She knew he was a thoughtful and considerate man, with a very definite romantic streak. It was possible that she was romanticizing him somewhat. The place where he lived and worked, Hawaii, was one of the most romantic places she could think of, and the circumstances under which she met him were the stuff of which romance novels were made. No wonder she couldn't stop thinking about him, but stop she must.

She was delighted with the gift he sent and knew he had gone to a lot of trouble to find out her schedule and to order it. However, it was Richard she was going home to, and Richard who would meet her at the airport when she arrived back in Buffalo tomorrow night. He'd checked his schedule before she left and knew he wasn't flying, so he said he would pick her up.

Adam was simply a delightful pen pal, someone to whom she could pour out her problems. E-mailing him was as cathartic as writing in a journal, and almost as impersonal. She doubted that she would ever meet him. If, someday, she ever got to Hawaii he would probably be long gone, transferred to some improbable place like the Hong Kong hotel.

When Susan arrived back at Buffalo airport the next day, Richard wasn't there to meet her. Instead, she saw her sister, Trish, waving to her from behind the crowd at the baggage carousel,

Hugging Trish, she said, "Thanks for picking me up, Sis, but..."

"...but where's Richard?" Trish finished.

"He did offer to meet me."

"He called me from the airport last night," said Trish simply. "He said he was taking a flight out to Frankfurt and remembered at the last minute that he promised to meet you. Since you didn't have your car at the airport and would be expecting someone, I said I'd come get you."

"Thanks Sis." She grinned. "I hope you're feeling strong tonight. I went a little wild in the British wool shops, and my suitcases are full to bursting."

"In that case," said Trish thoughtfully, "maybe we'd better get a luggage cart."

"Pregnant!" screamed Susan, her face alight with joy at her sister's obvious happiness. "You're going to make me an auntie again." Impulsively, she leaned across the front seat of the car and hugged a beaming Trish.

49

Trish laughed. "Now I know why I didn't tell you this inside. It's bad enough that the whole parking lot can hear you; I don't think everyone in the airport needs to know."

"Somehow," said Susan thoughtfully, as they drove along the highway toward Tonawanda, "I never thought you'd have another child. Tommy is almost six, and after all that time I figured you'd called it quits."

"I thought so too. Ted and I always planned on having two children. That's why we had the boys so close together. But lately we've been thinking how much we'd love to have a little girl. Ted is especially eager. He says every father needs a little girl to spoil."

Susan shot her sister a troubled look. "I hate to mention it, but what if this one is also a boy?"

Trish reached over and patted her on the arm. "Don't worry, Suz," she said, using her old childhood nickname. "We won't throw him out with the bathwater. We'll love him as much as the other two, and definitely call it quits this time."

"You never did tell me when this baby's due."

"The first week in March. The worst possible week for one of Buffalo's famous winter storms." Trish shivered involuntarily. "Thank goodness we live less than a mile from the hospital."

Susan wasn't even fully unpacked when she sat down, cup of tea in hand, to write a message to Adam. The e-mail was quite long, telling about her trip to London, including a watered-down version of the radio DJ's pursuit of her, then returning home to the news of her sister's pregnancy and thanking him for the teacup and the corsage.

Dear Adam:

...and what amazed me most of all is how cognitive you are. How did you know that I'm a tea drinker? What you couldn't possibly know is that the first thing I do when I get home from work is make a pot of tea. If there's an e-mail from you I read it while I'm enjoying my first cup (or cuppa, as the British say). Reading your mail and drinking tea are

inexplicably linked in my mind, so your gift couldn't have been more appropriate....
Susan

Adam read the message with a smile on his face, well satisfied with the results of his impulsive e-mail a couple of weeks earlier to his friend in London.

He called the hotel kitchen and ordered a pot of tea. He re-read the message while sipping the tea.

Later that day he went down to the hotel gift shop and poked around the souvenirs until he found what he wanted, a pink and white teddy bear with a removable flowered lei around its neck.

A few days later a parcel arrived at Whispering Wood Lane on Grand Island addressed to: *Trish's Baby, c/o Susan Jeffrey.*

The next e-mail to arrive for adam@bayhotels.com from Buffalo was from Trish.

Dear Adam:

Thank you so much for the pink teddy bear. It now sits on the window sill in our empty fourth bedroom, soon to become a nursery. I'm leaving it there as a talisman in hope that the fates who decide such things will think that it is a little girl's bedroom and arrange things accordingly.

I don't know who you are or what you mean to my sister, but, thank you for that too. She's had a difficult time these last few years, and your e-mails always manage to bring a smile to her face....
Trish Macpherson

Adam read the message with mixed feelings. He was pleased that his e-mails made Susan happy and delighted that she thought enough of their correspondence to discuss him with her sister. However, the fact that Susan had a difficult time these last few years bothered him. She was always so upbeat in all her notes. Even when she wrote about problems in her office, it was only in passing and only after the problem had been solved.

51

He realized he didn't know anything about her life before she became a travel agent. He didn't even know if she had a family other than her sister Trish. A couple of times she mentioned a man named Richard, but he really had no idea how large a part this Richard played in her life.

It was time to ask some questions.

Susan sat at her kitchen table watching the squirrels in her backyard. The early October sun, already low in the sky, slanted through the trees giving the orange and yellow leaves of autumn a gilded look.

In her computer was a message she had just written to Adam. Re-reading it, she'd scrolled down through at least ten pages. She hadn't decided whether or not to send it. In this e-mail she'd bared her soul, telling Adam things she never shared with anyone else, some of them not even with Trish.

She told him about losing her parents in a car crash eight years ago when she was just twenty. She wrote about Trish, married only a short while and expecting her first child, opting to take the family home in Clarence, a suburb of Buffalo, as the major part of her inheritance. Although Trish told her she was welcome to live with them as long as she wanted, Susan felt out of place living with Trish and her husband, Ted. Shortly after Timmy was born, she moved out and used part of the insurance money she inherited as a down payment on her small house on Grand Island.

At first she missed her home terribly, almost as much as she missed her parents. For a while she even resented the fact that Trish had sole ownership of the house she'd always considered home. However, after a couple of summers living on Grand Island, she loved it so much she couldn't even consider living anywhere else.

She told Adam about investing the bulk of the money from her inheritance and living on the rest while she took the travel agents' course at Niagara Community College. She worked for a large travel agency for a couple of years and then, when the opportunity arose, used her inheritance to finance the opening of her own agency, Harbor Square Travel.

She very proudly told him that she'd owned her own agency for almost three years and made a profit almost from the beginning.

Then she told him about Richard. That was the hardest of all, but it actually helped to clarify her own thoughts. Trying to justify her relationship with Richard, putting it down on paper how she felt about him in the beginning and how she felt toward him recently, and helped to make up her mind about her future with him.

She still enjoyed going out with him and still considered him a good friend, but she knew she would never marry him. She didn't, however, tell Adam that, preferring him to think she was in a stable relationship.

Dear Adam:

....so that's the story of the life of Susan Jeffrey. Not very interesting, I'm afraid. I've arrived at the ripe old age of 28 unmarried, with a mortgage and a small business that is paying its way but will never make me rich. I haven't done anything special with my life.

What I really like to do is travel, and I'm lucky to have a job that lets me do that with very little strain on the budget.

I can't believe I've written as much as I have. It's gotten dark since I started this letter, and I'm on my second pot of tea. But now, turnabout is fair play. I want to know all about Adam Joffrey, your family, how you came to be in the hotel business and what wild and wonderful places you lived and worked before Hawaii.
Susan

Adam dropped heavily into his desk chair, exhausted after a long day of union negotiations. He flipped on his computer and sat up straight when he saw the message from Susan. Seeing the size of the file, he whistled to himself and temporarily saved it. He called the kitchen for a pot of tea. He would need some sustenance before he read this one.

He shook his head in disbelief when he came to the line, `I haven't done anything special with my life'. Here was a girl who was struck by the tragedy of her parents' deaths, then felt compelled to leave the home in which she'd grown up because it no longer belonged to her. Then she bounced back by going to college and eventually opening her own business doing a job she loved and was obviously good at.

He wondered what she would consider a special event in her life and rather hoped it would not involve one Richard Penrod the Third.

A week later, Adam spent most of one evening hunched in front of his computer. It had taken him several days of thinking before he replied to Susan's letter. Even then he was thankful for the computer's correcting abilities, because he did a lot of rewording before he was satisfied with what he wrote.

He sensed from the day he first spoke to her on the phone that he wanted to get to know Susan Jeffrey better. Most men in his position would have simply pressed the matter and found a way to meet her, but Adam was wary from experience.

His family was one of the richest in California, and he was often pursued by women who were more interested in his money than himself.

He wanted to pursue his relationship with Susan, but he wanted to do it as plain Adam Joffrey who worked his way up to his present position, not as the heir apparent to the Bay Hotel chain.

He did not, however, wish to deceive her, so he stuck to the truth...with certain deletions.

He told her about his childhood; what it was like growing up in San Francisco, learning to sail on the bay and spending his summers working as a caddy at a golf course in Monterey. He didn't tell her that his father was a member of the yacht club where he sailed, and was also a director of the exclusive golf club where he caddied and that he later became a member himself.

His family, he told her, were all hard workers, and some of them were also involved with the hotel business. His father had been a hotelier all his life, and Adam, having grown up in the business, made it his career. So had his brother, Chris, who was assistant manager of a hotel in Hong Kong. His mother was in the advertising business in San Francisco. He neglected to mention that she was a vice-president of the Bay Hotel Corporation with responsibilities for advertising and promotion. His sister, Beverly, and her husband ran a winery in the Napa Valley. Again, he neglected to mention it was one of the largest California wineries whose brand name she would be almost certain to recognize.

...as you can see, my mother belonged to the ABC school of naming children, Adam, Beverly, and Christopher. We once brought home a stray cat and named it Donald, saying that it was the natural progression of names in our family. My mother was not amused...!

Telling her about himself and his career was a little easier. He graduated from Berkeley with a degree in Business Administration, majoring in Hotel Management. He worked in hotels all over the US; New York, Chicago, Houston, Denver as well as San Francisco, and in two hotels in foreign countries, London and Frankfurt, before coming to Honolulu almost four years earlier.

...this is the longest I have ever been in one place, and I expect I'll be here awhile longer. I like Honolulu, and I seem to be doing a good job here, so hopefully, it will be a long stay. I hope to still be here when one Susan Jeffrey, of Harbor Square Travel, decides to visit Hawaii. When that happens, I'll pull some strings and see that she gets the best room in the house, ocean view, corner suite. The question is...when?
Adam

Those e-mail letters signaled a change in their relationship. Where before, Susan tried to be upbeat and interesting, she now wrote about what was troubling her and explored things she had never been able to talk about to Richard, or even Trish. She even asked Adam's advice about business, including a legal problem she was having with a client. He gave her such good advice about that problem that she was able to settle it without having to go to court.

It worked both ways. Based on her experience in London, she helped him plan a Murder Mystery Week at the Honolulu Bay Hotel to boost business in one of the slowest weeks of the year.

The first Friday in December, Susan thought fleetingly of the same day a year earlier when she ventured out in the ice storm. It was the day she had e-mailed the Honolulu Bay Hotel and received the phone call from Adam. Actually, it was the only time she'd talked to him. All their contacts since had been by e-mail. She wondered if he remembered.

He did.

Shortly before she was ready to go home, Jacey arrived in her office carrying an exotic Japanese-looking flower arrangement. The center flower was the stately Hawaiian flower the Anthurium, flanked by two splashy Bird of Paradise flowers. Long spiky green leaves and an interesting piece of driftwood completed the arrangement in a low flat ceramic bowl.

"It's that sexy-voiced man again," said Jacey. "The one who sent you the crystal bowl last spring." When Susan just sat there, staring at the flowers, she prompted her, "You know, the Hawaiian."

"Oh, I know who you mean," said Susan softly. "I should have known he wouldn't forget. I'm overwhelmed. I've never seen such beautiful flowers. Jacey, you've outdone yourself this time."

"I didn't have much choice in the matter. He called about two weeks ago so I'd be sure to have the correct flowers in stock. Then he followed it up with an e-mail and attached a picture describing exactly what he wanted and what time he wanted it delivered."

Susan gasped as she looked at the clock, and the significance of the time dawned on her. Just a year ago, it had been five minutes before five o'clock when she answered the phone and heard Adam's voice for the first time.

Adam was so much on her mind all day Saturday that she almost forgot she was having dinner with Richard. Richard called her earlier in the week and suggested dinner tonight. She hadn't really wanted to go, because she was always so tired by the time she finished working on Saturday, but he insisted, saying he was going to be out of town for a while.

She imagined he was going to tell her that he wouldn't be around for Christmas and New Years. As he hadn't been around during the holidays for either of the past two years, she intended to tell him it was no big deal.

He arrived promptly at seven carrying a bouquet of long-stemmed roses. As she arranged them in a vase and set them on the dining room table, she glanced guiltily at Adam's Hawaiian arrangement in the place of honor on the coffee table. Richard didn't even notice it, even though he dropped his driving gloves on the table almost touching the ceramic dish.

Susan had a strange premonition as she finished arranging the roses and added water. Richard almost never brought her flowers, and she couldn't help wondering what prompted them today. Probably, she thought uncharitably, they were to soften her up for whatever bad news he had this time. She had a feeling this was no ordinary dinner date.

She was even surer of this when he announced a few minutes later that they should be going, because he had made reservations for eight o'clock at Justine's.

Justine's, in the Buffalo Hilton Hotel, was one of the city's finest dining rooms, very conservative and very elegant, and not the type of place she and Richard usually frequented.

He was very distracted. Twice she tried to talk to him in the car, but his mumbled responses showed his mind was obviously elsewhere. Finally she gave up, and they drove the rest of the way in silence.

It was a beautiful, clear, cold night when they arrived at the restaurant, a definite contrast from the stormy early December of a year earlier. They were led to a high-walled private booth at the rear of the room. The soft plush seats in the curtained alcove and the muted music playing were made for seduction. Somehow, she didn't think that was what Richard had in mind.

The waiter came, and Richard ordered a bottle of her favorite German white wine. Susan's eyebrows shot up. He was being extra nice to her tonight. She wondered what was up and when she would find out. After three years, she knew Richard well enough to know something was wrong.

They finished their main courses and were scanning the dessert menu when Richard abruptly passed the menu back and said, "We'll just have coffee."

Susan settled back in the seat and waited. She was about to find out whatever was on Richard's mind.

When their coffee came, he made an elaborate ritual of adding cream and stirring. Then he said, so softly that she wasn't sure for a moment she'd heard him, "Susan, I'm getting married."

Her heart lurched, and for one crazy moment she thought he was proposing to her. Then she realized he'd said "I" and not "we". She shook her head in disbelief and opened her mouth to say something, but nothing came out.

"I'm sorry to spring it on you like this. I've spent the past few weeks agonizing over how best to tell you, but I guess there's really no easy way to say it."

"Who?" Her voice sounded in her ears like a squeaky croak, but, if Richard noticed, he gave no sign.

"Her name is Birgit. She's a flight attendant for Lufthansa."

"When?" Susan wracked her brain for a sentence longer than one word but couldn't find any.

"Between Christmas and New Years." He smiled wryly. "I can use the tax break."

"How long?" *Good*, she thought, *that's two words. An improvement, at least.*

"How long?" he repeated, frowning. "You mean how long have I known her?" Susan nodded. "We met last New Year's Eve at a ski resort in Switzerland."

Susan looked down at her coffee, now cooling rapidly, and remembered how lonely she had been last Christmas and New Years. She'd consoled herself then by thinking that

Richard made a sacrifice by flying the long-hauls over the holidays and giving a married pilot the chance to spend Christmas with his family.

Then she remembered how he had come back in January and they drifted back into their old relationship. Her fist clenched as it lay on the tabletop.

Richard reached across to hold her hand but instead caught his sleeve on the handle of the cream jug and overturned it. As the cream spilled across the tabletop, spreading under the centerpiece and toward her side of the table, Susan picked up her napkin and dropped it in the mess, then stood up abruptly.

"I'd like to go home," she said, suddenly getting her voice back. "It appears this evening is over."

CHAPTER 4

At three a.m., after lying awake for hours, Susan finally gave up on sleep and got out of bed. The furnace was turned down for the night and the house was cold, so she wrapped herself in a warm quilted robe and put on a pair of fuzzy slippers. She made a pot of tea and sat at the kitchen table watching the snow blowing underneath the streetlight.

Then she started replaying the evening in her mind and recalling incidents from the past few weeks to see if there were any warning signs. She couldn't find any.

She spent some time explaining the evening to herself and finally realized she was doing the explaining to someone else in her mind, and that someone was Adam. Somehow, she thought he would understand. Actually, she didn't really care if he understood. She just needed to tell someone.

She made another pot of tea, and sat down at the computer.

Her fingers flew across the keyboard, her thoughts twining themselves around her grief and anger. *Oh, Adam, I wish you were here,* she thought. *This is what friends are for.*

She told him about the three years with Richard: the bad things; his working over Christmas and spending New Years on a skiing holiday, leaving her alone, his constant traveling and never being there when she needed him, and most of all, his reluctance to make a commitment. To be fair she also told him about the good times; how much fun he was to be with, the great parties he gave, and his reasons for working most holidays.

Then she told him what happened that evening, about Richard's elaborately staged farewell dinner.

Dear Adam:

. . .and I think I'm most upset by the fact that it had gone on for almost a year. Since last Christmas, eleven months ago, he's been seeing that woman at every opportunity; at least enough to fall in love and make plans to marry, and never said a word to me. He would never make a commitment to me, because he always said he wasn't

interested in marriage as long as his job took him away from home so much. Yet he made a commitment to her.

I'm not upset, darn it, I'm angry. The more I think about it, the angrier I become. I am also furious, livid, and fast working myself into a rage.

How could he do this to me?

I just made another pot of tea. It's my third since three a.m., and it's almost six now. I think I'm calming down a little. A year from now maybe I'll look back on this and laugh. Maybe I'll even laugh at it a month from now.

I'm beginning to wonder if I'm so upset (angry, livid, furious...whatever) because Richard was the one to end it, not me.

If that's so, maybe I'm not a very nice person.

Oh Adam, I'm sorry to dump on you like this, but I really needed to get it off my chest. I have half a mind not to send it at all, but I probably will. After all, what are pen pals for? What an archaic name, pen pals. Cyberspace pals, maybe? Or simply cyber pals. I'm sure I don't know how to describe us.

Read it and delete it!
Susan

He didn't delete it.

Adam sat for a long time re-reading before he saved it. He felt her pain in every line. He wanted to phone her, he wanted to send her an enormous bouquet of flowers to cheer her up, and at one point he even considered calling the airlines and going to her...that night. Even as he reached for the phone, however, he knew that none of those things was the right thing to do. She had to work it out for herself. To her, he was a pen pal, nothing more. She said so herself.

So he would do the expected thing and e-mail her back.

He wrote what he hoped were all the right things. He sympathized, he commiserated, and he told her she really was a very nice lady, that what she was thinking was normal under the circumstances. He told her that, from his experience, the best antidote was work. He warned her about not getting involved with someone else right away on the rebound. He wondered if it was himself he was thinking about, not her.

Then he told her about Liana.

My Dear Susan:

. . .and it came to me as I was writing this message, that an amazing coincidence is involved here. Liana sailed out of my life with Michael Dodd the same day you came into my life.

I remember talking to you on the phone and being intrigued by that sexy voice of yours. I thought about you so much that day that I almost forgot my date with Liana that evening.

I wished afterward that I had forgotten it. Once she saw Dodd she never really looked at me again. So you see, I do know how you feel. Your experience was private, at least. Liana dumped me in the most public way possible, in front of about three hundred of our friends and acquaintances.

So take it from me, life goes on. And yes, you will laugh about it. Sooner than you think.

Merry Christmas!
Adam

The message from Adam cheered her immensely, especially the salutation. *My Dear Susan* he wrote; not just *Dear Susan,* but *My Dear Susan.*

She spent Christmas with Trish and her family. Trish, six months pregnant and not as light on her feet as usual, was grateful for the help with Christmas dinner and the planning for a New Year's Eve party. Susan suspected the party was more for her benefit than Trish's.

A friend of Ted's, a lawyer with whom his firm did business, was attentive to Susan at the New Year's party. He sat with her at dinner, kept her wine glass full, danced with her most of the evening, and kissed her at midnight. The next morning she couldn't even remember his name.

The winter slid by quietly. It was one of Buffalo's mildest winters on record. Susan hardly noticed. She lived for her work and Adam's e-mails.

On Valentine's Day a parcel arrived in Susan's office delivered by Express Courier. In the parcel was an exquisite porcelain cookie jar with a design of cupids and hearts around the rim and on the cover. Inside the jar was a small box of chocolate-covered macadamia nuts, a bag of chopped nuts and a recipe for macadamia nut cookies. The card read: *"Tea and Cookies go together, Love Adam."*

Susan was stunned. This was the first time he'd signed anything with *love*. Was he really feeling something for her despite the distance between them, or was it just a convenient greeting for Valentine's?

She took out one of the chocolate-covered nuts and popped it into her mouth, closing her eyes as she savored it. Susan always contended that if heaven had a taste it would taste like chocolate. She amended that. If heaven had a taste it would taste like chocolate and macadamia.

The Saturday after Valentine's Day Trish called her just before noon.

"Hi, Suz. How would you like company for dinner tonight?"

"I'd love it, as long as I don't have to cook."

Trish laughed. "I thought you'd say that, so I had already decided to pick up Chinese."

"I thought Ted didn't like Chinese."

"He doesn't. Ted isn't coming tonight. It'll be just us girls, so we can sit and talk for hours if we like. Timmy is playing in a Tiny Tykes hockey tournament this afternoon and Ted and Tommy are going to watch. Afterwards they're going with a few other players and their Dads to eat at McDonalds. I thought I'd drive out to the Niagara Outlet Mall and pick up a few last-minute things I need for the baby, then stop by your place on the way back. With the Chinese, of course."

"Just make sure you get a double order of garlic spare ribs. I love the stuff, and I've got no one to breathe on for a couple of days."

"You're on!"

"Wait a minute, Trish. Are you sure you should be driving now? Can you still fit behind the wheel?"

"Just barely. The seat belt has to be quite snug around my middle so the steering wheel can turn freely. But I have another three weeks to go, and I don't intend to be housebound all that time. So I'll just keep driving as long as I can."

"Be careful then."

"Don't worry, Suz, I'll be careful. This is precious cargo I'm carrying."

When Susan arrived home after work Trish was already there. The Chinese food was warming in the oven, and Trish had lit a fire. She was sitting on the sofa with her feet up, nursing a glass of soda water, and on the coffee table in front of her was a tray of cheese and crackers. On the kitchen table was a plate of homemade brownies.

Susan stood in the doorway taking in the scene. "I just realized what's missing in my life. I need a wife."

"Not a husband?"

"Nope, a wife. I'm a businesswoman, remember? I need someone to come home to, someone who'll cook and look after me, someone who'll take my clothes to the cleaners and bake me brownies and be waiting by the fire with a drink. And, at the present time, I've sworn off men."

Trish heard the pain in her sister's voice and, perhaps for the first time, realized how lonely Susan was and how much Richard's marriage affected her.

"Well," she said, "being a wife is something I'm good at. Next to being a mother, it's probably what I do best. Right now I'm yours for the evening. So get yourself a drink, sit down, and put your feet up and tell me about your day."

"If you were a really good wife you'd get me a drink." Susan bantered.

"If I weren't almost eight and a half months pregnant, I would." She reached down and patted the mound in front of her. "Right now I plead my belly and blame your soft sofa. I think it's going to take a block and tackle to get me out of here."

Susan poured a glass of wine and stretched out in the opposite corner of the sofa. "Here's to you," she said, lifting her glass. "Judging by the smells coming from the kitchen, you're a pretty good wife, even if you aren't mine. And here's to that bundle you're carrying. I'm getting pretty anxious to be an auntie again."

"Not half as anxious as I am. I don't seem to have the energy this time that I had before. I was in my early twenties when I had the two boys, and it was a piece of cake, but I'm finding that having another baby at thirty-one is a different story."

"You're all right though, aren't you Sis?" asked Susan anxiously. "I mean, there's nothing wrong, is there?"

"No, of course not. It's just that I haven't the energy to do much. I tire easily. At the mall today I couldn't walk more than ten minutes before sitting for a rest. Also, I swear this baby is sitting right on my bladder. Between resting and running to the bathroom, I got hardly any shopping done."

Susan sat for a few moments staring into the fire. "What you just said makes me aware that my biological clock is ticking away relentlessly. Here I am twenty-eight years old, twenty-nine in a few months, and I've got no prospects. I've just ended a three-year relationship that's kept me out of circulation for so long that I don't know any single men anymore. Even if I met Mr. Right tomorrow, assuming a normal courtship period and a nine-month pregnancy, I'd be thirty-one when my *first* child is born."

Trish fished the lime slice out of her soda water and bit into it. "Forgive me for changing the subject, but how is Adam these days?"

Susan smiled indulgently at her sister. "I don't believe for a minute that was a subject change. For your information, my dear Sis, Adam is not one of my prospects."

"Then why do you get all soft and gooey-eyed when you say his name? How come he sends you expensive cookie jars and chocolate-covered macadamia nuts? Which, incidentally, I haven't had the privilege of tasting."

"OK, OK, I saved you one. I knew I'd never hear the end of it if I didn't. And I do not get `all soft and gooey-eyed' as

65

you so graphically put it. Adam is a very special friend who has done his best to help me keep my sanity these past few months. But he's just a pen pal, someone I e-mail when I'm lonely. There couldn't possibly be anything between us. He lives in Hawaii, half a world away, and loves it. I live in Buffalo and own a business with employees depending on me. From reading between the lines and from what Betsy Braddock told me, I gather he's a handsome playboy who likes to take out rich and beautiful women. He certainly can't be very well off with the job he has, so maybe he's looking for a rich wife. I'm not rich, and he knows it, so that puts me out of the running."

Trish's eyebrows shot up. "That was quite a speech. Methinks you protesteth too much. What I'd really like to know, is how you feel about him. But I think I smell cardboard burning. If we don't eat soon everything will be dried out, especially that double order of garlic spare ribs."

As they ate at the kitchen table by the window it started to snow. Large wet flakes drifted down and stuck, swiftly piling up in the corners of the window. Susan, gazing out, thought idly that her backyard would look nice tomorrow with the fresh snow down.

The two sisters talked late into the evening in front of the fire, neither noticing how much snow was coming down. Trish finally looked up and glanced at her watch when a heavy gust of wind rattled the windows.

"Oh my, I hadn't realized how late it is. I'd better get going."

The phone rang. Susan answered it. "Hi Ted. Yes, she's still here." She passed the phone to Trish. "It's Ted."

Trish's eyes widened as she talked to her husband, and Susan gathered from her side of the conversation that Ted was telling her to stay the night.

Trish confirmed this when she hung up. "Ted just got home and was upset that I wasn't home yet. He said the roads are terrible. It took them over two hours to get home from the hockey rink. The airport is closed, and the roads around the open areas have huge drifts. He was glad I was still here and wasn't stuck on the highway somewhere. So, Sis, I guess you've got a houseguest for the night."

While Trish cleaned up the kitchen and stacked the dishes in the dishwasher, Susan put fresh sheets on the bed in the spare bedroom and found a cotton granny nightie that was full enough to fit her sister.

Neither of them was sleepy, so they got ready for bed, then curled up together under a blanket on the sofa to watch the late news on TV, much as they used to do when they were teenagers and were minding the house while their parents played bridge at a neighbor's..

Susan made hot chocolate while they watched the news. Trish drank hers despite her comments that she really shouldn't drink anymore, that she was already wearing a path to the bathroom.

Trish was sitting cross legged on the sofa with a pillow behind her back. "I think the baby has dropped even lower in the past few days. My bladder has squished to the capacity of a teaspoon. Thank goodness it's only three more weeks."

"Susan." Then a few seconds later she heard again, "Susan!" She came awake with a start as she recognized Trish's voice and felt her shoulder being violently shaken. Squinting at the clock radio on her bedside table, she saw it was 3:10. Trish was standing beside her bed with the bottom of the cotton nightie bunched between her legs.

"Susan? Are you awake? I just got up to go to the bathroom and my water broke."

Susan was on her feet in a flash. "My God, Trish. Are you sure?"

Trish smiled thinly. "Take a look at your bathroom floor, and you'll know how sure I am. I'm just going to call Ted and ask him to come get me, but I thought I'd wake you first."

"Call Ted and tell him what's happened, but don't ask him to come. I'll drive you to the hospital, and he can meet us there." While Trish phoned her husband, Susan swiftly dressed in jeans and a warm sweater and went looking for something for Trish to wear. She found a fleece-lined sweat suit in a drawer. The pants had a drawstring waist, and the top was large and long. It would have to do.

She found Trish next to the phone, doubled over clutching her stomach. She'd just hung up when the first pain struck. Swiftly, Susan helped her sister out of the soaked nightie and into the warm sweat suit, then put heavy socks and slippers on her feet.

"Ted said to take the Envoy, not your car, because there may be drifting on the road." Ted had taken Trish's minivan to the hockey tournament, because it easily held all the hockey gear, so Trish had driven to the mall and then on to Susan's house in Ted's 4-wheel drive.

They were just going out the door when the phone rang. Susan rushed back and picked it up. It was Ted, sounding almost hysterical.

"I just found out the bridge on the I-90 between Buffalo and Grand Island is closed. A transport truck overturned on the approach and blocked all three lanes. Don't leave yet until I find you an alternate route. I'll call the police and ask them."

They came back inside, a white-faced Trish sitting on a kitchen chair just inside the door. She was bundled in a blanket against the cold but her teeth still chattered.

She was having pains every five minutes.

A few minutes later Ted called back. "The police say most of the side roads are impassable. The only one plowed is the I-90. I just talked to Trish's doctor, and he says to take the I-90 in the other direction off Grand Island and go to the hospital in Niagara Falls. He'll call ahead, so they'll be expecting you." He paused, and Susan thought she heard a sound like a sob or a hiccup, but when he spoke again his voice was controlled. "Susan, the Envoy's got four-wheel drive, so you should be able to get through almost anything. Just drive slowly and be careful." He paused again. "Oh, hell, I'm scared witless. Just tell Trish I love her, and I'll be there as soon as I can." Abruptly, he hung up.

Susan stared at the dead phone for a minute, bemused. She had never heard her calm, laid-back brother-in-law in such a panic before, but she supposed he had never been in a situation that was so out of his control before.

She started the SUV and brought it as close to the door as possible, only then realizing how deep the snow was.

With Trish, still wrapped in the blanket, safely belted into the car, they started down the street. Susan drove slowly for the first while until she became accustomed to the larger vehicle.

The snow was deep on Whispering Wood Lane, but the Envoy easily drove through it. On Whitehaven Road leading to the I-90 it was more difficult. In the open areas the road was blown clear of snow, but in some places waist-high drifts angled across the road. Susan had to drive carefully around them, sometimes not even sure she was on the road.

Occasionally she heard Trish draw in a breath sharply and shift uncomfortably on the seat, so she knew the pains were still coming steadily. Her own arms were beginning to ache from fighting the car in the drifts.

Finally they came to the highway, and Susan swung on to it, relieved when she saw it had been plowed. She picked up speed and, for the first time, really felt they were going to make it.

As they drove down one slippery hill, the car started sliding toward the edge that dropped off sharply. Struggling to keep the car on the road, Susan swung the wheel sharply and gunned the motor. The Envoy wheeled over too fast to control it; sideswiped one snow bank piled up by the plow, and came to rest in another.

The impact threw Trish forward against the seat belt, and she started to cry.

Susan opened the door and stepped out into the icy wind that almost blew her off her feet. The left front tire was flat. She felt like crying, too, but realized there was too much at stake here for her to lose control. Her sister's life, and that of her unborn baby, was in her hands. She was totally responsible. At this hour there was no one traveling on the road, in either direction. She tried calling AAA on her cell phone, but all she got was a recorded voice, "All our operators are busy." There didn't appear to be any help coming from anywhere.

Fortunately, the experience of living so far out of town and owning an old car long ago taught her how to change a tire. Changing the tire was a long, slow job, with almost-frozen fingers and the blizzard raging around her, but she got it done.

They were in open country, and the road was clear, so they covered the next few miles swiftly.

Shortly before the turnoff to the hospital there were more drifts across the road. They were impossible to go around, so Susan gunned the motor and rammed the car through. One drift was deeper than she thought, and the car slammed to a halt. Both of them were thrown forward violently.

Trish, who had been whimpering softly, started to sob and thrash her head from side to side. Between sobs, Susan heard her talking to herself.

"I'm sorry, Baby, I'm sorry. I know I should have stayed home. Hang in there, kid...please, baby. Oh, it hurts!"

Susan rocked the car out of the drift, and this time, going slowly, she was able to get through it. The exit that led to the hospital was just a few yards away, and she turned gratefully into it.

Trish suddenly slid forward in the seat, her legs sticking straight out in front of her. "Susan," she rasped. "Hurry, the baby's coming."

Susan stepped on the gas and leaned the car heavily into the next corner. There was a bang and a hard jerk on the wheel as the spare tire she'd just put on, blew out. She used almost her last reserve of strength to keep the car from going off the road.

Dejected, she put her head down on the steering wheel, feeling like crying herself.

Trish started screaming and banging her fist on her sister's arm. "Hurry! Hurry!" Susan jerked the car into gear and hurtled down the road without even thinking about the flat tire. She saw the hospital lights about two blocks away.

As she turned into the hospital drive, the SUV gave a heavier lurch, and a piece of rubber from the tire hit the windshield. They were riding on the rim alone.
Just as she pulled up to the emergency entrance there was a ringing metallic sound and Susan looked up to see the wheel rim weaving across the hospital lawn through the snow.

The front of the Envoy crunched down on the axle and stayed there.

Later, when Susan looked back on that moment, some things would be crystal clear, and others would be fuzzy and indistinct. She remembered the wheel rim rolling across the snow. She remembered the dawn lightening the sky to a pale pink and realizing that the snow had stopped. The commotion as Trish was lifted from the car onto a stretcher was rather vague. Someone was asking her questions, but she didn't remember answering them. All she felt was an overwhelming relief that she'd gotten there in time and the actual delivering of Trish's baby was someone else's responsibility.

She pulled herself out of the car and, on shaking, rubbery legs, walked into the hospital. A nurse was just coming out of an examining room with a big smile on her face.

"Are you Susan? Congratulations! Your sister just had a baby girl. Two and a half minutes later and you wouldn't have made it."

Susan's legs abruptly gave way. She was thankful there was a chair right beside her.

Dear Adam:

. . .and as much as I love Trish's two boys, I'm very sure that this baby will be extra special to me. I was so physically exhausted and emotionally wrung out after that wild ride to the hospital that I almost felt as if I had given birth to her myself. They've even given her my name. She was only an hour old, and her Daddy hadn't even seen her yet, when Trish told me she was naming her Jennifer Susan.

We've already decided that when she's old enough to understand, some snowy February night on her birthday, we're going to tell her the story of the night she was born. We're betting it will become her favorite story.

It will probably still give me the shivers even then. I can still hardly believe I was only two and a half minutes away from being the midwife at my niece's birth. I'm not sure I could have coped. Trish says I would have, but I'm eternally thankful I wasn't put to the test.

I suppose in your land of perpetual sunshine it's a little hard to imagine battling blizzards and snowdrifts and taking over two hours to drive fifteen miles.

Thinking back, I don't know how Trish stood it. I was exhausted and worried, and yes, terrified, but Trish was all those things and had the pain to cope with as well. She claims she was confident all along that I'd get her there in time, but I think she was a little shaken at how close it was.

Susan

P.S. I had saved Trish one chocolate-covered macadamia nut, (all I was willing to part with) and took it to her in the hospital the next day. She thinks they taste like heaven too.

Adam smiled when he saw the e-mail in his inbox. Because it was an attachment and not just a note he could see it was one of her "marathon letters." Some of Susan's e-mails were short and hurried, but every couple of months she would sit down and write page after page in word processing and then just attach it. Usually she wrote a "marathon" after something momentous happened. He recalled the e-mail after her trip to London and the one after Richard left.

He wondered what happened in her life now to warrant this letter and hoped it was a happy occurrence. He felt a frisson of apprehension and hoped it wasn't an occurrence that involved a man.

By the time he finished the e-mail, Adam's hands were shaking, he had paled under his tan, and the back of his shirt was soaked with sweat. He had been with her in imagination every mile of that stormy, dangerous trip. He was terrified for her, and his heart ached at the thought of what might have happened if they had gone off the road.

Susan verbalized her fear mainly of the possibility of having to deliver her sister's baby by herself. Adam's fear centered instead on the hazardous road conditions and the risk to their lives if they had gone off the road in the storm.

"You're one gutsy lady, my Susan," he said to himself.

Later that day he left the hotel and walked down the street toward the new International Marketplace. He tried to restrain himself when it came to buying Susan gifts, sending her things only on special occasions like the anniversary of the day they first spoke on the phone and, more recently, on Valentine's Day. He could afford to buy her anything he wanted to, but he didn't want to jeopardize their special relationship. For the first time in his life a woman was relating to him simply as Adam, not as Adam Joffrey, heir to the Bay Hotel chain. He didn't want to tempt fate.

This, however, was an extra special occasion, and he wanted the gift to match the event.

What he really wanted to send both Susan and her sister were medals for bravery, and he finally thought of the perfect gift. He would send them each a shark's tooth. In Hawaiian history, only the bravest warriors were allowed to wear a shark's tooth. The tooth was earned by an act of bravery above and beyond what was expected of them.

He went to a little jewelry store he had done business with before. Peter Lee, the owner, came out from behind the counter to greet him.

"Mr. Joffrey, it's nice to see you again. What can my shop offer you today?"

Adam explained what he was looking for. Peter nodded gravely and said, "I think I have what you're looking for. It just came in yesterday and is not on display yet."

He brought out a matched pair of shark's teeth that had been made into earrings. They were set in gold and hung from gold rings, and the sharp serrated edges of the teeth had been dipped in gold to outline them and to blunt their edges. He removed the earring hoops and replaced them with tiny rings, then threaded a gold chain through each one making two perfectly matched pendants.

They were exactly what Adam wanted, so he asked Peter to gift wrap them.

While they were being wrapped, he glanced idly around the store. His eyes lit up when he saw a display of children's jewelry. There, with the tiny gold hearts and initials, was a little white fish tooth hung on a delicate chain. It wasn't a shark's

73

tooth, but it was a real tooth. He imagined little Jennifer Susan wearing it and someday asking her mother where it came from.

A smiling Adam walked out the door a few minutes later with three gift wrapped parcels.

The parcel arrived by Express Courier at the office, like the last one, late in the afternoon. Inside were two identical gift wrapped boxes with cards, one read *Susan* and the other *Trish.* A third, very tiny, box in the same gift paper read *Baby Jenny.* Underneath these was a larger box that rattled interestingly when shaken. Its card read: *For everyone except Jenny Sue.*

A note on hotel stationery, tucked between the gifts, was stapled to a page torn from a tourist information brochure.

For the two most courageous ladies I know, and, of course, little Jenny Sue, the cause of all the fuss.

Shame on you, Susan, for only saving your sister one piece of chocolate macadamia. You have my permission, Trish, to claim ownership of half this box.
Love Adam.

Susan's eyes lit up at the news that the large box was chocolate-covered macadamia nuts. She could hardly wait to sample them. She picked up the brochure page and read the story Adam circled. It was a story of the ancient Hawaiian custom of the king hanging a shark's tooth around the neck of the bravest warrior following a battle.

She read the note again and shook her head in amazement at the name Jenny Sue. Trish started calling the baby Jennifer and then shortened it to Jenny, but Susan called her Jenny Sue right from the beginning. It touched her that Adam chose that contraction of her name as well.

She glanced at the clock and reached for the phone.

"Hi Trish. If you're going to be home, I thought I'd drop by with a couple of gifts."

"Where else would I be with a two-week-old baby who's breastfeeding every two hours?" grumbled Trish good-naturedly. "And please don't buy her any more gifts, Suz, you're spoiling her."

"Nonsense, Trish. How can I spoil her that young?"

"Well, it's never too early to instill good habits."

Susan laughed. "Relax Sis. These gifts aren't from me. In fact, one of them is *for* me. There's also one for you and one for Jenny Sue."

"Jenny Sue?"

"That's what he calls her."

"He?"

"Adam. The gifts are from Adam."

"Adam sent baby gifts? Susan, I think you're reading that man wrong. You called him a playboy, but buying a baby gift is a very thoughtful and domesticated thing to do." She paused for a moment. "Did you say there's also a gift for you and me?"

"That's right." Susan laughed. "But I wouldn't get too excited if I were you. I think he's sent us a couple of shark's teeth on a thong as medals for bravery." Then almost as an afterthought she teased, "Oh yes, he's also sent a huge box of chocolate-covered macadamia nuts."

"Chocolate covered macadamia nuts!" shrilled Trish. "Susan Jeffrey, don't you dare open them before you get here. I want at least two out of this box, and the only way I can do that is to get mine first."

Susan laughed and hung up after saying she would be there in half an hour.

"Susan," said Trish in an awed voice, as she looked at the pendant she held in her hand. "This is exquisite. And to think there are two of them, exactly alike. Do you have any idea how much they must have cost? They're set in 14KT gold and the chains are the same."

"I know," said Susan quietly with a remote look in her blue eyes. "Even Jenny Sue's necklace is real gold. Who would give a baby gold jewelry?"

"Not a poor reservations clerk, that's for sure. Are you sure he's really who he says he is, that he hasn't misrepresented himself to you?"

Susan sighed. "Right now I'm not sure of anything. He was a res clerk when I first talked to him a year and a half ago, but he may have been promoted since. He has never mentioned getting a promotion, but he may have gotten one in the four months between the time I first spoke to him and when we started to write."

"From what you say, he seems to move in social circles that are far beyond even the means of an assistant manager. You say he belongs to a yacht club and spends his weekends sailing and scuba diving. That kind of lifestyle wouldn't leave much room in the budget for expensive gifts or grand gestures. And he seems to be a master of the grand gesture."

"He sure is," said Susan fervently, as she fastened the pendant around her neck. "And I've loved every one of them."

The correspondence between Susan and Adam was very sporadic throughout the spring and early summer. When Adam did e-mail he mentioned being very busy, that this was a record year for tourism in Hawaii.

Susan was also very busy. She thought it was a record year for tourism anywhere. Everybody seemed to be going somewhere. She managed to get a week away by herself, but even that was partly business.

A local seniors' club, during the winter, asked her to speak at one of their monthly meetings. One of the travel benefits she told them about was the savings in traveling as a group and the fact that a large group could qualify for the services of an escort. An escort, she told them, could look after all the troubling details of luggage handling, dinner reservations, and sightseeing tours. Many seniors would travel only when there was an escort.

Several weeks later a spokesman for the club called and asked Susan if she would arrange a bus tour through northern Ontario, including a train trip to James Bay on the Polar Bear Express. On the return trip they would like to spend a couple of days in Toronto and attend a play or a concert.

As this was not a packaged tour but one she was planning from scratch, Susan wanted to personally drive the route and choose the hotels. Early in June she took a week off and drove through Ontario. Her business took only a couple of days, so she spent the rest of the time just relaxing.

One very short message from Adam said he was going to San Francisco to be Best Man at the wedding of his brother Chris.

Then a postcard arrived from San Francisco with a picture of the Golden Gate Bridge partially covered in fog.

Then a postcard from London.

...and another from Paris.

...and another from Frankfurt.

...and another from Rome.

They all had a picture on the front of the Bay hotel in that city.

Susan imagined Adam travelling from city to city, taking advantage of his employee discount to stay at the first-class Bay Hotels. She wondered if he had bought a Eurail Pass. If he'd mentioned his trip to her, she would have recommended it as the most economical way to travel Europe.

She hoped he was having a good time but felt a little envious. She also felt a little sad, because she felt their relationship, such as it was, was waning.

By early September she hadn't heard from him, except for the postcards, in over two months.

Then came an e-mail with a San Francisco domain name.

Dear Susan:

It seems like ages since I've written to you or heard from you. I have been in Europe for the past six weeks, moving from city to city and hotel to hotel until I sometimes forgot which one I was in.

I hadn't really intended to do that, but while I was home for my brother's wedding, my father, at the request of the Board of Directors, asked me to go to London on business. There had been a fraud problem at the London Bay Hotel, and they needed someone with a business degree and hotel experience to put the books in order. I was happy to do it as I hadn't had a vacation in a couple of years and thought I *would do some traveling on the continent while I was there. I might have known they wouldn't let me get away with it. The Board suggested that I take a day or two at each hotel and check the books to make sure that what occurred in London was not occurring in the others.*

So, of my six weeks in Europe, I had less than two weeks on my own. I enjoyed the trip, but, for the first time while traveling, I was lonely. It would have been nice to share it with someone. It would have been nice to share it with you.

I envy my brother Chris. He and his new wife, Anne, are very much in love. They had a month-long honeymoon in my suite at the Honolulu Bay Hotel before heading back to Hong Kong. He'll probably be there for at least another year.

It seems that Chris and I have more in common than we thought. We are both long distance writers. He and Anne were friends in college and started e-mailing each other when he was transferred to Hong Kong. Their romance had been mostly long distance. Our mother says it's a family trait. She writes to friends all over the world. Only she uses a pen and paper, not a computer keyboard.

I'm writing this on my father's computer. Tomorrow I head back to Honolulu and work again. . .
Adam

Susan was overjoyed to receive another message from Adam, not just to hear from him but the fact that he missed hearing from her.

She was, however, more confused than ever about Adam and his position in the hotel. She knew he had a business degree in hotel management but presumed it was a community college course like her travel agent's course. Now she realized he had a university degree in business and accounting. What was a man with those qualifications doing working as a reservations clerk?

Then he mentioned that his *father* asked him to go to London to audit the books. His father must be an executive with the Bay Hotel chain. If the Board of Directors approved his auditing the books in London and the other cities, they must trust his ability. Why then didn't they give him a better job in the corporation?

It was all very confusing and very mysterious. She felt there was something she was missing.

A couple of weeks later she was awakened early on the morning of her birthday by the ringing phone. She covered her head and tried to ignore it, but the ringing persisted, so finally she reached over and pulled it into the bed with her. Glancing at the clock she saw it was just seven o'clock.

"Hello," she muttered sleepily, certain it was Trish or one of her boys on the other end of the line.

"Good morning, birthday girl," said a sexy, husky voice.

Susan's eyes flew open, and she sat bolt upright in bed, wide awake. She hadn't heard that voice in two years, but she recognized it in an instant.

"Adam," she breathed.

Adam laughed delightedly. "So you did recognize my voice. I wondered if you would."

"I've never forgotten it," she said, in her sleep-befuddled state not realizing what that admission implied.

Adam caught the implication, and his heart leaped.

"I really missed your e-mails this summer," he said gravely," and I really missed writing to you. When I noticed the date earlier today and realized that tomorrow is your birthday, I just got the urge to talk to you." He laughed. "But I guess it's now today, isn't it?"

Susan laughed with him. "It's a very early today, seven a.m. to be exact. That makes it, let me see, one o'clock in the morning in Honolulu. You haven't been to bed yet, I take it."

"No, it's still last night here. I don't usually stay up this late on a weeknight, but I stayed up tonight so I could catch you before you went to work."

They talked for a few more minutes before Adam brought up what was really on his mind.

"Susan, you and I have been writing for almost two years. I've enjoyed it, but I think it's time we changed our relationship."

Susan's throat constricted painfully, and she couldn't have said anything if she wanted to. *Oh, Adam,* she thought, *why did you pick today to tell me you wanted to end it? Why couldn't you have just written me a "Dear Jane" message? Then I could have cried in private.*

"I think it's time," Adam went on, "that you and I meet face to face."

Susan expelled a long-held breath and fell back on the pillow, a grin lighting up her face.

"Susan?" said Adam anxiously, "are you still there?"

"I'm still here, Adam," she said, trying to keep the delight out of her voice. "I'd like to meet you too, but dating would be rather difficult for us. After all, Buffalo and Honolulu are not exactly within driving distance."

"Obviously, we're going to have to meet either on your turf or mine. Since I've been away all summer, I really can't justify taking another trip right now." Adam hesitated a moment, not sure how to put his next suggestion. "I know you want to spend Christmas with your family, but could you possibly take another week off later in the winter?" he asked hopefully. "I once promised you the best room in the house if you ever came to Honolulu and that offer still stands."

"Oh, Adam, I don't know what to say. I'd dearly love to come, both to see you and to see Hawaii, but I'm going with Trish and Ted and the kids to St. Pete's Beach for Christmas, and I'll only be back from Florida a little over a month, and I'm off again. The senior citizens group I took to northern Ontario last summer asked me to arrange a cruise for them and to escort it myself. We leave the second week in February for a ten-day cruise on the Pacific Venturer from Los Angeles to Acapulco." Susan rambled on, hearing the whine in her voice, desperately wanting to meet Adam but frustrated by the responsibilities of family and job.

Adam was silent for a moment, frustrated by the same needs and responsibilities. Then in a blinding moment of clarity, the solution came to him, so simple, yet so perfect. He would go on the cruise with her.

"Uh, Susan," he began tentatively. "I have to be in San Francisco again in February for the Bay Hotels' annual meeting. I could take some vacation time then, fly down to L.A., and meet you on the ship."

"You mean go on the cruise with us?" she asked breathlessly, her heart hammering at the thought.

"Yes, if you don't mind. I've never been on a cruise. I tend to spend my vacations either at home with my parents or trying out other companies' hotels for research purposes." He pondered a moment. "Actually I could even call this a business trip. A cruise ship is really just a floating hotel and they must have some of the same problems that we do."

Her heart was really doing flip-flops as she realized he definitely intended to go on the cruise. "I'll make the reservation for you if you'd like, and simply include you as part of my group. That way it will be cheaper for you, because you'll get the group rate."

"I can hardly wait," Adam murmured through the phone. "I'm starting to get excited about this trip already."

Susan hesitated a second. "What kind of a cabin do you want, Adam?"

"What options do I have?"

"You can have a single cabin, or I can arrange for you to share with someone else."

"With one of your seniors?"

Susan laughed. "That's rather a daunting thought, isn't it?" She was silent for a moment, remembering what he must make in his job at the hotel. She wondered if he could afford a cabin of his own.

She heard Adam sigh, then say wistfully, "I think it would be wonderful to share a cabin on a cruise ship with you."

Her breath caught in her throat as she thought through the implications of that. She was about to pretend she hadn't heard him when she remembered again the probable state of his bank account. Perhaps he was subtly telling her he couldn't afford to go as a single.

"Er...ah...Adam," she cleared her throat, and then went on. "As the group's escort I get a cabin to myself, of course. I guess you know that because it must be the same situation when groups book into hotels. Also I'm allowed to bring along a companion to share my cabin, at a very nominal daily rate. That would cut the cost considerably. But are you really certain you want to do that? We don't really know each other very well, you know." She stopped talking abruptly, realizing she was babbling while there was silence on the other end of the line.

Adam listened intently on the other end, relief washing through him as he caught two bits of information. First, that Susan had a cabin to herself, and second, that she was not averse to sharing it with him. He knew that was true when she put the onus on him to decide. If she didn't want to she could have simply said, "No!"

CHAPTER 5

Susan shook her head to clear it. She watched the bags come tumbling down the chute onto the baggage carousel, then glanced around the huge airport terminal looking for the dark-haired man. He was gone. She wondered how long she'd been standing here day-dreaming, but figured it couldn't be more than a few minutes.

Retrieving her single suitcase, she plopped it on its wheels and started pulling it across the terminal. An experienced traveler, she'd learned a long time ago to travel with only one suitcase, one with wheels and a strap to attach her carry-on bag so she could handle it herself.

She scanned the terminal building looking for the Adventure Cruises' assembly point. It was eleven-thirty a.m. In less than three hours she would be meeting another flight with the thirty senior citizens she was escorting on the cruise.

She checked her bag at the Adventure Cruise desk and inquired which exit in the terminal the buses to the ship would depart from. She also arranged to have one bus held empty for her group so all thirty would travel together. Younger travelers didn't mind fending for themselves, but she knew from experience that seniors preferred to stay together as a group, and they tended to get upset if things didn't go as planned.

Her tour group arrangements made, she went in search of the restaurant, the Pacific Room, where Adam suggested they meet for lunch. Her nervousness surfaced again as she thought of Adam. She wondered what he looked like and if she would be disappointed. The thought that he might be disappointed in her was scary. They knew each other well, Adam and she. After two years of e-mailing, baring their souls and comforting each other when they were sad, they knew each other better than most friends who lived in the same city. In about ten minutes, she thought with an uneasy feeling, they would meet face to face for the first time.

She pulled a battered red sun hat out of her tote bag and put it on, being careful not to disarrange her hair. Adam would be looking for a blonde lady with a red hat. She scanned the men sitting on benches near the restaurant entrance. Adam said he would wear an orchid in his lapel. There was no one fitting that description nearby so she went into the restaurant.

Choosing a table well off to the side, she sat facing the restaurant entrance. For some perverse reason, she wanted to see him before he saw her even if she had the advantage of only a few seconds.

She glanced around at the high-ceilinged room hung with a profusion of plants and stared out the window at the view across the end of a runway, to the freeway and the city beyond. Neither the plants nor the view registered. She nervously pushed back her cuticles with her thumbnail. For the first time in her life she wished she smoked so she would have something to do with her hands. A waiter approached, and she ordered a mineral water with lime.

She glanced at her watch. Adam was ten minutes late. Maybe he wasn't coming after all, and that would solve the whole problem.

She went over in her mind the options she had if the meeting with Adam turned out to be a disaster. She could always take Charles Courtney up on his offer. Charles was the president of the seniors' group and was her main contact with them. He was the only one of the group who knew about Adam and the circumstances of their meeting. Charles was traveling as a single and had a cabin to himself. When Susan, at one of their meetings, hesitantly told him about the addition to their group, he immediately understood and offered to share his cabin with Adam if it became necessary.

She remembered him saying with a twinkle in his eye, "I can't see him wanting to bunk with me once he gets a look at you. But you might want a few days to get used to him."

Then she thought of Grace Cole, a wealthy but lonely widow also traveling as a single. Grace had offered to share her cabin with Susan right at the start, and was actually disappointed when she found out that Susan's escort status entitled her to her own cabin. If sharing with Adam became intolerable and *she* had to get out, she knew Grace would be glad to have her.

Adam entered the restaurant breathlessly, having rushed through the terminal and up the last flight of stairs without waiting for the elevator. He spotted the blonde lady in the red hat immediately. She was seated off to the side with her head down, the hat brim obscuring her face. She was nervously picking at a fingernail. Adam could understand her anxiety. He was feeling not a little of it himself.

He crossed the restaurant swiftly and slid into the chair across from Susan's. She looked up, and startled blue eyes collided with twinkling brown ones. A smile lit up his face.

"Hello, Susan," he said, and promptly fell in love.

For a moment her throat constricted, and nothing came out. Then she managed to whisper, "Hello yourself, Adam," and just as promptly fell head over heels in love.

"That was you in the arrivals area," she said, so drenched in euphoria her voice was shaky.

"Yes it was," he said as he reached across the table and took her hand in his. "I thought the blonde lady was you, but there was no red hat, so I wasn't certain. I didn't have time to investigate, because I was already late for an appointment."

"And you were to wear an orchid in your lapel. Instead you're trying to kill it." She grinned and looked pointedly at the orchid corsage crushed in his fist.

He followed her gaze and laughed, opening his hand and smoothing the petals. "Isn't this awful? I guess I've lived in Hawaii so long I've forgotten what the rest of the world is like. In Honolulu, street vendors sell miniature orchids about so big," he held his thumb and forefinger about two inches apart, "and everyone wears them in their lapels, or the ladies wear them in their hair. This," he said, holding the large elaborate corsage out to her, "was the best the florist in the hotel could come up with. I couldn't really see myself wearing it, but I hoped you would."

Susan slowly took off her hat and smiled at him. "I was thinking of buying a silk flower earlier to dress up this hat. Now

I'm glad I didn't. I'd much rather use a real one, and an orchid is about as dressy as you can get."

She pinned the corsage to the hatband and plopped the hat back on her head, tilting it rakishly to one side. Catching his eye and surprising a look of admiration, she laughed joyously. He laughed too and, reaching across the table, caught her hand again in his. They sat there, staring into each other's eyes, his thumb absently caressing the back of her hand.

He noticed she wore the gold-tipped shark's tooth and chain he'd sent her when Jenny Sue was born. He supposed she had worn it to please him.

"You're a beautiful woman, Susan." He paused a moment, then went on, "I knew from your e-mails you were a beautiful person inside, and despite the square dance lady's less-than-flattering praise, I just knew the packaging had to be superb. You have too much self-confidence to be otherwise. And I was right."

Susan's throat constricted, and, for the second time in the few moments since they met, she was speechless. Finally getting her voice back she said hoarsely, "And you're a beautiful man, Adam, in every sense of the word."

The highly-charged moment was interrupted by the waitress asking if they were ready to order. Adam looked at Susan questioningly. She shook her head.

"I ate on the flight, and I'm really not hungry, but I'll have a coffee and keep you company if you want something."

Adam ordered a ham and cheese on rye for himself and coffee for both of them before turning back to her, still holding her hand.

"I'm starved," he admitted. "I flew from Frisco this morning on the 7am shuttle, and all they served was coffee and danish. Since then I've been in meetings all morning."

"But I saw you at the baggage carousel earlier this morning," said Susan with a puzzled frown.

"Yes," said Adam with a shamefaced grin. "That was between meetings. I knew you were on that flight, and I was trying to get a look at you before you saw me."

Susan burst out laughing. "And I was trying to see you first. That's why I sat off to the side...."

"And then you missed me when you looked down and started fiddling with your nails."

This time it was Susan's turn to look shamefaced. "That's a nervous habit left over from childhood. I used to bite my nails badly, and my mother was always warning me that I would wear my fingers down to the knuckles. She once showed me a picture of the statue of Venus de Milo, and said that's what I would look like before I was thirty."

He smiled at her. "Well, you still have your arms, so I guess your mother's warnings were successful."

"You must have had your second meeting here in the airport," said Susan. "There wasn't enough time for you to go somewhere and get back."

"You're right. It was here, at my request. The meeting was with a group tour operator who was booking bulk space for next winter. I told him that if he wanted the contract signed today, to meet me in the airport to go over the last-minute details. I guess he wanted it signed badly enough to show up."

Susan was puzzled. It was very unusual for a large tour operator who booked bulk space to cater to the whims of hotel staff. In most circumstances, Adam would have gone to the man's office or taken him out to lunch and given him a sales pitch to secure the contract. Adam must have more clout in the company than she previously suspected. Meeting him hadn't cleared up the mystery.

The waitress arrived with his sandwich, and Adam stopped talking and dug into his food.

Susan took advantage of the fact that his attention was elsewhere and studied him over the rim of her coffee cup. His black wavy hair was thick and glossy, worn a little longer than was usual with most businessmen. His dark-brown eyes were remote while his attention was on his food, but she had seen them twinkle with humor, shine with admiration, and grow alert with interest. She wondered what they would look like clouded with passion or alight with love. She felt her face growing hot and dipped her head so her hat partially hid her face.

Adam reached out a finger and slowly lifted the brim of her hat until he could see her eyes. He stared into them a few seconds, his own as confused as hers. Abruptly he set down his coffee cup and stood.

"Let's go for a walk. We can probably both use the exercise." He reached for her hand, and she gave it to him without thinking. It felt right in his.

They walked for about an hour, through the different levels of the terminal building, up and down escalators, completely oblivious to the throngs of people rushing by.

Not once did he let go of her hand.

They talked about their families and what they had done that winter. Adam told her about his trip to Europe last summer. She told him about Trish and her family and their Christmas trip to Florida and about Jenny Sue.

"Her first birthday is the day after I get back from the cruise," she said. "After what we went through the night she was born, I don't think I could bear to miss it." Her hand went to the gold-tipped shark's tooth and she rubbed it absently as she walked.

Adam saw the gesture, and his heart leaped. She was wearing his gift because it was important to her, not just to please him because they were meeting today. He knew that from the familiar way her fingers caressed the gold pendant.

Shortly before two o'clock they went back to the arrivals area to await the flight from Buffalo with the 30 senior citizens in her group. Due to the advance preparations, the transfer to the ship was made smoothly. Adam stood back and admired how efficiently Susan did her job.

On the bus on the way to the ship, Susan used the intercom to give her group a few instructions. She told them the cabins had been pre-assigned and that when they arrived at the cruise terminal they should all follow her and go through the group check-in.

"You will each get a key card. This card will open your stateroom door, and it will also be used as a credit card to charge drinks at the bar or purchases in the on-board stores.

You do not need to carry any money on board ship; for everything you do or buy, even getting your hair done in the salon, you will use this card. At the end of the cruise, all your on-board purchases will be charged to your credit card."

"At the same time," Susan went on, "you will get your table number in the dining room. I've reserved four tables for eight at the first sitting. As the first night at sea is always informal, you will not need to change for dinner, so I suggest you use the time between to acquaint yourselves with the ship. Just wander around and learn where things are. Most people like to find out the quickest way from their cabin to the dining room and the main lounge."

"What about our luggage?" asked an anxious-looking woman a few rows from the front.

Susan smiled. "One of the joys of traveling by ship is not having to worry about your luggage. It will magically appear in your cabin sometime between now and when the ship sails. When we meet at dinner I'll also give you my cabin number. Please feel free to call me at any time if you have any concerns."

The Pacific Venturer was a magnificent ship. Even Susan, who had been on a cruise before, felt a thrill of excitement when the bus pulled onto the dock in San Pedro and she saw the big white ship towering over them. Part of the excitement, she knew, was caused by the presence of the dark-eyed man seated next to her. The next ten days, she was sure, would be a turning point in her life. She'd thought this cruise would be an exciting, but pleasant, interlude in her life, but any hope of her heart surviving unscathed had been dashed the moment she saw Adam.

When the check-in was finished and all her group were safely on board, Susan decided to take her own advice and learn her way around the ship. Adam went along, keeping up a running commentary on the differences and similarities between a ship and a hotel. He was the one who studied a diagram of the ship and discovered a stairwell in the stern that connected most of the main public rooms.

"Ha!" he said triumphantly. "Just like in a hotel. Find the service stairs, and you'll get where you're going and avoid all the traffic." He led her up and down them, in and out of the various lounges and bars, to prove his point. Finally they collapsed in lounge chairs on the deck and watched the last stragglers board the ship.

They still hadn't gone to their own cabin. Neither, if asked, would have admitted that all the running around they had done was simply an excuse to avoid doing that.

Adam leaned back wearily and closed his eyes. It had been a long day for him, starting with the early morning flight from San Francisco, and the stress-filled meetings that morning. He hated doing business that way, but he had no choice if he was to take the next 10 days off. He wondered that morning if he was out of his mind to take this trip, but now that he was here, had met Susan and talked to her, he wouldn't have it any other way. This could be the single most important thing he had ever done. He smiled to himself at the thought.

Susan glanced over at Adam and saw him smiling with his eyes closed. She thought he had dozed off and took the opportunity to study him without being observed.

He was easily the handsomest man she had ever seen. He was so good-looking that it made her a little uneasy. She kept expecting him to finish saying his lines and walk off the stage. Except this stage was her life and she was involved with the players, not just watching.

He was still wearing the suit she had seen him in that morning at the baggage carousel. It was an expensive suit that fitted him so well she knew it had been tailored just for him. He'd taken off the jacket and hung it on the back of the lounge chair. His tie had long since been removed and stuffed into his jacket pocket. The fine white cotton shirt that hugged his wide shoulders was unbuttoned halfway down his chest, showing a dark crop of curly chest hair. His short sleeves showed a finer crop of the same dark hair covering his arms. There were the beginnings of dark circles under his eyes. She guessed he hadn't had much sleep in the past few nights.

Had he been working hard to get caught up on his work so he could take these few days off? Or had he been as worried and apprehensive about this meeting as she was?

She was startled out of her reverie by a blast from the ship's whistle. Adam's eyes popped open, and he looked at her questioningly.

"That was probably the fifteen-minute whistle," she said, glancing at her watch. "They should start pulling in the gangway and loosening the lines in a few minutes."

"Do you want to stay up here and watch us leave port, or," he grinned, "do you want to check your cabin and see if your bags have 'magically appeared?'"

"That was rather grandstanding, wasn't it?" she laughed. "But I needed to get their attention and reassure them or, instead of exploring the ship, they would sit in their cabins and fret until the baggage turned up." She got to her feet and held out her hand to him. "Let's go stand by the rail and watch the activities. If my bags haven't arrived by now there's nothing I can do about it. They're not going to stop the sailing to look for them. I'll just have to share yours. Unless," she grinned wickedly, "it's yours that have gone astray."

"Heaven forbid," groaned Adam. "Given the choice, I'd rather see you wearing my jockeys than me wearing your frillies."

Susan gripped the rail, staring unseeing at the hive of activity on the dock. She tried to tamp down the rising heat of desire spiraling through her. Her mind was filled with visions of this very virile man, standing with his arm around her at the rail, wearing nothing but jockey shorts. There was the very real possibility, practically a certainty, that sometime in the next ten days she would see him like that. It would be difficult to avoid since they were sharing a cabin.

She wondered what she had really gotten herself into.

So preoccupied was she that she didn't notice the faint tremble in Adam's hand as he gripped her shoulder. Her back was to him, so she didn't notice the strained look on his face. If she had she would have known that Adam's thoughts paralleled hers almost exactly.

They stayed at the railing, both lost in their own thoughts until the ship was well out to sea. Adam stirred, murmured something about living in Hawaii having thinned his blood, and retrieved his jacket from the lounge chair. He was

91

just about to suggest that they go to their cabin when the ship's speaker announced that dinner for first sitting would commence in five minutes.

By unspoken consent they started toward the dining room, both of them relieved to be putting off yet again the moment when they would be alone together in their cabin.

Most of the seniors' group was already seated when Susan and Adam arrived. Charles Courtney beckoned them over to two empty chairs on his left. On Charles' right was Grace Cole with a beaming smile of welcome. Also at the table were two widowed sisters, Maudie North and Clara Singleton, and a married couple, Birdie and Clay Terdak. The Terdaks were both in their 80s and the oldest couple in the group. Susan went around the table introducing everyone by name to Adam.

The conversation soon became quite lively as experiences were shared in finding their way around the ship. The Terdaks discovered the lounge where bingo was played every afternoon in the hour before dinner. Maudie and Clara found the casino and declared their intention of playing the "slots" the instant the room opened for business. Grace Cole, a self-confessed compulsive shopper, could hardly wait for the ship's boutique to open.

Charles shook his head at the others' activities and said he intended to secure a front-row seat in the theater and, with a glass of port in hand, enjoy the dancers in the Vegas-type show.

"I understand their costumes are superb," he said. "Not to mention their legs."

Grace, next to him, snorted and said, "You men!"

Charles laughed and said, "Of course there are a couple of good-looking young men in the show as well, so there's something for you to look at too, Grace, if you'd care to share my front-row seat."

"If you'll also share your port with me, then yes thank you, I'll watch the show with you."

Susan watched this byplay with amusement. She'd suspected that Grace had more than a passing interest in Charles, and now she thought that the interest was probably returned. It might prove an interesting cruise for more than just Adam and her.

By the time dessert was served the table companions were on a first-name basis.

"Adam," asked Maudie, "are you a travel agent like Susan?"

"No, I'm not, Maudie. I'm in the hotel business. So I guess you could say I'm in the overall travel industry."

"How nice that you have that in common. You were lucky to be able to get the time off to accompany your wife on a business trip."

Susan gasped and threw a panic-stricken look at Adam. He gave her a wicked grin and leaned over to whisper in her ear. "Shall we play along or tell the truth? It's up to you."

"They have to know sooner or later," she murmured. "So go ahead."

He stroked her cheek with his knuckle. "I'll be discreet."

Maudie watched this byplay with a puzzled look on her face.

"Maudie," said Adam gently, "Susan and I are not married." He reached over and clasped Susan's hand where it lay on the table gripping a crumpled napkin.

Glancing swiftly from Susan to Adam, Maudie's eyes widened in surprise. "But, your last names are the same, and you certainly aren't brother and sister."

"No, we aren't brother and sister," said Adam patiently. "Neither are our names the same. Susan's name is Jeffrey, while mine is Joffrey. Just one letter different, but I must admit it confused me too in the beginning."

"How long have you known each other?" Maudie was clearly embarrassed, but her curiosity was getting the better of her.

"We've been friends for just about two years now, although we first came in contact with each other longer ago than that."

"Oh, dear," said Maudie, clasping her hands to her pinkened cheeks. "I didn't really mean to...I mean, I know young people today do things differently...but I hope you don't think...Oh, dear."

Adam laughed. "Don't worry about it, Maudie. I'm sure young people today aren't all that different. Each generation has its own way of doing things and its own form of rebellion. Take yourself for instance. You're a beautiful woman, so I'm sure when you were a young girl you were a real heartbreaker. Did you ever go to parties against your parents' wishes?"

"That I did!" Maudie chuckled. "And a wild one I was too. My mother, God rest her soul, despaired of my ever finding a decent husband."

"Maudie! How could you say such a thing!" interrupted a shocked Clara. "You were never like that!"

"You don't know what you're talking about, Clara. Younger sisters never know what their big sisters are up to, and just as well!"

The Terdaks had been making plans for the rest of the evening with a couple at another table so missed that conversation, but Grace Cole was listening avidly. Charles, the only one to know the full story, followed the byplay with an amused smile. He'd been wondering how Susan would break the news to the others about her relationship with Adam. Sensing that she didn't want to answer any more questions just now, he got to his feet and offered Grace his arm.

"I think, my dear, we'd better adjourn to the theater if we expect to get anywhere near the front-row seat I promised you. Susan, we'd be pleased if you and Adam joined us."

Susan glanced at Adam and nodded, and they followed the older couple out of the dining room. Adam's hand at her waist as he guided her through the throngs of people in the hallways felt warm and firm as if it belonged there. A warm glow surged through her as she thought about how skillfully he deflected any more questions about them by turning the focus of the conversation back on Maudie. She supposed that kind of diplomacy was an asset in the hotel business.

They were sipping their after-dinner drinks and waiting for the show to start when Grace leaned over and touched Susan's pendant.

"What a beautiful pendant. I was noticing it during dinner. It's a real tooth isn't it?"

"Yes it's a shark's tooth with the edges tipped in gold."

"Did you pick it up on one of your trips? One of the things I like best about traveling is shopping in so many new and different places."

"Er...ah...no," said Susan hesitantly. "The pendant was a gift from Adam about a year ago."

"For your birthday?" persisted Grace.

"Actually," put in Adam, "it wasn't a gift at all, but a medal for bravery. Maybe someday, if we have a couple of spare hours, I'll tell you the whole story."

"I can hardly wait," crowed Grace. "I'll just bet it's a terribly romantic story."

"It depends on how you look at it," said Adam with a humorous glint in his eye. "It's about a stormy night and a girl named Jenny Sue."

"Jenny Sue?" repeated Grace looking from Adam to Susan.

Susan started to giggle and was about to tell Grace who Jenny Sue was when the Cruise Director picked up the microphone and walked on stage.

Susan saw and heard very little of the show. She was acutely aware of the tall handsome man seated next to her who, even that late in the day, still smelled faintly of a tropical lime after-shave. His arm rested on the back of her chair, his fingers occasionally flexing and brushing her shoulder. She was intensely aware of every touch. His other hand held hers loosely as it rested on the arm of the chair. She was leaning on her elbow, and her arm was going to sleep, but there was no way she was going to move it, not while Adam still held her hand.

The show ended and they stood.

"Susan...."

"Adam, I...."

They both stopped and looked at each other warily. Adam grinned crookedly.

"I was just about to suggest a walk on the deck, but I think we've put it off long enough." He took her elbow and started leading her through the lounge toward the door. "Come on Susan, let's go to our cabin."

CHAPTER 6

Susan stood self-consciously in front of the door to cabin D51 while Adam fumbled in his pocket for the key card. He opened the door and stood aside for her to enter.

The cabin looked appallingly small.

Although Susan had previously been on a cruise and knew what to expect, and been in an even smaller cabin before, she was, nevertheless, momentarily shocked by the size of this one. The room seemed even smaller with Adam's presence in it. His size seemed to shrink the available space.

"I can see why they don't advertise king-sized beds," said Adam dryly.

Susan looked at the two twin beds, already made up for the night. The room steward had obviously been by while they were in the lounge. The beds were at right angles, one underneath the window and the other along the side wall. The opposite wall had a built-in dresser with four drawers and a mirror above it. Across the back wall were a clothes closet and the door leading to a tiny bathroom.

She noticed with relief that their bags had arrived. Her large, flowered, tapestry, soft-sided case was there, along with a dark brown leather case and a matching garment bag.

She started to drag her suitcase across the floor, but Adam deftly took it from her and effortlessly set it on her bed.

Opening up her suitcase and taking out a pair of cotton pajamas and matching robe and her toiletries bag, she looked around the cabin in dismay. This wasn't going to work.

Adam turned around from hanging some clothes in the closet and caught the look on her face. He dropped the lid on his bag and came to stand in front of her.

"This is going to take some getting used to," he said, squeezing her shoulder. "Suppose I make it easy for us and go for a walk on deck. I'll be gone at least half an hour. That should give you time to shower and do whatever else you have to do without me around." He dropped a light kiss on her forehead and was gone.

Susan stood there staring at the closed door with a bemused expression. The kiss had been so fleeting it was hardly there but she could still feel it as if his lips branded her. A feeling of warmth suffused her at his thoughtfulness in leaving her alone.

Swiftly she stripped off her clothes and turned on the shower in the tiny bathroom. The shower curtain billowed into the room from the water pressure and soaked the bathroom floor, and, when she emerged a few minutes later wrapped in a bath towel, Susan knew there was no way she could have showered and dressed in dry clothes in that small space. She was glad to have the cabin to herself to get ready for bed. She put on the plain cotton pajamas and robe she had brought, knowing she would feel very uncomfortable wearing anything slinky or sexy in front of Adam.

She mopped up the bathroom floor and went back in to brush her teeth. Replacing the toothbrush she automatically picked up the pink plastic box of birth control pills and popped one out. Her mind went back to the soul searching she had done several weeks ago....

Shortly after Adam had decided to go on the cruise, she was cleaning out her medicine chest and found an empty pill box. She was about to throw it out when thoughts of a handsome, dark-haired man in a small ship's cabin crossed her mind. She put it back on the shelf.

She left it there for a couple of days. After all, there was no possible way she was going to make love with a man she didn't know after being with him only ten days. She and Adam would meet, become friends, and then go back to being pen pals again. It would all be very platonic.

Then one night he called to confirm that he had booked his flight and would definitely be there. His warm sexy voice unsettled her so much that she had trouble sleeping that night. The next morning when she saw the pill box still on the shelf, she was filled with a myriad of thoughts. If there was any attraction between them at all, ten days in a small cabin might force things to a head. Add to that a few glasses of wine with dinner and the sheer romanticism of a ship at sea, and anything could happen. He might even turn out to be a cad who would trick her into sleeping with him, or worse still, force her.

That morning she ripped the prescription number off the box and put it in her handbag. She took it to the drugstore later that day and got two months' supply.

For another few days the pill box lay on the bathroom shelf while Susan's conscience warred with her common sense. Then one evening, getting ready for bed, she saw the pill box and realized that she was at the point in her monthly cycle where she had to take the pill today or forget about it for another month. Not allowing herself to think about it, she swallowed the pill with a few sips of water and was committed.

Now as she took the pill, she smiled at the thought that this gentle, soft-spoken Adam, who held her hand most of the day, could ever be a cad.

By the time she unpacked and put away her clothes, Adam had been gone almost an hour. She took off her robe and slipped into bed, leaving the bathroom light on so he wouldn't stumble around in the dark. She tried to stay awake, but the busy day caught up with her, and she soon fell asleep.

With the ship's air-conditioning loud in the room, she didn't hear him return, rummage in his bag for a robe, and disappear into the shower. She didn't see him sitting on the edge of his bed in the faint light spilling from the bathroom, watching her sleep. She didn't know that he reached over and picked up a handful of blonde hair as it lay strewn across her pillow, feeling its texture and letting it run through his fingers.

When Susan opened her eyes, early morning sun filtered through the porthole, and the ship's motion drew lazy patterns of sunlight on the walls. She lay quietly in her bunk for a moment, enjoying the sensation of being gently rocked. Then the memory of last night returned and she jerked her head toward Adam's bunk. Her heart leaped when she saw him laying there, his head not two feet from hers, sound asleep.

Silently she pushed back the covers and sat up on the edge of the bed, shivering slightly in the air-conditioned coolness of the cabin. Adam didn't move. He lay on his stomach, one hand pillowing his head, the other gripping the blanket around his shoulders. He must have been cold in the night and tried to cover himself. She smiled when she saw that he had pulled the covers up off his feet, and they were bare from the ankles down. The regulation bunk blanket was no match for his long length.

She pulled the blanket off her own bed and laid it over his feet. He moved under the covers and she thought he was waking up, but he only snuggled farther into the blanket and went on sleeping. His hair, that yesterday had been neatly combed, was a riot of black waves sticking up in all directions. She imagined it took a lot of effort to keep it looking businessman-neat. His hair looked soft and silky and she wanted to touch it but didn't dare. She didn't want him waking up to find her staring at him while he slept or, worse still, touching him.

She picked up a clean set of underwear and a pair of pale green striped shorts with a matching top. Hastily dressing in the bathroom, she discovered it really was big enough to get dressed in as long as the shower wasn't on and the floor was dry.

Quickly brushing her hair and putting on a minimum of makeup, she picked up her key card and headed for the dining room. First sitting breakfast had started half an hour earlier, and she would bet that most of her group were already there. One thing she'd discovered on her trip through Ontario last summer was that seniors were notoriously early risers. Even those who weren't early risers would be up by now courtesy of the three-hour time difference.

For Adam the three-hour time difference was in the other direction, and that's why he was still asleep, and why she hadn't wakened him.

She was right about the early rising seniors. Three of the four tables were filled, and Charles Courtney, who had just arrived and hadn't started his breakfast yet, was sitting alone at the fourth.

Susan walked around the tables, spending a few moments at each, greeting each of the group members by name and asking if they had slept well or enjoyed the previous night's show or if there were any problems.

She reminded them all of the captain's cocktail party that night and that it was usually quite formal.

"Tonight's the night to wear the dressiest outfit you've brought with you," she said. "Some evenings on board ship are quite casual, but not this one. This is your night to shine. There might even be some unattached men around," she teased. Of the 30 seniors, 22 of them were women, a sad, but accurate, distribution of the sexes at that age.

She noticed, as she approached the third table that Edna Mayberry got swiftly to her feet, leaving her breakfast only half finished, and left the dining room. Edna, a plump, pretty woman in her fifties, was on the trip with her husband, Tom, who was at least ten years older. She stopped briefly at the service table and picked up a small tray that had obviously been prepared for her. The waiter argued with her for a moment, his expressive hands whirling as he indicated the table and another waiter standing nearby, but Edna shook her head and kept on walking.

"What was that all about?" asked Susan of the others still at the table.

"Her husband's not feeling well," said Maudie, who tended to appoint herself spokesman for whatever group she was with at the moment. "So she asked the waiter for some tea and toast to take to him."

"Why didn't she call room service?" asked Susan. One of the perks of being on board ship was the ability to order breakfast served in your room if you wished.

"I guess she didn't want to bother anyone," answered someone else at the table.

Susan sighed. That was another trait she'd discovered about seniors. Most of them were so used to doing things for themselves that they hesitated to ask for help and often turned it down when it was offered.

Shaking her head, she sat next to Charles Courtney. Almost instantly, juice, coffee, toast, and a bacon omelet were set in front of her. Surprised, she glanced at Charles, whose eyes danced with amusement.

"I figured by the time you were finished with your socializing breakfast would be over, so I ordered for you."

"Thank you," she said gratefully. "You even remembered the bacon omelet."

"How could I forget? Until that bus trip last summer, I never would have believed someone could eat a bacon omelet for breakfast for five days straight, and then eat one for lunch one day as well."

"Yes, well," said Susan with an embarrassed grin, "I guess it is one of my favorite foods. I'm lucky I don't have a weight problem."

"You're lucky you don't have a cholesterol problem. When you get to our age," he indicated the rest of the group, "the arteries start to get clogged, and we're limited to two eggs a week with bacon absolutely forbidden." He sighed and put down his coffee cup. "But enough of the vagaries of an old man's diet. How are you and Adam getting along? Any problems last night?"

Susan finished the last of her omelet before she answered. "No problems that weren't easily solved. Actually Adam was very considerate. He went for a walk on deck and didn't come back until I was asleep. Then he was still asleep when I left the cabin this morning."

"Don't tell me he's a slug-a-bed?"

Susan smiled at the old-fashioned expression. "No, I don't think so. It's probably the time difference. He had a three-hour time difference, as well, coming from Hawaii, but in the opposite direction from ours."

As they were leaving the dining room, Charles stopped and said, "Just remember what I said, Susan. If the situation gets a little sticky, send him over to bunk with me."

"Thanks, Charles. I'll remember that."

Susan spent the next two hours keeping score for a shuffleboard tournament. She glanced up from her notebook once and saw Adam watching her. He was leaning on the rail wearing white shorts and a white polo shirt that showed off his tanned good looks to perfection. His hair was slicked down like it was yesterday with the bare suggestion of a wave. Susan felt an almost overwhelming urge to go over to him and mess it up to bring back the riotous waves she had seen this morning while he was still asleep.

He watched for a few minutes and then left, saying he was going to try to find a late breakfast.

She didn't see Adam the rest of the morning, although she kept looking for him everywhere she went. She spent half an hour with the purser arranging a private cocktail party for her group the next evening; choosing a location, the small bar just forward of the main lounge, and selecting the hors d'oeuvres to be sent from the kitchen. Then she browsed in the boutique for a while. Grace Cole came into the boutique while she was there and, after laughing for a few minutes at the sayings on a display of T-shirts, they went to the dining room for lunch.

The Mayberrys were both on hand for lunch, but Tom looked very pale and shaky and barely picked at his lunch. His wife kept giving him worried looks. Susan wondered briefly if the problem was something more serious than seasickness. She made a mental note to talk to them privately later and remind them a doctor was on board.

She was just leaving the dining room when she saw Adam on the other side of the room just working his way toward the table. Knowing he would be in the dining room at least half an hour, she thought this would be a good opportunity to go back to the cabin and change into her swimsuit.

She was a little uneasy at the thought of Adam seeing her in the black swimsuit that Jacey insisted she buy. It left little to the imagination. The one-piece suit was cut high on the thighs, the back dipped below the waist, and the front was cut almost to the navel but was held together across the bust with a bit of gold chain. She knew it looked good on her, but it was blatantly sexy.

She braided her hair in one long pigtail to keep it from tangling if she went swimming and slipped into a lacy cover-up. She scribbled a note for Adam, "Gone Swimming", on the notepad by the telephone, picked up her tote bag, and headed for the pool on the aft deck.

She found a lounge chair near the railing, checked her watch, and picked up the paperback book she brought with her. Fifteen minutes later she decided she had enough sun on her unprotected skin and took a plastic bottle of sunscreen out of her bag.

She had oiled her arms, chest, and throat and was starting on her shoulders when the lounge chair creaked as someone else sat on it. Startled, she looked up to see Adam grinning at her. If she'd thought he looked good before, she now revised her opinion upward. He looked devastating in a swimsuit. Every inch of him that was showing was tanned to a deep bronze. Her skin looked so pale and colorless next to his.

"Let me," he said reaching for the sunscreen. "I'll put it on the parts you can't reach." She passed over the bottle and obligingly turned her back. There was dead silence for a moment, and then Adam let out a long low wolf whistle. "Oh, my, there's a lot more parts you can't reach back here than I thought at first."

He dribbled the sunscreen in a line from one shoulder to the other and started to work it in with both hands. His thumbs rubbed the ridge of her spine, and his fingertips lightly caressed the side of her neck. She shivered as his touch unleashed a curl of desire deep in her stomach. She was about to protest when his hands moved on and applied the lotion to the rest of her back.

"Lie down," he whispered, "and I'll do your legs too."

"I..uh...don't really need it on my legs. I'm going in swimming soon anyway, and it'll only wash off."

Adam looked at the bottle of sunscreen, clearly marked *waterproof* and at the long expanse of leg exposed by the black swimsuit.

"You're right," he said briskly. "You don't need any on your legs. But let's go in right now before you burn."

Susan took a few unsteady steps to the pool and just jumped in. She surfaced in time to see Adam do a jackknife off the board and slice cleanly into the water with hardly a ripple. He started swimming laps in the pool, and she soon joined him, needing to work off the nervous energy that surfaced just being around him. After a few minutes she stopped and clung to the side of the pool, out of breath. Obviously she was not as fit as Adam.

She watched him for a while until she heard someone call her name. A plump woman named Lily, whose last name Susan could never remember, was coming toward her across the pool deck. Lily eased herself gingerly into a deck chair, sighing with relief. Susan could see that her fingers were knobby and swollen with arthritis and surmised that her knees, under the voluminous dress, were probably also painful.

"How are you, Lily? Is the heat getting to you?"

"Oh my, no, my dear. The heat is the best thing there is for arthritis. I've been lying here in the sun just baking these old bones." She looked past Susan to the pool. "Your Adam sure likes to swim, doesn't he? You young people have so much energy. I'm sure I don't know where it comes from."

Susan was about to protest that he wasn't "her" Adam, but decided to leave it alone. She really wasn't prepared to explain their relationship.

Lily talked for a few moments then brought the subject around to the real reason she'd sought out Susan. She was worried because tonight was formal, and she hadn't brought a long dress.

"Don't worry about it," said Susan. "A cocktail-length dress is fine. Not everyone wears a long dress, and in fact, the dress I'm wearing tonight is only knee-length. They only use the term 'formal' anyway so the young kids won't turn up in jeans. Just wear what you're comfortable in."

Lily smiled her thanks and got painfully to her feet.

Susan turned around, still clinging to the edge of the pool, and bumped into Adam. He snaked his arm around her shoulders and pinned her to the pool wall.

"Gotcha," he whispered, sending little frissons of excitement through her. "I've wanted to put my arms around you all day, but I wasn't expecting it to be this wet or this public when I succeeded." He pulled her against him, and she felt his full length, from his bronzed, muscled chest to the roughness of his legs intertwined with hers. The breath whooshed out of her, and she would have sunk below the surface if he hadn't been holding her so tightly.

"Adam, I think it's time we got out of this pool before we wrinkle up like prunes."

"You go ahead. I'm going to swim for a few more minutes."

"I would have thought you'd be tired after all the laps you've swum so far."

"I would have thought so too, but one part of me obviously isn't. If I get out of the pool now, I'm going to embarrass both of us."

"Oh," said Susan, as she swiftly left the pool. She hoped anyone who saw her would think her face was pink from sunburn.

She commandeered two lounge chairs in the shade when Adam finally got out of the pool. He toweled himself dry and scooted his chair a little closer to Susan's before he sat down.

"So what did you do after you finished refereeing the shuffleboard game this morning?"

"Refereeing! I'll have you know I was keeping score. Although I must admit it was a bit difficult at times."

"The way they were yelling at each other I thought I might have to come rescue you, but you did quite well as a peacemaker."

"Thank you. One thing I've learned in dealing with seniors is never to underestimate the seriousness of an incident. I try to put myself in their shoes. When someone has been involved in sports all their life and are now reduced to participating in only one sport, they can take that one sport pretty seriously."

"Seriously enough to challenge most of your calls?"

"That was pure frustration. When the eyes aren't quite sharp enough to see the other end of the court, and the legs aren't quite energetic enough to walk the distance after every play, you have to rely on someone else to make the call. When you've been self-sufficient all your life and all of a sudden age creeps up on you and makes you dependent on someone else, it can be very frustrating. Most of my group were very independent until just a few years ago; some of them have traveled a lot more than I have. But now they're afraid to travel alone. The memory's not so good anymore, so they might forget the name of their ship or the time of their flight. They're afraid to go sightseeing alone because they might not be able to read the signs and might get lost. And most of all they're afraid they'll get sick on the trip and no one will know or care."

Adam shook his head in wonder. "You really care for them, don't you?"

"Yes, I do. I got to know most of them last summer on the bus trip, and I've seen them several times since. But it's not only this particular group. I've always been a `people lover.' Back in school on career day I always said it didn't matter what I did as long as I could work with people. A lot of the other kids said that because they thought it was expected of them, but I really meant it. And I think you're like that too, Adam. You wouldn't be in the hotel business if you didn't like working with people."

Adam reached over and squeezed her hand, then continued to hold it, rubbing her fingers absently as he talked. "You're right. I do like working with people. It's fascinating to watch the many different kinds of people who go through my hotel in a week. I like to think of the hotel as a filtering system. We take in a group of stressed and uptight people and a week or two weeks later we send them back home, relaxed and happy with all the stresses and problems filtered out."

"That's a lovely thought," said Susan dreamily. "One of these days I'm going to take a real vacation and see what it's like. When I travel as an escort I'm usually too busy to get filtered."

"Speaking of your job as escort, where are your charges now?"

"Enjoying themselves, I hope. They can't get into too much trouble when we're at sea, so I let them have their independence onboard ship. What they don't know is that I have an unobtrusive roll-call three times a day at meals. If someone doesn't turn up for a meal, I want to know where they are and why. And if I don't get a satisfactory answer, I track them down. Keeping track of them onboard ship is easy. My job will get tougher when we start shore excursions and I have to make sure everyone is back onboard before the ship sails."

"Well, Ms. Jeffrey, if it will lighten your load and spring loose any more free time for you, I hereby offer my services as your assistant. With the two of us splitting the job, round-up and roll-call will take hardly any time."

"Thanks, I appreciate the offer, even if I'm certain you'll regret it before the week is out."

They talked for a while about the next day's shore excursion at Cabo San Lucas and the private cocktail party for their group in the evening. When the shadows started to lengthen, Susan stood and gathered her tote bag and cover-up.

"It's getting late. I'd better go shower and change for the Captain's party. What about...." she trailed off and looked at Adam doubtfully.

He smiled up at her, understanding her embarrassment. "I'm going to move to a chair in the sun for a while. I'll give you half an hour before I come down."

Susan had almost reached her cabin when she noticed Hattie Bromsgrove standing in the open door of the cabin she shared with Lily. Susan sighed to herself and tried to hide her exasperation. Hattie was a querulous and sour-faced woman who, on the bus trip last summer, constantly complained. That afternoon when Adam commented on how much she seemed to care for her group, she almost answered "Except for Hattie Bromsgrove." She had no doubt that Hattie had been watching the corridor for her return.

"Oh, Miss Jeffrey, I'm so glad I caught you. Lily and I have a little problem with our shower. It's leaking, and the constant drip is very annoying."

It can't be bothering Lily very much, thought Susan, *or she would have mentioned it earlier.* Nevertheless, she followed the older woman into the room. The shower was dripping slightly, Susan conceded, but so was the one in her own cabin, and she certainly couldn't remember hearing it outside the bathroom.

"It is dripping a little," said Susan, as she tried to tighten the faucet handle. "But with the air-conditioning on you won't be able to hear it."

"We never turn the air-conditioning on," said Hattie, her eyes round in horror. "It's very bad for the sinuses, not to mention Lily's arthritis."

"Well, why don't you just close the bathroom door? You won't hear it then."

"We always leave the bathroom door open at night and the light on in case one of us has to get up. We don't want to fall and break anything in the dark."

Susan sighed again, this time in defeat. "OK, Hattie, I'll talk to the steward and ask him to send a plumber."

By the time she found the steward and explained the problem, most of the half hour Adam promised her was gone. As she let herself into the cabin she fervently hoped Adam's idea of half an hour was as long today as it was last night.

She stripped off her swimsuit and put on a robe, then got out fresh underthings and the dress she intended to wear.

Stepping into the bathroom, she frowned when she remembered how the shower soaked the whole room last night. Instead of hanging her robe on the inside of the door, she tossed it on the nearest bed. The cool water felt good, because her skin was dry and itchy from the pool chemicals. Swiftly, ever mindful of Adam's return, she washed her hair and toweled it damp-dry. There was still no sound in the cabin, so she wrapped a towel around her, sarong style, tucking the end underneath one arm, and stepped out of the bathroom.

Adam, wearing a robe, was leaning against the dresser, his arms crossed and sporting a huge grin.

"Oh! Why are you...I mean, I didn't hear you...I thought you were still out on deck."

"You've been down here almost forty-five minutes. If you've been in the shower all that time, you must be turning into a prune."

"Yes, well, I got sidetracked by Hattie Bromsgrove," said Susan shortly.

Adam, still grinning, ran his eyes over her from the tips of her polished toes to her still-wet hair. Susan was uncomfortably aware that the towel was a bit on the skimpy side and barely covered the essentials.

"The shower was running so I know you didn't hear me come in," Adam apologized. "But when I noticed your frilly underpinnings and your robe still here on the bed, I was too consumed by curiosity about what you would be wearing when you finally emerged, that I couldn't have left if I'd wanted to." He stepped forward until they were almost touching. "And I didn't want to."

Susan looked wildly around to locate her robe. She tried to step around the edge of the bed but couldn't without touching Adam. His hands came up and caressed her bare shoulders.

"Your skin feels like satin. I still want you in my arms, more even than this afternoon, although," he grinned that soul-melting grin again, "you're still wet." Her wariness at his touch changed swiftly to an awareness of anticipation and curiosity. The dying moments of the setting sun reflecting off the clouds and diffused through the porthole gave the cabin a rosy glow. His face was in shadow, disguising the tired lines that had been there earlier.

His hand coasted up the slope of her neck and lifted her chin as his mouth descended. A feeling of breathless wonder surged through her, for a moment so long in coming and so achingly awaited.

"It is more private here, definitely more private." His lips touched hers briefly and parted, his tongue brushing gently along her lower lip. Her eyes dropped closed, and she gave in to sensation, a glorious fire that licked along the nerve endings, curled through her chest, speeding up her heartbeat, and sending a tingling weakness to the far reaches of her fingers and toes.

His fingers touched her cheek, moving over each feature in her face as if cataloguing it in memory. As his middle finger slowly caressed her parted lips, she unthinkingly flicked his fingertip with her tongue. Adam went rigid and groaned.

"You are...without...a doubt...the most beau...ti...ful... and sexy...and tantalizing...." Adam's words came in a whisper, punctuated with tiny kisses that moved from one corner of her mouth to the other.

A searing heat leaped through her leaving her knees weak, and she gasped, just as Adam pulled her roughly to him for the most soul-stirring, blood-rushing kiss she had ever known.

She had known the instant she saw Adam he was someone special. She guessed his kisses would be very special. Now she knew for sure. She had never in her life been kissed like Adam was kissing her. All her past romantic entanglements were merely rehearsals for this one.

The absolute wonder and surprise of it caught her off guard. Somehow her arms came up around his neck, fingers tangled in his hair, causing the waves to spring free. Somehow the towel, once tucked under her arms, slipped down and caught on her hips.

Her unexpected abandonment released the deep well of passion within him, causing it to spill over until he was mindlessly spinning out of control. His hands were on her breasts, gently caressing the soft slopes and moving farther down to span her waist. Like a man drugged, his mouth broke from hers and buried itself in the curve of her neck as his arms wrapped tightly around her. They were touching every inch from the knees up. His arousal was evident, and he didn't try to hide it.

"Susan," he said hoarsely, as he feathered kisses along her jaw. "What have we unleashed?"

Reality intruded with a jarring impact as first static, then a double chime, and finally the cruise director's voice came over the ship's intercom system.

"Ladies and gentlemen, the casino is now closed and will reopen at nine p.m. following the first sitting dinner. The captain's cocktail party will commence in the main lounge in half an hour. Please line up at the doors...."

Susan stared, dumbfounded, shaking her head to clear it. She blushed hotly when she followed the direction of Adam's gaze and realized that she was bare from the waist up, and only a precarious twist of the towel away from being completely nude.

She picked up her robe and put it on, turning away before slipping off the towel, and tying the belt before darting a glance at Adam. He hadn't moved, and he looked as unsettled as she felt.

With a wan smile, she said, "The shower's all yours."

Adam grimaced. "I guess it's almost roll call time." He stepped into the bathroom and said, almost as if he were talking to himself, "Getting dressed in a monkey-suit and going upstairs is the last thing I want to do right now. But it's your job, and I guess duty calls. However," He stuck his head out the door and caught her eye in the mirror. "We will continue this discussion later." The bathroom door closed with a thunk.

What discussion? Susan wondered as she plugged in the hairdryer and attacked the snarls with a brush. *If that was a discussion, I don't think I could stand an argument with him.*

With her hair dried and swinging silkily blonde against her shoulders, she paid more than usual attention to her makeup. Adam finished showering, and she heard him humming as he shaved. It gave her a funny feeling, sort of shaky and weak-kneed, to listen to such personal and domestic sounds.

She slipped on the dress she had chosen for that night, a formfitting tube of bias-cut, apricot silk, that hugged her curves to mid thigh, then flared out in a full ruffled skirt that ended at the knee. The tiny straps that held up the top were highlighted with seed pearls, and her only jewelry was a long, opera-length, rope of pearls.

The effect was stunning, as she could see in Adam's eyes when he opened the bathroom door. He stood there in the doorway, frankly staring. She stared back. He had put his robe back on, but it was damp and clung to his muscled shoulders. His dark hair was a riot of waves and curls, still wet from the shower. She found herself wishing he wouldn't slick it down so severely. The blatant desire in his eyes was more than she could stand. If he made a move toward her, she would forget about her thirty charges, forget about dinner and the captain's cocktail party, and forget about anything except this exciting man who stood damp and half naked in her bathroom doorway.

She grabbed up her purse and started out the door before she could change her mind. "Everyone gets to shake the captain's hand tonight, so the lineup is pretty long. I'll go get us a place in line and you can come along when you're ready."

As she predicted, the line was long, extending through the lobby and into the library. Most of the women, she noted, wore short cocktail dresses, although a few, mostly the older ones, wore long gowns. A scattering of the men were in black tie. She found a place at the end of the line behind two couples discussing the merits of various cruise ships. They were all very well traveled and were trying to impress each other with stories of where they had been. Susan smiled to herself at their attempts at one-upmanship.

Several couples joined the line while she was listening to the conversation in front of her. She turned when she heard her name and saw Grace Cole and Charles Courtney directly behind her. With them was Edna Mayberry. She greeted Grace and Charles then turned to Edna.

"How's Tom tonight? Still not feeling well?"

"Oh, he's feeling fine now," said Edna. "But he didn't want to stand in line all this time, so he's sitting in one of those chairs just outside the lounge. He'll join us when we reach him."

"Good. I'm glad he's feeling better."

"And what about your man, Adam?" asked Charles in a low voice so only Susan could hear. "Where is he tonight?"

"He'll be along soon," she said. "I had first dibs on the shower, so he wasn't dressed when I left." She felt her face grow hot as she realized how intimate that sounded. Charles smiled at her in amusement and, helpfully, changed the subject.

They were still discussing what they had each done that day when Susan caught a glimpse of Adam through the crowd milling in the lobby. Her breath caught in her throat. Every time she saw him he looked better than before. No matter what he wore, he always looked wonderful. Tonight, he

113

looked magnificent. The formal suit he wore fit him so well that it had to be custom tailored. The finely pleated white shirt and the black bow tie gave him the conservative look of a banker or a corporation president. Again, Susan felt a twinge of unease that she really didn't know this man. Then his jacket fell open as he put something in his pocket, and she saw that he was wearing a cummerbund in a bright Hawaiian print. She laughed out loud. Adam heard her laugh and caught her eye across the room. He smiled and came toward her, and her unease disappeared in a welter of anticipation.

Other women eyed him with interest as he crossed the room. Susan felt a burst of happiness, and just a little smugness, because he was with *her*. When he reached her, he took her hand, and with a solemn look on his face, bowed from the waist.

"Good evening, Madam," he said, affecting an upper-class British accent. "Do you mind if I crash the queue?"

"Not at all, Sir," she said, suppressing a grin and playing along, much to the amusement of Grace and Charles. "In fact, I thought I saw a big, Hawaiian kahuna lurking around a few minutes ago, and I may be in need of protection."

"First of all, kahunas do not lurk, they swagger. And according to ancient Hawaiian folklore...oh, hell!" he broke off and stared ahead of him at the captain and cruise director just inside the lounge doors.

"What's wrong," she asked, looking anxiously around.

"The captain is a friend of my father's," said Adam flatly. "I suspect we're in for a few questions. Hang tight, sweetheart." Susan was so bemused by the endearment that the implications of Adam's knowing the captain didn't even register.

When it was their turn, Amy-Ann McDonnell, the cruise director, stepped up to introduce them to the captain.

"Captain Sinclair, I'd like you to meet Miss Susan Jeffrey, tour escort for our seniors' group, and...."

"Adam Joffrey!" boomed the captain. "How are you? I didn't know you were on board. I don't recall seeing your name on the passenger list."

"It isn't," said Adam. "I booked rather late, so I'm sharing Miss Jeffrey's cabin. How are you Edmund, and how is Fiona? Is she with you this trip?"

The captain ignored Adam's obvious attempt to change the subject. He glanced from Adam to Susan and frowned. "You say you're sharing an escort's cabin. Surely we can do better than that. We have one of the large suites on `A' deck unoccupied right now, Adam. I'll get the purser to arrange to move you...."

"No thank you, Edmund, Miss Jeffrey and I are quite happy where we are now. Thank you for the offer, though."

Captain Sinclair seemed to notice Susan for the first time as she watched this bewildering exchange with a frown.

"Er, ah, Miss Joffrey, you say you're escorting one of our groups. Good. Good. I hope you're quite comfortable and everything is to your satisfaction. Please contact the purser or Amy-Ann if you have any problems."

Susan smiled and said, "Thank you," not bothering to tell him that he had gotten her name wrong. He had already turned his attention back to Adam.

"Adam, my boy, you'll dine with me at my table, of course."

"I'm sorry, Edmund, but with Miss *Jeffrey's* position as escort, it is necessary that she dine with her group."

"I quite understand Miss Jeffrey's position, but you, yourself...."

"Am on this cruise specifically at her invitation and unofficially as her assistant. I am therefore obliged to stay with the group in case my assistance is required. And now, Edmund, we've held up your reception line long enough, Susan and I will move along and avail ourselves of your ship's hospitality."

"Of course, of course. Nice to see you again, Adam." Pointedly ignoring Susan, he turned to greet Charles and Grace who had been watching the exchange avidly.

Susan's mind was in a whirl as they walked across the lounge. She had intended to seek out some of her group and sit with them, but when Adam picked up two glasses of white wine from a passing waiter and steered her toward an unoccupied corner, she went without protest.

All her speculation and misgivings about Adam boiled to the surface when she sat and turned to face him.

"Who are you, Adam Joffrey?"

"Very simply, I'm Adam Joffrey, hotelier, and manager of the Honolulu Bay Hotel."

"Manager!" Susan gasped. "How...when...?"

"Yes," said Adam, with a puzzled frown. "I've been manager there now for about five years. What did you think I did?"

"I don't...I don't know what I thought. When I first spoke to you two years ago, I thought you were the reservations clerk. Then after a while I realized you were older than I first guessed, and more experienced, so I thought you must be a sort of assistant manager." Susan frowned, trying to sort her way through her earlier misconceptions. Her wine glass tilted alarmingly in her nerveless fingers until Adam reached over, took it, and set it on the table.

"Then," she continued, "you did some things that were puzzling. Like spending the summer in Europe, and sending me those expensive gifts. They didn't fit with what I thought you were. Yet not once," she said accusingly, "did you ever mention that you were the manager."

"I guess I just assumed you knew," he said lamely. Then he laughed. "I never dreamed you thought I was the reservations clerk." Then his eyes softened, and he reached out and stroked her cheek. "Is that why you offered to share your cabin with me? Because you thought I couldn't afford the trip otherwise?"

She nodded mutely.

"Susan, that's the nicest thing anyone has ever done for me."

"Oh, Lord, what you must have thought." Susan went on as if she hadn't heard. "And then there's that tacky plastic buffalo I sent you."

Adam shifted closer and put his arm around her. "I wish you could see the credenza behind the desk in my office. That little plastic buffalo has a place of honor there. And do you

116

know why? It was a gift from the heart, from a wonderful girl who didn't know me but appreciated what little help I had given her and thanked me with a unique and wonderfully humorous gift. I treasured it then, and I treasure it even more now."

There was something else nagging at Susan and she figured she might as well get it all said. She remembered that it was his father who had sent him on the trip to Europe. "What about your father? What does he do?"

"My father is manager of the San Francisco Bay Hotel." Adam paused for a moment, remembering that he'd never told her just how wealthy his family really was. It seemed a time for honesty. "He's also the chairman of the board of the Bay Hotel Corporation, my mother is a vice president in charge of advertising and promotion, and my brother, my sister, and I are all major stockholders and members of the board. Chris is manager of the Hong Kong Bay as well. Bev used to work in personnel, but, since the birth of her first child, she hasn't held a regular job. She's an active member of the board though." He smiled at her. "The annual meeting of the corporation is held every February. That's why I was in San Francisco last week. I'm also on the long-range planning and acquisitions committees and those meetings ran overtime, which is why I was so rushed yesterday morning to the point of having to schedule a meeting at the airport."

To Susan, all this was mindboggling. She suspected there was more to Adam than he was letting her know, but she had no idea his family was so well off.

"Is it a totally family-owned business?"

"No, but it is a family-run business. Bay Hotels is listed on the New York Stock Exchange, but family members still hold a controlling interest. We had to go public several years ago, because property acquisition was too prohibitively expensive to be financed by the family alone."

"What about your Board. Is it all family?"

"No indeed. We have quite a few who aren't family. For instance, all the property managers are on the board. That was mainly my influence. I figured that no one knows the hotels and their problems better than the hotel managers, so they should have some input into how they are run. So far it's worked really well."

Susan was still trying to assimilate that when she noticed the people around them were leaving. The cocktail hour was over, and dinner would be served in a few minutes in the dining room.

She looked ruefully at her wine glass, still sitting untouched on the coffee table, and asked lightly, "We didn't really enjoy much of the captain's hospitality, did we?"

"No, we didn't," said Adam, a closed look coming over his face. "The captain was most inhospitable; to you anyway." He got to his feet. "A fact I will not soon forget," he muttered under his breath.

CHAPTER 7

Susan chose to sit at a different table this time, hoping to get to know more of her group.

Tom and Edna Mayberry were at the table, as was Maudie, this time without her sister, Clara. Lily was seated next to Maudie, *without Hattie Bromsgrove, thank heavens*, thought Susan uncharitably. The other two seats remained empty through the soup course.

Susan listened halfheartedly to the conversation at the table. Her mind replayed what Adam told her. She was sure that he had never mentioned that he was the hotel manager. That she would have remembered. She knew she would have remembered, because of the incongruity of the reservation clerk's job when compared with his age, his obvious maturity, and the business degree. Now that she knew how wealthy he was she was a bit embarrassed. He could afford to stay in the most expensive suite on board, but instead, he was sharing her cabin.

Well, she thought belligerently, *sharing was his choice. I offered in good faith, and he accepted under false pretenses. All he had to do was tell me he could afford his own cabin.*

He'd told the captain that he didn't want his own cabin, but she wondered if he only said that to be polite because she was standing there. Later tonight, she must give him the option of moving out if he wished. It would probably be for the best. The attraction between them was so strong, as they found out this afternoon, that she was certain they couldn't live together for the next week without eventually ending up in bed. When the parting came, as it must, at the end of the cruise, it wouldn't hurt as much if she could keep things light and casual between them.

She had a suspicion that wasn't going to be easy.

She looked over the four tables, mentally cataloguing them, trying to pinpoint who was absent.

Adam caught her eye. "Roll call?" he commented with a lift of his eyebrows.

She nodded. "I've just realized who's missing; Mr. and Mrs.Rafferty." The Raffertys were a very shy and quiet-spoken couple who were known to everyone as Mr. Rafferty and Mrs. Rafferty, because that was how they addressed one another. No one really knew their first names, because they were never used.

"I'll give them until the end of the salad course, and then I'll go look for them."

"No need," said Adam quietly. "Here they come now."

A red-faced and glowing Mrs. Rafferty slipped into the empty seat, followed by a perspiring Mr. Rafferty with a self-satisfied look on his face. Susan peered at them for a moment and knew instantly why they were late, realizing, with a pang, that she and Adam had come perilously close to being late for the same reason.

She knew the intensely romantic atmosphere on board a cruise ship often had a positive effect on the libido and, particularly in the case of an older couple, could rejuvenate a flagging sex life. Realizing how shy the couple was, she hoped no one at the table would be crass enough to ask why they were late.

Glancing at Adam out of the corner of her eye, she caught the ghost of a smile as his gaze lingered for a moment on the latecomers. He, too, surmised what had kept them in their cabin half an hour after the dinner bell sounded and decided not to mention it.

Neither of the Raffertys contributed much to the table conversation until Maudie, with a mischievous glint in her eye, asked if they had enjoyed the captain's cocktail party.

Mrs. Rafferty looked startled for a moment, glanced at her husband, then down at her plate and answered, "We didn't go. Mr. Rafferty and I don't drink."

"You didn't miss anything," said Maudie, watching Mrs. Rafferty's face pinken again. "If I were rooming with anyone more interesting than Clara, I probably wouldn't have gone either." She looked speculatively from Adam to Susan.

Susan, to forestall any more questions from Maudie, turned to the Mayberrys and asked them about previous trips they had taken. That sparked a lively conversation on where they had been and the problems encountered. Tom Mayberry, seemingly recovered from his earlier illness, told about a trip to Paris where the hotel room walls were so thin that he was sure they were only layers of wallpaper with bugs in between.

"I was sure about the bugs, anyway," he said. "I could hear them scurrying up and down between the walls all night."

Susan shivered. "One thing I can't stand is bugs. I stayed at a resort in Mexico once that had cockroaches. They were huge things almost two inches long. The local people referred to them laughingly as `la cucaracha' and said they were harmless, but I was never comfortable in that hotel and couldn't wait to leave."

"Unfortunately," said Adam, "bugs are creatures you have to learn to co-exist with in the tropics. In the big hotels we do a pretty good job of keeping the population down with a stringent extermination program, so the average guest seldom sees anything. But underneath it all, they're still there. We never get rid of them entirely."

After dinner, most of the group went to the theater to watch the show. Adam, however, said he wanted to try his luck at the blackjack tables in the casino.

Susan wavered between staying with her group, as she thought she should, and joining Adam in the casino. Duty won out, and she went to the lounge with the Raffertys and Maudie and Lily.

She was also not very sure of her feelings toward Adam. He had deceived her, and she felt angry and embarrassed. She needed a little distance and time to think.

Adam did not come back to the lounge and, when the show was over, Susan said good night to the others and went to her cabin. He wasn't there, and she wasn't sure if the nagging feeling was relief or disappointment. At least it gave her a chance to shower and get into bed in private. She tried to stay awake until Adam came in, but the tensions of the day caught up with her and, when he finally came back to the cabin, she was sound asleep.

A shrill ring intruded on her dreams. Susan groaned and turned over. Surely it wasn't time to get up yet. It was still dark. Another ring sounded, abruptly cut off, and she realized she wasn't back home on Grand Island and that wasn't her alarm clock.

Sleep fled as she heard Adam speaking into the phone and knew from the tone of his voice that there was trouble.

"We'll be right there," he said as he hung up and reached over to snap on the bathroom light. Seeing Susan awake, he answered her unspoken question as he struggled to pull on the pants of his suit from last night, "Edna Mayberry. She thinks Tom is having a heart attack."

"Oh, no!" A horrified Susan threw back the covers and was out of bed in an instant.

Not bothering with shirt or shoes, Adam headed out the door, calling back over his shoulder, "Call the doctor will you? I'll go see what I can do."

The doctor's phone rang several times before a sleepy voice answered. Susan tersely informed him of the emergency and gave the Mayberry's cabin number. Pulling on her robe over her pajamas, she followed Adam out the door.

High drama met her in the Mayberry's cabin. Edna was standing in her nightgown, still holding the phone in one hand, the other gripping the front of her gown and twisting it. She was emitting a high keening noise as she watched the two men on the bed.

Adam was on his knees on the bed, straddling the older man's hips. His fists were locked together as he pressed rhythmically on the thin chest, using his weight when he leaned forward as leverage. A gray-faced Tom Mayberry lay unmoving beneath him.

Susan rushed across the room, her swimming class lifesaving lessons coming back in a flash. Swiftly she tilted Tom's head back and pinched his nose closed. Adam stopped momentarily while she blew in the first breath, watching the chest rise. Then he resumed the CPR, timing his movements with hers.

Running footsteps sounded in the corridor. The ship's doctor rushed into the cabin and dropped his bag by the bed. He told them to continue what they were doing while he prepared and then injected a powerful heart stimulant. He took over from Susan while Adam continued his rhythmic pressing.

Edna stopped keening when the doctor arrived, but she still stood there with the dead phone in her hand. Susan gently pried her fingers loose and replaced the phone. Edna was shivering, whether from cold in the air-conditioned cabin or from fright, Susan didn't know - probably a bit of both. She took a blanket from the other bed and wrapped it around the woman, rubbing her arms and back to warm her, and making soothing noises.

She heard a grunt from the doctor and a cry of triumph from Adam and, looking over, saw that Tom was breathing on his own. Wordlessly, she pointed this out to Edna who drew a shuddering breath of relief and started to cry. Susan held the older woman while she sobbed.

A steward appeared in the doorway pulling a portable oxygen tank on wheels. The doctor strapped the face mask on his patient and, after checking his blood pressure, started to draw blood into a couple of vials. Adam stretched, trying to get the tension knots out of his shoulders.

"I think we got it in time," he said to Susan, at the same time patting Edna reassuringly on the shoulder. "He stopped breathing only seconds before I came in the door, and with the CPR and mouth-to-mouth started so soon there should be no problem. Even the doctor was here well within the four-minute time limit." He sat on the bed next to Edna and put his arm around her. She had stopped sobbing and was wiping her eyes on the blanket. Adam reached over and grabbed a handful of facial tissues and gave her.

"That was quick thinking on your part," he said, "to recognize what was happening and call us right away."

Susan felt an overwhelming love for this special man. He had just saved a man's life, and instead of taking credit, was being complimentary and reassuring to the man's wife.

The doctor pulled a chair up to Tom's bed and intently checked his vital signs.

"I'd like to take Mr. Mayberry to the ship's hospital," he said. "We have a heart monitor and an ECG machine there. We also have a defibrillator if needed. But first I want to make certain his condition is stable enough to move him, so I think I'll stay here awhile before I call for the stretcher. Mrs.

Mayberry, why don't you go with this young lady back to her cabin and try to rest. You, sir," he said to Adam, "if you could stay awhile, I'd appreciate the company."

Adam nodded. Left unsaid was what the doctor actually meant; that if Tom Mayberry went into cardiac arrest again, an extra pair of hands, trained in CPR, would be useful to have around.

Back in her cabin, Susan couldn't get to sleep again. She put Edna into her bed and then crawled into Adam's. His scent, clinging to the pillow, tantalized her until all thoughts of sleep fled. She heard Edna tossing and turning and finally, knowing that neither of them would get to sleep again that night, she called the room steward and asked for a pot of tea and some toast.

She sat cross-legged on the bunk, wrapped in Adam's bedclothes, drinking tea and listening to Edna talk about her husband.

"We should never have come on this trip," said Edna morosely. "Tom wasn't feeling well a week ago, and, although he seemed to perk up and get better the last few days before we left, I should have known there was this possibility."

"Edna," soothed Susan. "We can't live our lives acting on possibilities. There are just too many of them. Probabilities, maybe, we should look at seriously. But possibilities, not a chance. It's possible that I could have a heart attack, or you, but neither of us would consider canceling a trip because of that possibility. You say he's never had any heart problems before, so there's no way you could have predicted this."

"I should at least have insisted that he have a checkup before we left."

"Did you? Did any of the others? Some of them are older than Tom by quite a few years. Don't berate yourself, Edna; it's something that couldn't have been predicted or prevented."

Edna sighed. "Thank you, Susan. Thank you for putting it in perspective. And thank you for caring."

Susan reached over and patted the older woman's hand.

124

"We all care about you. That's what groups like this are all about. That's why people travel together, so you're never alone. I bet that by noon today you'll have 28 other people falling over themselves to help you out. Your big problem now," she went on, "will be deciding whether to go home as soon as possible or stay on board."

"I want to go home," said Edna firmly.

"So would I, in your place. But you have to look at it from a practical point of view. Traveling home from Mexico is not always easy. There are no direct flights from these small coastal towns where we'll be stopping. Tom may not be well enough to stand the stress of flying over the mountains in a small plane and then changing planes, perhaps twice more, before he arrives home. There's a good hospital onboard ship, and a week's rest, at sea, could put him in far better shape for traveling. Also, from Acapulco, where we disembark, there's a direct flight home."

"I...I guess I never thought of it like that. Traveling is tiring even when you're well, and immediately after a heart attack, what he probably needs more than anything is rest."

"Why don't we wait until you speak with the doctor and see what he says?"

Edna nodded and lay down in the bunk again. Susan did the same and, within minutes, both were asleep.

Adam stepped into the cabin just as the early morning sun crept into the corners, banishing the shadows. He spoke to Edna for a moment, returning her cabin key and telling her that her husband was in the ship's hospital if she wanted to go and see him.

"How is he?" asked Susan after the other woman left.

"Not good," he answered wearily. "He arrested again shortly after you left, and it took longer to bring him back that time. We thought for a while we had lost him. He wasn't really in fit condition to be moved, but we did it anyway. Jim has a new heart drug that minimizes damage after an attack, but it has to be started within a couple of hours to do any good and he should be on a monitor."

"Jim?"

"The ship's doctor. When you go through a night like we did, you get on a first-name basis pretty fast. But the reason I came to get you is that we're sailing by something you absolutely have to see. Why don't you throw on some clothes while I shower, and I'll meet you on deck on the port side in about ten minutes."

What Adam wanted her to see was the jagged line of rocks of Cabo San Lucas. They were just coming up to the extreme end of land where the Baja peninsula marched majestically into the Pacific Ocean.

Susan leaned against the railing, enthralled by the towering rocks with the surf beating against their exposed side. She felt, rather than heard, Adam come up behind her.

"The ocean and the weather have been wearing these rocks down for a million years," he said. "Can you imagine how awesome they must have been when they first broke off?"

"Broke off? From what?"

"The coast of Mexico. A million years ago this long peninsula was part of the mainland. Then a massive earthquake ripped up the San Andreas Fault, and the Pacific Ocean rushed in, leaving a peninsula almost a thousand miles long, joined at the top by a narrow strip of land."

"Is that the same fault that goes through San Francisco?"

"One and the same. The San Andreas goes north from here almost 2000 miles."

"Do you think it could ever happen again?"

Adam shrugged. "Who knows? Some experts say the part of the fault that runs from Los Angeles to San Francisco is overdue for a big one. Those same experts say that the San Francisco earthquake of 1906 and the big one in 1989 were both small ones compared to what could happen someday. The ancient seer, Nostradamus, is supposed to have predicted that someday the entire west coast of California will fall into the sea."

Susan shivered. "That's an awful thought."

"But geologically very possible. If you look at a map of California you can see that a massive earthquake along the

126

San Andreas could split the peninsula another thousand miles north. That would put most of Greater Los Angeles underwater."

Neither said anything for a while. They were too preoccupied with keeping their balance on the pitching deck. The ship was rounding the cape, and the currents from the Pacific Ocean on the one side and the Sea of Cortez on the other warred for dominance.

Susan arranged for about half of her group to go on a sightseeing boat trip to view up close the spectacular arched rocks or "Los Arcos" and the nesting places of the sea lions. The others elected to stay on dry land for a while and do some shopping in the town of Cabo San Lucas.

Susan returned to the ship late that afternoon, tired, but happy. The boat trip to Los Arcos had been awesome. Not even the pitching of the small boat in the currents could dim their amazement at the towering rocks. At one point the boat cruised close to shore, and Susan took several pictures of the sea lions basking on the rocks. After the boat trip she took several members of the group on a quick tour of the shops before catching a tender back to the ship.

After dinner, Adam excused himself from the group, saying he was tired after his sleepless night.

"I'm going to check on Tom Mayberry before I turn in," he said quietly to Susan. "See you in the morning." He dropped a kiss lightly on her forehead and was gone.

Susan roamed restlessly around the ship after dinner. She went into the lounge and watched the show for a while, but her mind wasn't on it. Wandering into the casino, she bought a roll of quarters, but, after putting a few into an unresponsive slot machine, she tucked the rest into her purse.

Thinking she needed fresh air, she headed for the deck.

The sky was beautiful. A million stars splashed across the heavens, ten times brighter than they looked back in the city. The moon hung just out of reach beyond the ship's bow, lighting up the ocean and the ship so even the smallest detail was sharply etched. Leaning on the railing, Susan watched the moon carve a silvery track across the dancing waves as the ship cut through the night. Off to the left was the darker smudge of land with an occasional light winking through the darkness.

She had some thinking to do about Adam.

Now that she knew who he really was, a lot of things that puzzled her fell into place. The trip to Europe, the rich friends, the expensive gifts, were all out of character unless one had money...a lot of money.

She knew he had a lot of money, but something else seemed out of character. Why was he sharing her cabin? Why had he let her think he *had* to share her cabin because he couldn't afford one of his own?

She *knew* he hadn't told her he was the hotel manager. She would have remembered that. He also let her go on thinking he was a reservations clerk when he could have cleared up that misconception with a few words.

One thing was certain, Adam Joffrey misled her. Maybe he thought it was amusing to go slumming with a travel agent. Maybe he just wanted a bed partner for his vacation.

That scenario didn't sound right either. This was the fourth night of a ten-night trip, and not once during that time had he tried to get her into his bed. The one time things got a little hot and heavy was as much her fault as his.

So far, damn him, he'd acted like a perfect gentleman.

Trying to gauge her feelings for him was also getting her nowhere. She suspected she was already half in love with her cyber pal of two years, before they even met. She was prepared to like him regardless of his looks. The reality of Adam, of the tanned good looks and the lithe, athletic body, was stunning. The more she got to know him, the more she liked and respected the man.

If only he hadn't deliberately deceived her.

Sighing, she left the railing and started back to the cabin. She thought briefly of moving in with Grace. Instead she straightened her shoulders with determination. It was her cabin and she wasn't going to be forced out of it. Let Adam move. She was sure the captain's offer of a suite on A Deck was still valid.

Back in the cabin she quietly undressed for bed. Adam had turned down the air-conditioning and it was hot in the room. He was, as usual, asleep on his stomach, but tonight, for the first time, he didn't have a death grip on the blanket. The warmth in the cabin caused him to throw back the covers, and he was bare from the waist up. Her eyes were drawn to his finely muscled shoulders. *Swimmer's shoulders*, she thought, remembering how they felt under her hands yesterday. She longed to touch him again but didn't dare.

It was too warm to wear the utilitarian cotton pajamas so she rummaged around in her drawer for something a little lighter. She pulled out the pink satin teddy with the cocoa brown lace that she bought two years earlier for Jacey and smiled to herself. Several times she'd started to gift wrap it for Jacey, and every time the vision of herself wearing the teddy in a Hawaiian hotel overlooking Waikiki Beach came to mind, and she put it back unwrapped. Eventually she bought something else for Jacey.

When she packed for this cruise the pink teddy was one of the first things into the suitcase. On a hot night like tonight it would be the perfect thing to wear. With a glance at the soundly sleeping Adam, she put on the teddy. He would never see it, she told herself.

Susan drifted out of a delicious dream with a feeling of warmth and contentment still with her. She tried to turn over in bed but found herself imprisoned by the bedclothes. Opening her eyes, she saw Adam sitting on her bed, slowly stroking her hair. In her sleep she had curled herself around his warmth.

"Good," he said. "I'm glad you're awake. Our breakfast should be here in a few minutes."

"Our breakfast?" she repeated, with a sleepy-stupid glaze still in her eyes. "But we usually eat in the dining room with the others."

"Not today. I thought we needed a little time to ourselves. Do you realize we've hardly had five minutes without an audience since we boarded the ship."

"But Adam," she protested, "that's my job. I'm here to look after my group, not on vacation."

"I realize that," said Adam calmly, "and I'm not stopping you from doing your job. But, we're not going ashore until nine o'clock this morning, and I think the old folks can manage breakfast without you for one morning." He grinned and rose from the bed as a knock sounded on the door. "I decided I needed you this morning more than they did."

The steward entered with a heavily laden tray which he placed on the low table between the two beds. He picked up a coffee pot from a cart outside the door and added it to the tray.

"Will that be all, sir?" he asked Adam, his eyes studiously averted from Susan.

"Thank you, that will be fine," answered Adam as he closed the door, amusement dancing in his eyes as he noticed the blush creeping up Susan's cheeks. She had just realized what a cozy scene they presented. She, still half asleep lying in the bunk, and Adam in his robe.

Worse still, she was wearing the pink and brown lace teddy, the top showing above the sheet leaving very little to the imagination.

"Adam," she hissed, as the door closed behind the steward. "What will he think?"

"Nothing different from what he's been thinking all week, I imagine. After all, we've shared a cabin for four nights now. What's he supposed to think?"

Susan considered that for a moment and then laughed. "I guess you're right."

She sat up in bed, pulling the sheet around her so he wouldn't see just how scantily she was clothed.

"Well, Mr. Joffrey, I'm awake now. Let's have that breakfast you promised."

They finished the chilled, fresh-squeezed orange juice and the Eggs Benedict and were starting on the coffee before either spoke again. Susan scooted backward on the bunk until her back was against the wall, intent on keeping the sheet firmly in place around her and, at the same time, not spilling her coffee. Adam leaned back on his elbow staring into his coffee cup.

A wave of happiness and contentment swept over her as she watched him. His wavy, black hair was still messy from sleep, not yet combed flat for the day, his lashes fanned out on his cheeks as he frowned into his coffee, and his robe was wrinkled and coming undone at the waist. At that moment, he wasn't Adam, the rich heir to a hotel chain. He was her Adam, who had been her friend for two years.

It didn't matter that he had deceived her. It didn't matter why he was here. It mattered only that he was here. He had chosen to come on this trip with her, and he had chosen to share her cabin. So far he'd behaved impeccably and helped her in her job. They had six more days left at sea, and she was going to enjoy them, and enjoy him, and hang the consequences.

He looked up while she was thinking, and she realized they had been staring at each other for a couple of minutes. Abruptly he sat up and put down his empty coffee cup.

"What are your plans for this morning?" he asked.

She felt a surge of disappointment; half hoping he would ask something more personal.

"At nine we're going ashore, and I have a bus chartered to take us to see the Mazatlan Flyers and then on to the Mazatlan Arts and Crafts Center. It's the largest shopping complex on this coast and *the* place to shop for Mexican crafts. We'll be gone all morning, but we'll be back on board in time for lunch at one o'clock." She quirked a smile. "The ship sails at four, but most of them will nap during the afternoon after their strenuous morning."

"Will you have lunch with me today?" he asked quietly.

Her hopes soared, but she forced herself to speak calmly. "Don't I always?"

"Hah!" he snorted, "with me and thirty chaperones. Just for once I'd like you all to myself. We'll bring the group back here before one, and then grab a cab back into town. I'll call a friend at the el Presidente Hotel and make reservations for one-thirty in the dining room, and we'll have two glorious hours all to ourselves before we have to be back at the ship."

"Sounds marvelous. The el Presidente isn't a Bay Hotel is it?"

"No, it isn't, but the chef there is an old friend I've worked with before. He'll make sure we don't have any problems with *el tourista*."

Susan's heart sang as she scrambled off the bed, carefully taking the sheet with her, and headed for the shower. She was actually going to get some time alone with Adam.

On the bus during the ride to the Mazatlan Arts and Crafts Center, Susan repeated her warning about eating and drinking in Mexico.

"Don't drink the water or any of those colorful juices sold by the sidewalk vendors. If you get thirsty walking around in the heat, buy a can of soda and drink it from the can with a straw. Don't get a glass from a bar, and don't put ice in your drink. And, no matter how good it looks, don't touch the ice cream. Adam and I will be walking around the Center as well. If you wish, you can stick close to us, or you can wander off on your own. Just remember to be back at the entrance by 12:30. One other thing, keep your wallet in your front pocket and a tight grip on your purse. The local pickpockets love tourists."

Adam patted his wallet in his front pocket and smiled as he did it. His lady knew her stuff, all right. His smile widened into a grin as he realized he had thought of her as "his lady." There was no doubt in his mind that she was his. Now all he had to do was convince her of that.

They wandered through the Arts and Crafts Center buying souvenirs and haggling with the vendors. Susan bought wooden castanets for her two nephews.

"They'll drive my sister crazy," she laughed, "but what else are aunts for?" For Jenny Sue she bought a hand-carved wooden truck. "I'm afraid," she explained ruefully, "that with two older brothers, Jenny Sue has learned to like trucks better than dolls."

It was Adam who found the perfect gift for Jenny Sue, a rainbow-hued wind sock. "Put it where she can see it from her bedroom window and I guarantee she'll love it."

Susan was delighted with the wind sock. "I know just the place for it," she said. "We'll attach it to the fence post

132

outside Jenny Sue's window, and she can watch it whip around in the wind. What a marvelous idea. I'd never have thought of it."

Adam put his arm around her shoulders and squeezed. "One of my favorite things to do is buying gifts for my two special girls. It's something I've given a lot of thought to in the past couple of years."

Susan's heart lurched as she realized the truth of what Adam said. His gifts were always so perfect that they must have taken a lot of thought. Her head whirled as she thought about the implications of that. Did she mean as much to him as he did to her? That didn't seem possible, because he was very, very important to her.

Susan planned to buy a Mexican cotton dress, so she stopped and flipped through the racks in a couple of dress shops but couldn't find anything she liked. She came out of one store to find Adam leaning against a planter holding two cans of diet Coke.

"As recommended by my travel agent on the bus ride here today," he said with a cocky grin, handing her one of the cans. "Seriously," he said, as they walked companionably along, "you're very good at your job. You didn't go into a lot of explanations that no one would remember. You told them in a few words what to do and what not to do. And you even warned them about the pickpockets. See, I took your advice too." He laughed as he patted his wallet in his front pocket. "If any of your group gets into trouble, it certainly won't be your fault."

"Thank you. I appreciate your saying that." She got a warm rush of feeling at his compliment. "I was a bit worried about letting them wander around on their own in this huge shopping complex," she said anxiously.

"They're all adults," he said quietly. "You can't baby-sit them all the time. And," he went on, "you did give them the option of staying with you during the morning, and not one of them took you up on it."

"You're right," she said, feeling better about it. "I can't baby them all the time. I'm not their mother. In fact," she giggled, "some of them have tried to mother me."

They turned a corner in the Arts Center and walked down an alley lined with archways. They turned another corner into an open square and there, in a store window, Susan saw "The Dress". It was exactly what she was looking for, soft, almost sheer, white cotton, its low scooped neckline outlined in lace, full elbow-length sleeves trimmed in lace and lace inserts banding the three-tiered full skirt.

"Oh, Adam, this is it, the dress I've been looking for." She grabbed his arm and pulled him into the store. "I do hope it fits."

Five minutes later when she emerged from the fitting room, Adam caught his breath. The dress was perfect. It fit as if it were made for her, and, with her long blonde hair spilling over shoulders left bare by the wide-necked dress, she was so beautiful he couldn't take his eyes off her.

Seeing the look on Adam's face, the store proprietor murmured something in Spanish about the *"belle senora"*. Adam, without thinking, answered her in the same language. Immediately she launched into a voluble commentary in Spanish.

Susan turned around to see Adam looking a little discomfited as he listened to the woman. She thought at first he didn't understand and was surprised to hear him answer in Spanish. He turned and gazed at her, and a warm feeling crept over her at the glint in his eyes.

He said something to the proprietor who nodded vigorously and rummaged through a drawer behind a counter and came up with a delicate filigreed silver belt.

Susan held her breath as Adam clasped the belt around her waist and turned her around to face the mirror again.

"It's beautiful," she murmured. "It's the dress I wanted, and the belt is the perfect finishing touch."

"You're beautiful," he whispered, planting a kiss on her bare shoulder. "Leave the dress on. We'll carry your other things." His lips felt red-hot, sending a slash of desire through her to coil into a knot in her loins. She closed her eyes so he wouldn't see the effect his kiss had on her

When Susan emerged from the dressing room still wearing the white dress and carrying the dress she had worn earlier, Adam was just picking up his credit card and folding the receipt.

Susan intercepted him halfway to the door. "Adam!" she hissed. "You shouldn't have paid for this dress. I won't take you shopping with me again if you're going to do that. That's something...."

"Shh," Adam interrupted, nodding toward the door. "Not here. Let's go outside, and I'll explain."

Around the corner and barely out of sight of the store Susan stopped and folded her arms in front of her. "OK, explain!"

Adam grinned sheepishly. "I couldn't possibly have let you pay for it after what the lady said to me." He looked down at the floor. Susan smiled to herself with delight. Adam was actually embarrassed.

"Well, what did she say?"

Adam's dark eyes glinted. "She said that I must be a very happy man to be able to buy things for such a lovely bride. Then she wished me many happy years and many beautiful bambinos and gave me a discount on the belt because she was sure it wouldn't fit for very long."

Susan's cheeks flamed and she turned abruptly and walked away, not even noticing where she was going. Adam caught up to her and squeezed her shoulder. Sensing her discomfort he said lamely, "At least now you know why I couldn't let you pay for it. It would have ruined her day."

At one-thirty as Susan and Adam walked into the dining room of the el Presidente hotel, there was a commotion on one side of the room, a door burst open, and an immense man came toward them. A wide grin split his round brown face. Smothering Adam in a bear hug, he almost knocked him off his feet. Susan noted with amusement that the man was several inches taller than Adam's six feet, and outweighed him by about a hundred pounds. After they had gone through the macho ritual of pounding each other on the back, both men turned to Susan.

"Susan, I'd like you to meet a very good friend of mine. His name is Juan Hernandez, but his friends call him Tiny."

Tiny enveloped her hand in his huge one and favored her with another of his mile-wide grins. "If you're the one who has finally gotten Adam to come visit Mazatlan, you're my friend for life."

Bypassing a bewildered Maitre d', Tiny led them to a table by the window overlooking the ocean. He waved away a waiter approaching with menus and growled, "No menu. I will choose." Then he stalked back to the kitchen.

Susan suppressed her laughter as she watched a ruffled Adam put himself back together, tucking in the shirttails of his pale blue sport shirt and smoothing down his hair. His hair was curling up on one side where he had missed it, and Susan purposely didn't tell him about it.

The lunch was delicious, as Adam predicted it would be. They started with a cool jellied gazpacho, went on to several hot spicy dishes that Susan couldn't identify but which all tasted marvelous, and finished with a throat-soothing coffee-flavored ice cream marbled with Kahlua. Through it all a waiter kept their glasses filled with a strong, dark Mexican beer. Susan barely sipped at it, but Adam drank his with gusto.

He grinned apologetically as he noticed her almost-full glass. "Don't drink it if you don't like it. That beer has to grow on you. I hated it at first, but after being with Tiny for awhile, you learn to drink it in self defense."

"Where did you and Tiny get to know each other?"

"I first met him at the Chicago Bay Hotel. We were both still in school. I had a summer job at the hotel as Wine Steward in the main dining room, and Tiny was an apprentice chef. We share a love of baseball and spent many of our free afternoons watching the Cubs at Wrigley Field." Adam stared out the window, a distant smile on his face. "Then later when I was Assistant Manager at the Dallas Bay, I hired Tiny as Head Chef in our rooftop Garden Room."

Susan shook her head in disbelief. "Why would he leave a prestigious position like that for a resort hotel in Mazatlan?"

"I think he was homesick. Even though he went to school in the States, Tiny always had strong ties to Mexico. His family was here, and so was the girl he eventually married. Besides," he smiled, "you know the old saying, 'better to be a big frog in a small pond than a small frog in a big one.' And Tiny is a big man in Mazatlan."

"Tiny is a big man in any land," said Susan with a smile. They were silent for a minute as both watched the waves rolling in on the beach below their window. "I'm stuffed," said Susan, groaning as she patted her stomach. "Do we have time for a quick walk on the beach?"

"Sure," said Adam, standing. "Let's duck out this side door here, then we'll come back in and say good bye to Tiny before we leave."

At the foot of the steps leading to the beach Susan stopped to take off her shoes, grateful that, as a concession to the heat, she hadn't worn stockings. Adam rolled up his pant legs after doffing his shoes and socks. Leaving their shoes on the steps, they stepped out onto the burning sand. Adam took her hand in his and squeezed it gently as they ran across the hot sand to the cooler, hard-packed sand near the water. They walked along in silence, occasionally side-stepping quickly to avoid a wave that came farther up the beach. One wave caught them unawares, wetting their feet, and Susan, enjoying the cool feeling, picked up her skirt and waded farther in.

"I can't believe I'm actually wading in the Pacific Ocean," she said with a delighted grin. "We've been sailing on it for the past four days, but this is the first time I've actually wet my feet in it."

Adam laughed as another wave wet the bottom of her skirt, and she almost lost her footing trying to snatch it out of the way.

"You remind me of a child playing in the surf. I kind of take the ocean for granted and forget sometimes how much fun it is to play in."

He hitched his pant legs higher and waded in with her. Susan, remembering something she and Trish used to do as children, pulled the back of her skirt between her legs and tucked it into the front of her belt, making a pair of baggy shorts and effectively keeping her skirt out of the water.

Adam eyed the result with amusement. "I liked that dress when you first put it on this morning, but I think it's rather fetching that way too." In fact, he thought, he would probably remember her forever just like this, long blonde hair streaming in the breeze, sun-kissed skin glowing from a few days at sea, her Mexican dress with the skirt looped into the filigree silver belt, her long shapely legs with the surf breaking around the ankles, and a sparkle of childish delight in those incredible blue eyes. He shook himself out of his reverie and took her hand.

They ran hand in hand along the beach for several minutes, splashing in the surf and laughing and dodging the larger waves. Finally Susan, out of breath, slowed to a walk. Adam put an arm around her waist and held her against him as they walked another few minutes before reluctantly turning around to head back to the hotel. A parasailer floated by overhead, and a little farther out boardsailers scudded over the waves. Adam looked out to sea, past the boardsails and the sailboats, his gaze seemingly fixed on something even farther away.

"It's hard to believe that 2,000 miles straight out there are the Hawaiian Islands. That this little wave," he said as he kicked at the next wave that broke on the sand, "could have washed the sand on Waikiki in front of my hotel just a few days ago." He smiled down at her. "And Buffalo is 2,000 miles almost due north from here. We're a long way from home, you and me. But we're here. We finally made it!"

Suddenly he stopped, grabbed Susan around the waist, and lifted her in the air with an exuberance she hadn't seen before. "We did it, Susan Jeffrey," he shouted. "We finally did it. After two years of e-mailing and wondering, we've finally met." He put her down and pulled her close, wrapping his arms around her and burying his face in her hair.

"I was afraid to ask you before," he said, whispering into her hair, still not looking at her face, "but how did you really feel when we met? Were you disappointed?"

Susan's arms tightened around his waist. "Never," She murmured, so low he could barely hear her over the crashing surf. "You're everything I thought you would be, and more. I was afraid you'd be disappointed in me."

"Oh, Susan, how could you even think such a thing?" They rocked together in a contented embrace until a small child, screaming at a friend as he raced through the surf, broke the spell. "It's getting late. I think it's time we were getting back."

Their leaving was as boisterous as their arrival, with Susan getting a hug this time as well. Tiny exhorted them to return as soon as possible and presented Susan with a covered container of "goodies" to keep in their cabin.

"Just in case you get hungry," he said. "I chose the ones with no cream, so just keep the container closed tightly, and they should keep for a few days."

"Just what we need, more food!" said Susan wryly, as they got into a cab for the trip back to the ship. "The way they feed us onboard ship, I've already put on a couple of pounds since I left home."

"I can't see where," he said, as his eyes ran over her warmly. "So I guess you must have needed them."

He put an arm around her shoulders and pulled her closer to him. Susan settled her head on his shoulder with a contented sigh. She was almost asleep when a slight snore told her he had beaten her to it. That beer must have been every bit as strong as she figured. They rode the rest of the way back to the ship with Susan enjoying the warm feeling of Adam's limp body leaning against her.

CHAPTER 8

Susan checked her watch a couple of times on the trip back to the ship. They were cutting it a bit close; the ship was due to sail at 4 o'clock and, thanks to their walk on the beach, it was after 3:30 when they drove onto the dock.

She smiled to herself. She wouldn't have missed that walk on the beach for anything. It was the first time Adam really let down his hair and behaved as if he were having fun. It was worth a few anxious moments worrying about the time.

When they arrived back at their cabin, Susan wanted to wash the salt spray out of her hair. Adam was lying on his bunk with his eyes closed, and she thought he'd fallen asleep again. She undressed in the tiny bathroom and, not wanting to get her clothes wet, opened the door a crack and tossed them out.

She had just poured the shampoo on her head and, eyes closed, was working her hair into a lather when she felt, rather than heard, the shower curtain pulled aside. Her eyes flew open and Adam was standing there, gloriously nude, with an unreadable expression on his face.

"I thought you might need some help," he said hoarsely. "Salt doesn't wash out easily."

He turned her around, facing away from him and started working his fingers through her lather-laden hair. As he massaged her scalp, running his fingers along her nape and up through her hair, the pure sensuousness made her quiver and an ache of desire started deep in her belly. He squeezed some of the lather from her hair and dropped it on her shoulders. Susan watched for a moment as a ball of foam ran down her breast, caught on a nipple, and then dropped to the floor.

The spell was broken and she gasped as Adam turned the full force of the water on her head to rinse off the shampoo. When her hair was squeaky clean he pushed it to the front, picked up the soap and began on her back. Working the lather into her skin turned into a massage as Adam stroked and squeezed the muscles of her shoulders.

Susan leaned her forehead against the wall of the shower and groaned with pleasure; certain Adam wouldn't hear her above the pounding water. Again he rinsed the soap off, then lightly kissed her on the shoulder, patted her on one buttock cheek, and left as soundlessly as he had come.

Susan, her legs suddenly weak, held on to the shower head and let the water beat down on her. She couldn't believe what happened! It was like a dream. Other than his first offer of help with her hair, Adam hadn't said a word. Her bottom still tingled with the feel of his hand. A smile broke out, and she hugged herself with delight. The smile faded as another thought surfaced. Why hadn't he tried to make love to her? He certainly had the opportunity. Was there something wrong with her? She turned off the shower and looked at herself critically in the mirror. Other than her straggly wet hair, she didn't look too bad. Maybe he didn't like blondes. Maybe he liked his women with more veneer and sophistication. If so, what was he doing here, on this boat, and in her cabin? She sighed. Adam Joffrey was an enigma.

She wrapped a towel around herself and peeked out into the cabin. Relieved to see that Adam was nowhere in sight, she dressed quickly in a matching raw silk pants and vest with a long-sleeved silk blouse.

She found Adam in the bar nursing a scotch, staring grimly into the glass as he swirled the ice cubes. She was suddenly shy, not quite certain whether or not to mention the incident in the shower. She was still hesitating when Adam looked up and saw her, a smile breaking over his face as the grim look disappeared.

He downed his drink and stood. "I'm not interested in dinner," he said, "I'm still too full of Tiny's magnificent lunch, but I need some fresh air. Let's go up on deck."

The lights of Mazatlan were fading in the distance. The ship passed out of the harbor and was on the open ocean. El Faro, the second tallest natural lighthouse in the world, winked at them from the harbor entrance. The ocean-cooled evening breeze had a chill in it causing Susan to shiver.

"Cold?" asked Adam, rubbing her arms as if to smooth out the goosebumps. "Would you like me to get you a jacket?"

"No. I have to go in now anyway. Even though I'm not eating, I should go check out the dining room while the group is still all there."

"Roll call?"

"That too." She laughed.

She was almost at the door leading into the companionway when she heard Adam's low voice, pitched just above the background noise of the ship.

"Susan?"

She turned around, and her breath caught in her throat. He was standing in a bar of light from one of the lounge windows, and she had to curl her toes into the wooden deck to keep from running back to him. He was wearing a white linen jacket with the sleeves pushed up, dark pants that hugged his lean hips, and a dark shirt open at the neck. His hair was ruffled by the wind. He was the most devastatingly handsome man she had ever seen in her life.

"The Quarterdeck Bar, in an hour. OK?"

The Quarterdeck was a small bar tucked into the back of the sports center. By day it served cool drinks to people working out, but at night it was a cozy intimate bar with low lights and soft music that quickly became known as "the lovers' bar."

"OK," she whispered, and turned and ran the rest of the way to the dining room, arriving flushed and out of breath.

The others were contentedly eating dinner and regaling each other with stories of their bargains and bargaining in the Mazatlan Arts and Crafts Center. No one noticed her except Charles, who gave her a wide grin as he took in her flushed appearance. He waved her off as if to say everything was all right, but she shook her head and sat in an empty chair.

She had an hour before meeting Adam again, so she ordered a pot of tea and nibbled a roll. She tried to put her day in perspective, from her early morning breakfast in bed, to shopping in the Arts and Crafts Center, to lunch at the el Presidente Hotel, their walk on the beach, the episode in the shower, and Adam's request to meet her in the "lovers' bar". It was undoubtedly one of the most eventful days of her life, and she had a feeling it wasn't over yet.

The waiter placed two liqueurs in front of Adam. The Drambuie he'd ordered for himself and an Amaretto for Susan. He glanced up and saw her in the doorway trying to find him in the dimly lit bar. He didn't take his eyes off her as he passed his key card to the waiter to cover the bar tab, so he knew the instant she spotted him. Even in the shadowy darkness he saw her eyes light up. The thought that the look in her eyes and the smile that followed was for him alone did things to his equilibrium and his hormones. God! His hormones were acting up as they hadn't since he was in his teens. He didn't know how much longer he could sleep in the same cabin as Susan and keep his hands off her.

Susan threaded her way between the closely packed tables to the empty chair that Adam managed to save for her.

Adam forced his mind off his raging hormones and willed his voice to speak normally.

"Everyone present and accounted for?"

"Every last one, and they're enjoying themselves enormously. You wouldn't believe the shopping stories they're telling. If even half the tales of bargains and haggling are true, you and I are rank amateurs in the shopping department. Grace Cole practically bought the place out. Charles claims that half the stuff she bought she didn't even want, but, after haggling the price down for the sheer fun of it, the bargains were too good to resist."

Susan knew she was babbling. As long as they talked about her charges they could avoid talking about themselves. She picked up her Amaretto and gulped a large mouthful. The pungent liqueur took her breath away and made her cough, but at least it stopped her talking.

When she got her voice back she asked: "Were you waiting very long?"

"Yes...no." Adam looked up with a smile. "I did give you an hour, remember, so it's not your fault. I stayed on deck for a while longer, until it got too cold. I've been in here for about half an hour now, just sitting and thinking."

Susan leaned back in her chair with a contented sigh, enjoying just relaxing quietly with Adam.

"Thinking about what?"

"You."

Susan's body tensed with apprehension, and her eyes searched his, wishing she could see him better in the dim light.

"Why me?"

"Why not you? Would you like to know what I was thinking?"

"Only the good parts." Her voice quavered as she tried for a lighter note and failed.

"I was thinking," he said in a low voice, pitched so only she could hear, "of what it would be like to make love with you."

Susan's breath caught in her throat, and she would swear her heart stopped before it resumed hammering at twice the normal speed. She thought of waking up this morning and sharing breakfast with Adam, of kissing him on the beach, of how she felt as he washed her hair in the shower and how upset she was when he abruptly left.

"That's definitely the good part." Her voice quavered. "I... well; I was wondering the same thing earlier today."

Adam stood abruptly and reached for her hand. "Let's go," he said. "We have a few things to talk about."

Susan's mind was in a whirl as she followed Adam back to their cabin.

The door was barely shut behind them before he pulled her into his arms. His body pinned hers against the cabin door in a bruising, searing kiss. Time stood still as she wrapped her arms around his waist and hung on tightly. When he lifted his head and stepped back he was like a man in a daze.

"I'm sorry, Susan. Did I hurt you?"

She shook her head, unaware that they hadn't turned on the lights and he couldn't see her.

"I've wanted to kiss you like that," he said, "ever since this morning when I saw you in that pink lace confection."

Susan smiled to herself. So he had seen the pink teddy.

"But," he went on, "you've had responsibilities all day, and I told myself that I'd keep `hands off' as long as you were working."

"But I'm not working now," she murmured.

"Thank heavens for small miracles. I thought we'd never make it. Barring any other emergencies, maybe we can get a little 'hands on' time for ourselves," he finished hoarsely as he cupped her face in his hands. His lips slid across hers like warm satin. He flicked the corner of her mouth with his tongue and returned to gently tease it open. A warm feeling flooded through her as she wound her arms around his neck and instinctively pressed her body against his. She opened her mouth as he deepened the kiss and shivered with delight as their tongues tangled in the age-old thrust and parry dance of love.

His hands slid along her shoulders and down her back, stopping to massage the muscles before slipping farther down to cup her firm, round bottom. He pulled her tightly against him so she could feel his firm rigidness growing between them. A searing wave of desire ripped through her and she pressed herself even tighter, her pelvis rocking gently against his.

Adam lifted his mouth from hers with a gasp. "Tell me now if you want to stop," he said. "Another minute of this and I won't be able to."

He started kissing her again as if to prevent her from answering, but Susan didn't need words. Her answer was to start unbuttoning his shirt. Adam pulled her to him with a groan, trapping her hands between them.

"Susan, Susan, my love. I've waited so long for this, for you."

"My love," the words hung between them and went singing through her soul. She hardly noticed as Adam slipped the vest from her shoulders and started on the buttons of her silk blouse. What she did notice was the tremor in his hands, and that delighted her even more. Adam, who was always so reserved, so in control of himself, was actually trembling! Her blouse undone, Adam snapped the clasp on her bra and tossed both of them on the bunk.

The full moon had just risen above the horizon and shone through the porthole, moving back and forth as the ship rolled with the waves. Adam was speechless as the moon shone on Susan's bare breasts, highlighting their perfection

145

while her face above and hips below were in shadow. He traced a finger around one globe, letting it trail off her nipple. The nipple peaked as the moonbeam slid off it and, answering the roll of the ship, momentarily lit up Susan's face. The sheer longing in her eyes as she reached for him pierced his heart.

"It's not fair," she whispered. "You've got too many clothes on." She pulled his shirt out of his waistband and, leaning forward, rubbed her breasts against the crisp, curly hair on his chest, delighting in the feel against her erect nipples.

Adam, unable to stand it any longer, threw off his shirt and jacket and divested himself of the rest of his clothes in record time. Susan unabashedly stared when he stood in front of her nude, and Adam let her look, glorying in her enjoyment of him. Then he sat on the bunk and slowly slipped off, first her slacks and then the tiny scrap of lace that passed for underwear. He trailed his fingers down her soft stomach then followed with his lips, feeling her muscles tighten spasmodically at his touch.

Eyes closed, she was lost in sensation and gave no resistance when Adam stretched out on the bunk and pulled her down beside him. For a moment they just lay there, enjoying the feeling of touching skin to skin. Then imperceptibly Adam started to move, running his hand over the silky skin of her hip, dipping into the hollow of her waist, moving down to cup her buttock cheek before playing lightly up her spine, across her rib cage and coming to rest on the underside of her breast. He rasped his palm lightly across the nipple, and Susan shivered at the sensation.

Levering himself up on his elbow, he leaned over and traced the curve of her breast with his tongue. She gasped and reached for him as he hotly and wetly engulfed first one nipple then the other, sending shards of flame-tipped feeling deep inside her.

He slipped lower and buried his face in her belly as his hand crept between her thighs. He caressed the velvet-soft skin there before tangling his fingers in the damp tendrils. Instinctively her thighs parted, and his fingers slipped into the hot moistness. She moaned and pulled at his head. He moved

146

up until he was partly on top of her and kissed her with a mind-drugging thoroughness, his tongue emulating what his fingers were doing.

Susan moaned and reached for his rigid erection, feeling its pulsating hardness against her hip.

"Oh, sweetheart," he groaned, "don't touch me there, or it'll be all over much too soon." Susan nipped his shoulder with her teeth and ran her hand up his sweat-slicked belly and into the thick covering of curly chest hair, seeking out the flat male nipples and teasing them until they stood erect.

Adam rolled over completely on top of her and settled himself between her legs, lifting them high around his waist for comfort in the narrow bunk.

"This is a hell of a time to ask you," he murmured, "but are you protected? Because if not I can...."

"No problem," she whispered back. "I'm OK." She gasped as Adam moved slightly and with a groan sheathed himself completely in her hot wetness. The shock and the ecstasy reverberated through both of them, and neither moved for a minute as the reality of the experience engulfed them, the heat of their joining wrapping around them like a warm blanket.

Adam lifted himself on his elbows so he could see her face in the faint moonlight.

"I wish I'd left the light on," he whispered. "I would love to watch your eyes while we make love. Do you know you have beautiful eyes? As deep and blue as the Pacific Ocean on a summer day."

Susan started to answer, but Adam began to move rhythmically within her, and all speech fled. He moved slowly at first, each stroke being almost more than she could bear. A wave of heat and need spread outward from her center to the tips of her fingers and toes. Her back arched, her fingertips dug into his clenched buttock muscles, and an involuntary cry warbled through the cabin as she burst over the edge of ecstasy. Adam called her name, and every muscle tensed as with a final stroke he followed her over the peak.

Adam's head dropped to the pillow, and they held each other in the afterglow, absorbing each other's body heat as the tremors ceased and breathing slowed. They turned onto their sides, snuggled close together, legs still entwined, amazingly comfortable in the narrow bunk. There was so much to say, so much to discuss in their changed relationship, but neither wanted to talk now. The time for talk would come later. Adam pulled up the sheet and tucked it around them. Susan couldn't remember ever feeling so safe, so happy and so at peace. Just before she drifted into a deep sleep she thought she heard Adam whisper, "I love you, Susan Jeffrey."

The ship was rolling in a heavy sea when Susan came awake with a start. She was curled on her side on the narrow bunk, and Adam was wrapped around her spoon-fashion, his knees tucked into the back of hers and his arm around her waist. At first she thought he was still asleep, until she felt the soft sensation of his fingers spreading and closing as he rubbed the soft skin of her belly. It was that slight movement, rather than the movement of the ship, that awakened her. Her stomach muscles contracted involuntarily and told him she was awake.

He came up on his elbow and, nudging the tangle of silky hair aside with his chin, he kissed the hollow of her neck. She shivered with delight, that one kiss bringing back all the memories of earlier that evening. He brought his hand up to caress her breasts, the nipples peaking at his touch. Susan didn't know how she managed to turn over in the narrow bunk without knocking Adam on the floor, but turn she did, wrapping her arms and legs around him to keep him from falling off. The loving this time was slow, without the frantic pace of before. It was all the more wonderful for being savored at leisure.

"I've been wondering ever since I met you what it would be like to make love with you," said Adam. "I wasn't kidding when I said that earlier. The fantasy was great," he whispered into her hair, "but the reality is pure heaven."

"Um...mm," she murmured. "It's even better than chocolate macadamia."

Susan held him tightly, this time not just to keep him from falling out of bed. She wanted to remember forever the feel of his body against hers. She knew that no matter what

148

happened from now on between her and Adam, she would never be the same. She had fallen in love, totally and irrevocably, and she hadn't the faintest idea what she was going to do about it.

Susan drifted out of sleep to the sound of the shower. There was no movement in the ship, and she could hear sounds outside, shouts and the occasional bang on the side of the ship.

We're docked in Puerto Vallarta, she thought.

She glanced at Adam's empty bed and remembered him leaving her to return to his own bed in the night. They'd tried to sleep together, but the bed was just too narrow, and, after almost falling out a couple of times, Adam reluctantly returned to his own. It was the only way either of them would get any sleep. Susan remembered how lonely and cold she felt when he left, even though his head was only two feet from hers where the bunks came together in the corner. What she wouldn't give for a double bed right then!

A smile stole across her face as she listened to the shower. She rose from the bed and padded naked to the bathroom door.

"Need any help?" she purred silkily to a startled Adam through the clouds of steam.

Taking the soap from him, she lathered her hands and started working it into the hair on his chest. He stood motionless while she worked her fingers through the lather and moved only slightly when she flicked her fingernails across his flat nipples, making them stand up at attention. He leaned weak-kneed against the shower wall when she followed the line of hair lower, soaping as she went. Long before she started soaping his groin, he was fully and blatantly aroused. She ignored his rigid arousal, except for a quick kiss on the tip which elicited an agonized groan from Adam, and went on to soaping his thighs. She caressed his knees including an erotic spot on the soft skin at the back of his knee that pulled another groan from Adam.

By this time Susan was so weak-kneed herself that she had trouble standing up again. Adam helped her to her feet and pulled her against him. The slick feeling of soapy skin against skin was Adam's undoing. Getting a grip on her buttocks, he lifted her and entered her all in one motion as Susan wrapped her legs around his waist and hung on for the ride. The dual sensations of slippery skin in front and the hot shower pounding on her back sent Susan over the edge in seconds with Adam following immediately.

Adam let her go, and Susan slipped slowly to her feet, trembling in the aftermath, her blue eyes locked with his brown ones. Tenderly he caressed her cheek as the water rinsed the soap off them.

"I love you, Susan," he said. "I think this was fated from the first time we spoke on the phone over two years ago."

"I love you too," whispered Susan. "I can't believe we've only really known each other for five days. It's much too soon."

"We've only *seen* each other for five days." he said. "We've *known* each other for two years." Suddenly he laughed. "This is a funny place to do this, in a cramped shower, soaking wet, and looking like two drowned rats, but will you marry me, Susan?"

Susan stared at him for a moment, stunned. She had fantasized about an affair with him, but marriage seemed so out of reach.

"Hurry up and say yes, my sweet. I'm wet, and I'm starting to get cold."

"Oh, yes, yes, Adam. Of course I'll marry you." Grinning delightedly, she hugged him again, and it was another few minutes before they emerged from the shower and hurriedly toweled themselves dry.

Their shared shower that morning meant that Susan and Adam missed breakfast in the dining room, so they grabbed a quick bite from the buffet on the pool deck. Neither paid any attention to what they ate. They were totally absorbed in each other.

Adam couldn't keep his hands or his eyes off her. All through breakfast he was either holding her hand or putting his arm around her shoulders or running his fingers through her silky blonde hair. Susan was euphoric. There was a glow to her skin and a sparkle in her eyes that announced to the world her changed relationship with Adam.

There was a bus tour of Puerto Vallarta arranged for their group that morning, and they were to meet at 9:00 in the lounge near the gangway.

Susan was embarrassed when she and Adam walked into the lounge. She was sure her feelings were plain on her face and that everyone would know that she and Adam had slept together last night. It didn't occur to her that everyone presumed that was their relationship right from the beginning. She was amazed that no one noticed anything amiss, and only Charles gave her a long look with raised eyebrows then turned away with a wink and a grin when she started to blush.

She walked over to the bar to pour a glass of water while she collected her thoughts, then studiously avoided Adam's gaze while she went over the morning's itinerary.

"The bus will pick us up on the dock in about fifteen minutes," she began. "First we'll drive out into the countryside for a few miles so you can see a real Mexican farm, then we'll go to Mismaloya Beach where the movie `Night of the Iguana' was filmed. It was in Puerto Vallarta during the filming of this movie that Richard Burton and Elizabeth Taylor fell in love." Adam, off to one side, made a sudden movement as he shifted on his seat, and Susan almost lost her train of thought. She cleared her throat and went on, describing how they would drive through Gringo Gulch, a residential area where a lot of celebrities lived for part of the year.

"When we come back into the city we'll pay a quick visit to the Cathedral of Our Lady of Guadeloupe. Then we'll visit several factory outlets." She smiled at the interested look on some of the faces, especially Grace Cole's. "Mexico does a lot of brand name manufacturing under license," she explained. "You'll find stores here that sell brand names such as Ralph Lauren Polo, Ocean Pacific, Fiorucci and Caressa Jourdan shoes at much lower prices than stateside. We'll have you back to the ship for lunch, but if you're not all shopped out there's more to do this afternoon within walking distance of the ship. The round building you'll see on the dock is an Arts and

Crafts Center, and I understand they have some very interesting and unusual gift items. Then down on the beach just south of the dock there is a flea market. That's where you'll probably get your best buys on Mexican woven rugs and jewelry. Or you can just sit on the beach and sun. If you're really brave you might want to try parasailing." The hoots of laughter that greeted that last comment told her there would be no parasailing with this group.

Adam went along on the sightseeing trip, taking his duties as volunteer assistant seriously. Some of the older ladies needed a little help getting on and off the bus and Adam was there lending a hand and sometimes giving an unobtrusive boost where needed. The cobblestone streets and the foot-high stone curbs in the old shopping district of Puerto Vallarta were picturesque but made hazardous walking. As Susan watched Adam making several trips over rough sidewalks and up steps with an elderly lady on each arm, her heart swelled with pride and love. That this wonderfully caring man loved her made her happiness complete.

They returned to the ship in time for a late lunch. Some of the group decided on a nap afterward, but most opted for the beach or the flea market. Adam and Susan decided to stroll through the flea market. Susan wanted to buy a couple of the brightly colored woven blankets she glimpsed from the bus as they drove by. She thought Trish's two boys would like them for their beds.

They wandered through the market for almost an hour picking up a few souvenirs. Adam proved to be a very adept bargainer and Susan got the blankets at such a good price that she decided to buy a third one for herself. Adam good-naturedly carried all their purchases, sometimes lagging behind to look at a booth while Susan forged ahead. Once when she backtracked to look for him she found him staring intently at a display of Mexican silver jewelry. He looked up and saw her and beckoned her to come closer.

"I've finally found what I've been looking for," he said. "Just look at this. Isn't it perfect?" He picked up an intricately detailed silver ring, the wide band covered with a deeply

152

etched design of intertwined hearts and flowers. "Let's see how it fits."

He placed the ring on the third finger of her left hand. It fit perfectly. Still holding her hand, he lifted it to tilt her chin upward and dropped a kiss on her open mouth.

"That's to seal our engagement until I can replace it with a very special ring."

Susan swallowed convulsively and tightened her grip on his fingers. "There'll never be a ring more special than this one," she whispered.

Adam smiled. "Wait till you see the other one. My mother has a magnificent five-carat natural Alexandrite. It's my birthstone, and my father gave it to her the day I was born. She always said it was mine when I found the special girl to wear it. We'll stop in San Francisco on the way home to pick it up."

While Adam was paying for the silver ring, she felt the first stirring of unease. *We'll stop on the way home*, he had said. Didn't he know that she was flying home from Acapulco with her group? They had a stopover in Dallas-Fort Worth, and she had to be with them, because part of her duties as escort was to see that they got on the right flight.

She felt an even stronger uneasy feeling when she thought about what would happen after that. She and Adam had met and fallen in love, but what would happen when she was back in Buffalo and he was back in Honolulu? Their circumstances hadn't really changed. It looked as if they had a lot of talking to do. Last night before they went to their cabin, Adam said they needed to talk. Instead of talking, they made love.

Tonight she would have to keep her hormones under control until she found out just what he had in mind. She shivered even though the sun was still high overhead. Suddenly the world was not as rosy as it had been an hour earlier.

While walking back along the flea market booths toward the ship, Susan spotted a lovely ivory and gold woven rug that would look just perfect in front of her fireplace. Her mind was in a turmoil thinking of Adam and what the future held for them. She wasn't really in the mood for buying anything but stopped anyway.

"How much?" she asked the wizened little man tending the booth.

"Twenty dollar?" he answered hopefully.

Susan shook her head. Grace had bought one in Mazatlan for the equivalent of about $12. "How much in pesos?" she asked, hoping to get it for a better price in the local currency.

"No pesos," said the vendor. "Very fine quality. US dollar only. For you, lady, because is late in the day and ship leaves soon, fifteen dollar US."

"I don't think so." Susan shook her head as she checked the coin purse she was carrying. "I only have five dollars left."

"Five dollar!" shrieked the little man. "It cost me twice that." Susan shrugged and started to walk away, but the man, amazingly agile for his apparent age, ran ahead and blocked her way. "Lady, have pity on a poor man. I have to make a living. Twelve dollar, just for you if you promise not to tell another soul." He shuddered. "I couldn't afford to sell any more at that price."

Susan was so lost in her own thoughts she didn't notice Adam grinning hugely at this byplay. She was about to step around the man when she remembered the three dollars in change from the blankets that she stuffed into a pocket instead of opening her purse again.

"Eight dollars," she told the man. "And that's my final price."

"Lady, I have five bambinos and a sick mother-in-law," he whined. "For eight dollar I lose money. I give you for ten dollar and I break even." Susan shook her head, looked around for Adam, and started walking rapidly back to the ship.

They had gone only a couple of hundred feet beyond the market booths when they heard a shout, and Susan turned to see the little man running across the open space between the market and the parking lot. He was carrying the rug rolled into a bundle.

"Eight dollar, Lady. Quick, before anyone see us." He shoved the rug in her arms, grabbed the money, and was gone in just a few seconds. Susan stood there nonplussed, not quite sure how she came to purchase a rug for that price. Adam's laughter rang out as he clapped her on the back, almost dropping their numerous parcels as he did so.

"That's the best bit of bargaining I've seen in ages. You were marvelous, Sweetheart. Did you see the look on his face when he realized he wasn't going to get any more out of you?"

"I was? I mean, no I didn't," Susan stammered. "That poor man. Do you think I owe him some more money?"

Adam looked down into her troubled blue eyes and would have kissed her if they weren't in the middle of a parking lot in full view of anyone on the ship. "No, Sweetheart. He probably did quite well on the sale. Just not as well off you as he did off some of the other tourists today. Come on. We still have to put our costumes together for the masquerade dance tonight."

Susan resolutely put her misgivings out of her mind and enjoyed the rest of the afternoon. They stood on the stern and watched the ship leave the harbor of Puerto Vallarta. Susan sighed as she watched the picturesque town recede in the distance. Night of the Iguana may have put Puerto Vallarta on the map, but Adam had imprinted it indelibly on her heart. Elizabeth Taylor and Richard Burton may have fallen in love here, but she and Adam had declared their love here. Whatever happened in the future, these two exotic places, Mazatlan and Puerto Vallarta, would be forever enshrined in her memories of her love for Adam. She was becoming more certain than ever that memories would be all she would have. In the heat of the moment, Adam asked her to marry him, but he obviously hadn't thought about the problems involved, and they had yet to discuss them.

When the ship cleared the harbor, they went below to their cabin to ready their costumes for that evening. Some ships had a masquerade night midway through the cruise. This ship did and Susan warned Adam of this tradition before he left home. Some people brought outfits especially for masquerade while others created something onboard ship from supplies obtained from the cruise director.

Adam had brought his own costume, and she laughed when he tried it on. He brought baggy neon pink shorts, a wild flower-patterned Hawaiian shirt, a floppy cotton sun hat in the same neon pink, two huge white silk-flower leis, and a camera around his neck. He completed the costume by thrusting his bare feet into rubber beach thongs.

"*Voila*! A tourist. A strange species indeed, but I wouldn't be in business without them."

"Me neither. But I don't usually see them looking like that. I see them in a business suit when they pick up their tickets, complaining about baggage allowance and wondering what the weather will be like."

"We really do have a lot in common you know. We're both in the same business, the travel business, just at opposite ends. You in sending and I in receiving," he joked. "But," he said, his voice sobering, "right now we're in a paradox. We're caught in the middle. On the one hand we're acting like tourists, enjoying ourselves, but on the other...."

"On the other I have responsibilities," she sighed. "And one of them is that I promised the sisters. Maudie and Clara, that I'd help them with their costumes. Lily might need some help too; she's not very agile with her arthritic fingers."

"OK, I'll let you go for now," said Adam with an injured look that made Susan laugh. "But what about your own costume? I haven't seen it yet."

"Oh, I thought I would just wear my red skirt and white blouse. I could put a tinfoil crown on my head and go as the Queen of Hearts. That won't take long to put together."

"Uh Uh," said Adam, shaking his head. "I think I can do better than that. You go look after your 'responsibilities,' and I'll put your costume together. It'll be waiting for you when you get back."

"Thanks," she said giving him a hug before going out the door. "Just don't make it too outrageous. I have my reputation to uphold. And," she popped her head back around the door, "30 chaperones I don't want to shock." Adam chuckled as he shut the door. He'd been wondering how to broach the subject of the costume, and now he had the perfect excuse.

Helping some of her charges with their costumes took longer than expected, and Susan hurried back to her own cabin just as first sitting dinner was announced.

Adam was nowhere in sight, but spread out on her bed was a length of cotton fabric in a beautiful brown, gold and white print that she recognized from pictures as Hawaiian tapa cloth. On top of it was a sheet of paper with printed instructions on how to wrap the fabric and knot it as a Hawaiian *pareu*. Also on the bed were a white silk lei like the one Adam had worn, a red hibiscus flower on a clip for her hair, a green leaf fringe to tie around one ankle, and her beach thongs.

Grinning hugely, Susan tried on the *pareu*. She was wearing her underwear at first, but, realizing she might not always be able to keep it closed, she opted instead for her bikini. Then modesty persuaded her to put a discrete safety pin at the hip to hold it closed.

Surveying herself in the mirror, she was quite pleased. The outfit would have been more appropriate on a beach in Hawaii than on a cruise ship in Mexico, and her blonde hair looked a little out of place, but she didn't care. She was dressed to please the man she loved, and nothing else mattered.

The masquerade parade in the lounge after dinner was hilarious. Some people brought very elaborate costumes. There was a Marie Antoinette, a Napoleon and Josephine couple, a Joan of Arc, and a few southern belles. One was an upside-down man with his coat on his legs and his pants on his arms. Most were made with what they could find: a walking disaster covered in bandages splashed with red food coloring; a prisoner with black electrical tape stripes wound around a white suit. One man, who got a rousing round of applause, wore his wife's girdle and bra and a sign saying he was a model for a Wonderbra commercial. Another, whose bare legs showed beneath a trench coat, "flashed" groups of people, revealing an animal print bathing suit and cat's eyes painted on his chest.

Susan and Adam joined in the parade and, to their surprise, won a prize in the couple's category for "best national costume." Adam thought it funny that his tongue-in-cheek version of a tourist was someone's idea of how Hawaiians actually dressed.

They accepted their prize of a bottle of Champagne and promptly uncorked it, sharing it with Grace and Charles who were sitting with them. Neither Susan nor Adam had yet mentioned to anyone about their engagement. It was still too new to share with anyone else. When Grace spotted the silver ring and asked about it, Susan said merely that Adam bought it for her in the flea market that day. Neither mentioned the significance of the finger she wore it on.

When the parade and presenting of prizes was over, the band started to play. Susan, flushed with champagne, pulled Adam up to dance on the slanted floor. Discovering they couldn't dance in beach flops, they discarded them and danced in their bare feet.

The ship gave a particularly long roll that sent most of the dancers slipping and sliding to one side of the dance floor. Susan giggled.

"At least it's easier to keep your balance in bare feet."

"Better get used to it. In Hawaii we'll dance in bare feet a lot. You'll have to learn the hula for instance, and that's always done in bare feet."

Susan went still. This was the moment she had been dreading, the moment they'd both danced around all day.

"Adam," she said quietly. "I can't go to Hawaii with you."

"What?" He thrust her away at arm's length, scowling down at her fiercely. "You did say you would marry me."

"Yes, I did," she said with a quaver. "And I...but I never...."

"And where did you think we would live?"

"I don't know," she said miserably. "I haven't really thought about it." Which was a lie, because she had thought of little else since that afternoon. "Adam," she said, swallowing hard to hold back the tears, "I can't leave Buffalo. I have a business to run. I have a lease and clients and staff who depend on me. I can't just leave."

Adam swore under his breath and, taking her arm firmly, led her off the dance floor. They sat for a while longer with Grace and Charles, but the magic was gone from the evening. As soon as she could, Susan made her excuses and left. Adam followed soon after, but instead of going to their cabin he headed for the casino.

CHAPTER 9

Susan managed to hold her tears in check until she reached her cabin. They started slipping down her cheeks as she jabbed the card in the lock and jerked open the door. Sobs ripped through her as she fell on to the bed. She cried as she hadn't cried in years. Thoughts swirled through her mind: *Must have been the shortest engagement on record; knew it was too good to last; we're worlds apart in more than just where we live; it's my fault - - I shouldn't have encouraged him; it's his fault - - he should have known I couldn't leave Buffalo.*

Finally, all cried out, she rolled onto her back and stared at the dappled moon reflections on the ceiling. For hours she lay there, thinking of Adam and their relationship, trying to analyze it objectively and find a solution to their problem.

There was no solution. Adam was the manager of a hotel in Honolulu. He couldn't move to Buffalo, even if she was foolish enough to ask him to. Susan owned a travel agency in Buffalo, with a lease, a clientele she'd worked hard to build up and staff who depended on her. Her only family, her sister, was also in Buffalo. There was no possible way she could just leave all those responsibilities and move to Honolulu. This was one case where love did not conquer all. There really was no solution.

Just before she drifted into sleep she realized it was almost morning, and Adam hadn't returned to the cabin.

Susan woke with a start when the alarm went off. She couldn't even remember setting it. The ship was still moving, but slowly, and the rolling motion had stopped, so she knew they were in a harbor and about to dock. For a moment she couldn't even remember what port they were in; Adam and their short-lived engagement had crowded everything else from her mind. She stumbled into the shower and turned the water on full-blast, noticing on the way that Adam's bed had not been slept in.

The hot water cleared the cobwebs from her brain. "Manzanillo!" she said aloud. Then, "Manzanillo," she groaned as she remembered what she and Adam had planned for the day in the romantic port city of Manzanillo; shopping in the morning with their group and then a couple of hours in the afternoon, just the two of them, on the beach made famous by Bo Derek in the movie "10." Most of the seniors in their group, unable to enjoy the water sports and horseback riding into the mountains that the younger cruise passengers participated in, threw themselves wholeheartedly into shopping. The bargains in Mexico certainly were worth hunting for.

Today they planned a shopping trip by bus to several craft shops in downtown Manzanillo, followed by a flea market on the outskirts of town. Then they planned to stop for a drink at the terrace restaurant in the fabulous Las Hadas Hotel before returning to the ship for lunch.

The water beat down on her, washing away tears as she realized she was still thinking of herself and Adam as "we." Surely Adam wouldn't be coming with the group. Now that he knew she couldn't just pack up and blindly follow him home he would quickly lose interest.

She dressed hastily in yellow shorts with a matching T-shirt and tied her hair back with a yellow scarf. Yellow wasn't her best color, it gave her blonde hair a drab look, but she didn't care. She grimaced at herself in the mirror and tried to cover with makeup the ravages of a sleepless and tear-filled night.

Adam was not at breakfast, but, when the group gathered on the dock waiting for their bus, he came down the gangway to join them. His hair was still damp from the shower, and his long lean body looked terrific in tennis shorts.

He walked over to where Susan was explaining something to Maudie and waited patiently for them to finish, then with a proprietary arm around her shoulders led her along the dock until they were alone. Even barely touching her, he could feel the stiffness as she held herself away from him. He sighed. This was going to be a tough one.

"Susan," he began, "I'm sorry. I apologize for letting my natural caveman instincts come to the fore last night." He gave her an embarrassed grin. "I haven't behaved like that since I was an adolescent. It's not my style to run away from a problem, but that's what I did last night. I knew we had some talking to do, I just didn't know how serious that talk was going to be."

Susan had been silently staring out to sea as his apology rambled on. She lifted her eyes to his, pain showing in them, and what she blurted out horrified her.

"Where did you sleep last night?" *Oh, no,* she thought. *Now who's acting like an adolescent?*

Adam's heart suddenly soared. If she was jealous, then at least she still cared.

"I bunked in with Charles, but I think I put a crimp in his love life." Suddenly he smiled, that devastating smile guaranteed to turn her knees to water. "Did you know we weren't the only ones on this cruise to...er...ah, how shall I say it, start a romance?"

"Really?" Susan brightened, glad for the change of subject. "I sort of suspected he and Grace had something going, but had no idea it had gone that far. I'm glad. They're two very nice people who come on trips like this because they're lonely. They deserve another go at happiness."

"And what about us, Susan, do we deserve another go?"

She opened her mouth to answer but was stopped when someone from the group hailed her. Turning, she saw that their bus had arrived.

Susan went through the mechanics of escorting her group around the stores. Afterwards she couldn't have said where they went or what they saw; she was conscious only of Adam. She tried to ignore him, but he was always there, sitting across the aisle from her in the bus, helping the elderly ladies in and out of the bus and up the stairs into the shops and generally making himself useful. He helped Maudie choose a gift for her son and patiently tried on several sombreros for Lily who was trying to decide on one for her grandson. Whatever he did, Susan was painfully aware of him. He never spoke to her or touched her, but Susan knew where he was each minute.

At dinner that evening the chair beside Susan remained empty. Through the first course she kept glancing at the door, wondering if he was going to come and how she would react if he did. Then Charles gently tapped her on the shoulder. She saw the kindly sympathy in his eyes as he nodded toward the back of the room. She turned and looked, and there was Adam seated at the captain's table. He was several tables away across a noisy room, but she could still hear his voice above the others as he laughed at a remark made by someone at the table.

The rest of the meal could have been cardboard for all she tasted of it. Her ears strained to catch the sound of his voice again, and she wondered if any of the women at the captain's table were single, and if so, would Adam go dancing with them later. *The green-eyed monster,* she thought ruefully. *Yes, I'm jealous, even if it is my own fault that he's there and I'm here.*

After dinner, Susan found herself walking the deck with Grace Cole. They discussed the day's shore excursion and their purchases in the craft shops, but Grace obviously had something else on her mind. Susan wondered if it concerned Charles. She thought she might feel awkward if the older woman wanted to discuss her love life.

They wandered out onto the deserted pool deck. Grace sat in a lounge chair and patted the one next to her. The moon had not yet risen, and the sky was a brilliant canopy of stars. Music from the bar drifted faintly out the open doors. Susan sighed, thinking it was a night made for lovers, and her lover had chosen to be elsewhere.

Grace leaned back in her chair and said softly, "Did I ever tell you about my husband?" Susan shook her head, knowing Grace couldn't see her in the dark, but also knowing it was just a rhetorical question she was using as an opening.

"His name was John," Grace went on. "He was an executive for a steel company. He was a marvelous man, so loving - - when he was around. But he was a workaholic. Oh

163

we had our dreams. We used to talk about when he would retire, the fun we would have together, the places we would travel. I wanted to do all those things before we got too old. For five years I tried to get him to retire, but he always had an excuse - - one more year would give us a little cushion; then, another year would give him a larger pension; then it was the promise of a bonus if he stayed another year. He was the vice-president of his company, and once he stayed another year because he thought he had a shot at the president's job. Finally, he agreed to retire, and we started looking at travel brochures and talking of a tour of Europe."

Grace was silent for a while, and Susan turned in her chair. "Then what happened?" she asked, certain she knew the answer.

"He died two months before he was to retire. Our dreams were shattered. I was shattered. I know it sounds irrational, but I was also angry at him, angry at him for depriving me of his companionship in my old age. For several years I drifted through life until I joined the Senior Citizens Club. And that's when I started traveling. You see, I'd never traveled alone. Most of my traveling with John was business trips or conventions, and he looked after everything. By the time I got my life back on track again, my self-confidence had slipped, and I was too old to venture out on my own. That's why I like traveling with the group so much. They, and escorts like you, my dear, give me such a secure feeling. I can enjoy myself without having to worry about missed planes or getting lost."

Susan smiled, feeling happier than she had all day. This was why she enjoyed her job so much. Moments like this made it all worthwhile.

"But I've rambled off the subject a bit," said Grace with a laugh as she reached over and put her hand on Susan's arm. "I'm just an old lady, and you're probably wondering why I'm telling you all this. I just wanted you to know that life is too short to live with regrets. Grab your happiness while you can. We never know what tomorrow holds. I wanted to see the world with John, now I'm alone and filling my life by shopping and spending his money." Susan leaned back in the lounger and stared at the stars, mulling over what Grace said and trying to relate it to her own circumstances.

"You mustn't blame yourself," she said finally. "It was his decision to continue working."

"Yes, but I probably could have influenced him. He loved me enough that if I had said 'enough is enough, retire or else,' he might have done it. But I didn't insist. I have to admit I was quite comfortable the way we were. I enjoyed the comforts of a big house and the perks of being Mrs. Corporate Executive. So I didn't push him. I thought if we waited, that someday we'd have it all. But we waited too long, and someday never came."

"I doubt if you could have done anything," said Susan, thoughtfully. "I know what it's like to run a business, to have so much depending on you - - your staff, your customers, the business itself. Even your own sense of self is tied up in it. When you put that much of yourself into a business, you can't get out of it because it won't run without you."

"But that's just the irony of it all," said Grace with what sounded perilously close to a sob in her voice. "The company managed quite well without him. Another man got the presidency, someone else slipped into John's job, and life went on. Even me. Some people would say I've got it all now, a wealthy widow, traveling the world, living off my husband's pension and insurance. But, I'll tell you something, Susan, I'd happily live on a small pension in a senior's apartment if I could have John on this trip with me now."

The two women sat there for a while longer, listening to the night sounds of the ship. Then Grace got slowly to her feet, muttering to herself about the night air stiffening her joints. She paused for a moment to squeeze Susan's shoulder.

"Regrets, Susan, regrets...everyone has regrets. The small ones we can live with, but the big regrets turn to grief, and our lives are never the same again."

Susan stayed on the deserted deck for a long time, until the chilly night air finally penetrated her thoughts. She knew that if she let Adam go now she would regret it all her life. She'd thought about it last night and again this afternoon at the beach. The answer was the same... she was no nearer to a solution.

When Susan opened the cabin door, she was surprised to find Adam lying on his bed. He was fully clothed, right down to his jacket and shoes as if he was poised for flight, but he was there. He sat up quickly and tried to smooth down his hair, but it was curly and rumpled as if he'd been running his hands through it. Her heart thumped painfully in her chest as she drank in the sight of him sitting there sleepy-eyed. How was she going to live the rest of her life without this man she loved so dearly?

Adam smiled wryly. "Come on in. I promise I won't bite."

Susan looked around, a bit embarrassed and surprised to find herself still in the doorway staring at him.

She shut the door and leaned against it. Finding Adam here was unexpected, and she was unsure of what he wanted. Adam ran his hand through his hair again and rubbed his cheek, obviously uncomfortable with what he had to say.

"Susan, I'm sorry about the way I acted last night. I came on like a male chauvinist of the worst kind. I'm really not like that. I was just so caught up in us and our being together that I didn't think." He got up from the bunk and stood in front of her, close enough so she could feel the heat from his body but still not touching. "Of course you can't drop everything and follow me home," he said. "My sensible self knew that, but it wasn't my sensible self talking last night. That was a desperate man who saw himself about to lose something very special before he'd even got a good grip on it." He leaned forward and dropped a light kiss on her lips, still without touching her anywhere else.

"We have a very big problem, my sweet. I love you, and you love me. Agreed?"

She nodded.

"I asked you to marry me, and you said yes. Agreed?"

She opened her mouth to say something, changed her mind and closed it again, then nodded.

"But you live in Buffalo, and I live in Honolulu."

She nodded.

"So what are we going to do?"

166

"I don't know." She reached up and touched him, idly running her fingers through the hair on his nape, needing some physical contact while she talked. "I knew I was being unfair to you when I said I would marry you without thinking of the consequences. I know you can't move to Buffalo any more than I can move to Honolulu. I know you expected me to go back to Honolulu with you, but, Adam, I have responsibilities I can't turn my back on. I own a business, with a long-term lease and employees depending on me. I have a regular clientele, some of them with bookings up to six months in advance. The fact that Buffalo is my home and the only family I have left is there, is also a factor, but not a serious one." She brought her hand down until it gripped his and looked deep into his eyes. "Adam, I would leave my home and family for you, but I can't leave my responsibilities. I'd never be able to live with myself if I did."

Adam sighed as he gathered her in his arms, tucking her head under his chin. He understood perfectly what she meant. He had responsibilities too. One of the things he loved about her was her devotion to her business and her staff. Liana, and her selfish devotion to self, briefly crossed his mind, and he wondered what he ever saw in her. He hadn't known Susan then. He had never known a woman like Susan. He couldn't give up this woman he loved. Life wouldn't be the same without her. He couldn't, however, see a solution, any more than she could.

He knew for certain there had to be a way to do it. His arms tightened around her convulsively. There was no way he was giving her up now.

Susan could almost follow the progress of his thinking as his arms tightened around her. She cuddled against him, feeling a sense of security that she hadn't felt since she was a child.

"I know you have to go back to Buffalo," said Adam softly. "And I have to go back to Honolulu. But once we're there, and things are back to normal, let's see what we can work out. When two people are as determined to be together as we are, we'll find a way."

167

Susan tried to blink back the tears that had been perilously close to the surface ever since she'd returned to the cabin and found him there. They couldn't be stemmed any longer and rolled down her cheeks as she thought of the many times she had been over it in the past few days. She knew that once they went their separate ways, back to Buffalo and Honolulu, they would never see each other again. She choked back a sob.

Adam wiped the tears away with his thumb. "Don't cry, my sweet. We'll find a way. I promise."

Her chin quivered as she answered, "I...I don't know. I've been thinking about it since last night and...and I can't...I don't...I just don't know. All I know is that I want..." she broke off with a sob.

"You want...?" prodded Adam.

"You!" she wailed as tears started to flow. Adam pulled her away from the door and into his arms, heedless of the tears wetting his jacket shoulder.

He kissed her damp forehead and trailed his lips to her tear-filled eyes. Massaging the back of her neck and murmuring comforting words, he waited for the sobbing to trail off into hiccups and finally stop. When she finally lifted her head, he claimed her lips in a soul-drugging kiss. Without releasing her lips he divested himself of his jacket and led her to the bunk. A roll of the ship caused him to lose his balance, and he sat down heavily pulling her into his lap. He buried his face in her hair that smelled of sea breezes, loving the feel of its silky softness as he ran his fingers through it.

"We'll find a way, Susan," he whispered. "Somehow, somewhere, we'll find a way. We were meant for each other from the day we first talked on the phone. We'll find a way to be together. I know it."

She smiled at him tremulously through her drying tears, wishing she could believe him, but knowing realistically it was impossible. Then she made a decision, knowing it would make the pain of leaving even worse, but also knowing she'd never regret a minute of it.

For the next two days, she thought, *I'll pretend we can make a go of it. If this is all I'll ever have of him, I'll enjoy those two days and store up memories to keep forever.*

Her decision made, she shifted her weight on his lap, moving away from him slightly. Adam's grip on her shoulders tightened then softened and turned to a caress as he realized she was only giving herself space to unbutton his shirt. With a sigh that was perilously close to a sob, he fell back on the bunk, pulling her with him.

The bunks on the cruise ship were small, but they shared one that night, sleeping entwined, neither willing to be separated from the other.

Susan woke to a feeling of contentment. She pushed away other feelings that tried to surface and simply enjoyed the feeling of the warm body curled around hers spoon fashion. One knee was hanging in midair, and one foot was uncovered, exposed to the pre-dawn air-conditioned chill, but she'd never felt so warm and comfortable and, yes, happy in her life. Adam's arm was thrown around her, the only thing, she had to admit, that was keeping her from falling out of bed. His hand cupped snugly and possessively around her breast.

She didn't want to move and lose that wonderful warm closeness, but she knew she wouldn't go back to sleep, so she thought back over last night. Their lovemaking had been a toe-curler, the first time fast and desperate, the second time slow and delicious. It was made all the more poignant by the knowledge that last night was a gift out of time. Their time together was so short, and neither knew when, or if, they would be together again.

Her heart thumped painfully as she realized that today was their last full day together; tomorrow they would arrive in Acapulco. Tonight would be their last night together, and just the thought of it gave her a hollow feeling in the pit of her stomach. She would have to make it extra-special to give them both something to remember. She couldn't bear the thought of Adam going back to Honolulu and forgetting all about her. She knew she would never forget one minute of this cruise, the most enchanting ten days of her life.

She went over in her mind what they were planning to do today. The ship was stopping at Zihuatanejo, the tiny fishing village three miles from the tourist resort of Ixtapa. Some of the passengers on board were going horseback riding up in the hills, while others were going shopping and sightseeing in the town of Ixtapa. Ixtapa had been badly damaged in an earthquake several years earlier, but had since been rebuilt and was a resort town of glitzy five-star hotels, fancy restaurants, and expensive shops.

Susan thought her group would prefer the real Mexico to the touristy Ixtapa, so she arranged for them to have a champagne brunch on the beach just outside the village of Zihuatanejo and then a stop in the village for shopping before returning to the ship.

Her mind came crashing back to the bed with a start when Adam's hand, which had been tucked under her breast, started to move. His rough fingers moved over her nipple, making it stand upright and sending a jolt to her very core. With a moan she managed to turn over, brushing against him as she did and discovering, to her delight, that he was already fully aroused. He must have been awake while she was daydreaming. He buried his face in her neck and started nipping her ear and jaw line. She grasped his buttocks and pulled him tightly to her, realizing with a rush of warmth that she was as ready for him as he was for her. He raised himself up and pulled her under, with one movement sheathing himself within her and lowering himself until they touched along their full length. Claiming her mouth, he assaulted her senses with his tongue, his hands, and his body. Spiraling out of control she dug her fingernails into his buttocks and bucked beneath him, then filled the room with a keening cry. Aroused beyond endurance, Adam followed seconds later.

Susan gasped as she got her breath back, numbed by the shattering reality and the speed of what had just happened.

"Adam, I...I can't believe it, what just happened. I've never before...so fast. I don't know what got into me."

Adam chuckled. "What got into you was me.".

Susan giggled and bit his shoulder. As her stomach muscles contracted when she laughed, she realized that he was still inside her and still hard. She smiled as she brought her hands up and started massaging the back of his neck. This was another morning they just might be late for breakfast.

Zihuatanejo was a deep-water harbor, but the small wharf was made for fishing vessels and could not berth a cruise ship. For the second time this trip they anchored in the middle of the harbor and were tendered to the dock in the ship's lifeboats.

There was a bus waiting for them on the dock, and they were taken on a quick tour of the picturesque fishing village before going to the beach. There was still evidence in some parts of the village of the earthquake that devastated Ixtapa; there were piles of rubble where houses once stood.

"Why is the rubble still there years later?" someone asked. "Weren't the houses rebuilt?"

The guide shrugged expressively. It was easier, he explained, to build a house from scratch than to repair a damaged one, and somehow, once the new house was built, with a roof over their heads, clearing up the rubble was no longer a priority.

When a few people expressed incredulity at this, he grinned and shrugged again. "That's *manana*," he said. "It's a way of life here."

The beach where they were to have brunch was the kind of tropical beach everyone dreams about. The wide curving crescent of white sand was completely deserted and seemed to go on forever. At intervals along the sand were small thatched-roofed shelters, none of them occupied. About a mile away was a small hill that blocked their view of the town, and a rocky ridge that jutted out into the water. The waves that lapped gently against the sand swirled and foamed treacherously around the rocks. The ship, dazzlingly white in the sunlight, rode at anchor just offshore. It was the kind of scene often pictured in travel books but hardly ever seen in person.

It was several minutes before anyone in the group except Adam did anything but stare open-mouthed at the vista.

By the time everyone staked out a place on the sand and spread their towels to sit on, one of the ship's lifeboats was nudging in to shore. Kitchen staff from the ship swiftly beached the boat and started unloading coolers of food and drink. A barbecue had already been set up under one of the thatched-roof shelters, and tantalizing smells wafted across the beach. Soon barefoot waiters passed out tall glasses of *mimosas*, that delicious concoction of champagne and orange juice.

Within minutes of arriving on the beach, Adam shucked his shorts and shirt. Susan hardly had time to admire his tanned body in the tight white bathing suit before he plunged into the ocean and started swimming strongly out into the bay. She tried to keep him in sight, but several people came up to ask her questions, and she kept losing him in the waves. She knew he was a strong swimmer, but, not being comfortable in the ocean herself, she kept an anxious eye on him.

At one point she had to leave the beach and show some of the group the restroom and change room facilities. When she returned she scanned the water, but Adam's dark head was nowhere to be seen. Her heart thumped painfully, and she was giving way to a rising panic when she spotted him talking to some men near a small boat several yards along the beach.

Letting her breath out with a rush, she sagged weakly onto her towel, still shaking from her momentary panic at discovering Adam missing.

"You've got it bad, Susan girl," she muttered to herself. "How are you going to manage when he's 4,000 miles away?"

She watched him loping back along the beach. His hair, still wet from the ocean, curled around the edges as it dried in the sun. His tanned athletic body, moving gracefully as he ran, brought back memories of last night and made her want to reach out and touch him.

She patted the towel next to her, but instead of sitting down he grabbed her hand and pulled her to her feet.

"Come on," he said, laughing, "we're going to have some fun." He started back along the beach, still holding her hand so she had to run to keep up.

"Where are we going? Don't I need my shoes?"

"No shoes, but you can leave your shirt on," he said, plucking at the oversize T-shirt she wore as a beach cover-up. "It'll protect that soft skin of yours from the straps."

"Straps! What straps? Hold on there a minute." Abruptly, she stopped, digging in her heels and forcing Adam to stop as well. "Just what am I going to be doing that will require me to be strapped in?"

"Why, my sweet, we're going parasailing."

"Oh no, we're not!"

"But it's all arranged. See there?" Adam stepped from in front of her, and Susan saw a small motor launch pulled up on the beach with three young men in ragged shorts and shirts. They were laughing and talking together as they laid a brightly colored parachute out on the sand and started straightening out the ropes attached to a leather harness.

Susan's eyes grew wide with horror. "I'm not going up in that thing. How do I know they know what they're doing?"

"They know what they're doing. I asked a few questions on safety procedures before I paid them." He smiled down at her. "I parasail quite often in Hawaii, I know how it's done, and I would know by their answers if they were amateurs at this." His eyes darkened. "You know I wouldn't put you in any danger. If I wasn't absolutely certain this was safe, I wouldn't even consider it."

Reluctantly, she loosened her grip on his hand as one of the men, grinning hugely at her, came over to them carrying the harness.

"I'll go first," said Adam quickly. "You stay here on the beach and watch how much fun I'm having. Then you can have your turn."

"Not bloody likely," muttered Susan, as she watched two of the men expertly fasten the harness on Adam.

The boat accelerated swiftly, straight out from the beach. Adam ran a few steps along the beach then rose abruptly into the air as the boat picked up speed and the parachute billowed out above him. Susan gasped and closed her eyes for a minute. When she opened them Adam was far out over the bay, swaying gently beneath the parachute and waving to her.

She watched as he disappeared from view around the rocky headland toward the town and then reappeared a few minutes later on the other side of the bay. He was just a tiny speck hanging below the colorful parachute.

Charles and Grace joined her, watching Adam's progress around the bay.

"That looks like fun," said Grace wistfully. "I wish I had the guts to try it."

"I've got the guts, but not the legs unfortunately," grunted Charles. "I was watching the parasailers in Puerto Vallarta, and I don't think these old knees could take the landing."

Susan was about to ask what was so difficult about the landing when Grace yelled excitedly, "Here he comes!" They all looked up just as Adam skimmed over their heads, landed lightly several yards away, and ran with the parachute as it deflated.

"Beautiful landing," said Charles admiringly. "If I thought I could do it like that, I'd do it, knees or no knees."

"Oh no, you're not," said Grace. "I want you back in Buffalo in one piece. We've got...plans...." She trailed off when she saw Susan looking at her questioningly.

Adam jogged along the beach to where they were standing. His eyes were alight, his face glowing, and his hair was gloriously windswept.

He's happy, Susan thought with a pang. The only other time she'd seen him like this was on the beach that afternoon in Mazatlan. He was, she knew, a man who craved physical activity, loved sports and courted danger at times. *He must be awfully bored following me and my seniors around*, she thought.

Adam grabbed her, lifted her off her feet, and swung her around. "Wow-ee! That was great, just great. Now it's your turn."

"Adam, I'm not sure...."

174

He tilted her chin up and looked into her eyes. "Come on, sweetie, I want you to try it. It's a feeling like no other, and I want you to experience it. It's perfectly safe. You know I'd never let you do it if it weren't."

Susan looked into those brown eyes and knew she couldn't let him down. If there was ever a chance that she might be able to share Adam Joffrey's life, she knew she would have to share his activities as well. She gritted her teeth, clenched her fists, and said, "Let's go."

Adam kept up a running commentary as he helped strap her into the harness.

"When the rope from the boat to the 'chute tightens and pulls it upright, just start running. The 'chute will pull you off your feet a bit, and then you'll be airborne."

The harness was surprisingly comfortable. Two leather straps went between her legs and around each thigh, making a makeshift "seat." These were attached to a lifejacket and to the parachute lines. Adam finished buckling the front of the jacket and adjusted the lines position. One of the lines on her left side, within reach of her left hand, was bright yellow. Adam pointed this out to her.

"Don't touch the yellow rope while you're being towed," he said. "That's your landing rope. It spills the air out of the 'chute when you land so it doesn't drag you." Seeing her look of alarm, he brushed her hair back from her face and kissed her on the lips. "Don't worry about the landing. I'll catch you and run the last few feet with you. Now listen carefully. When you're about 20 feet above the beach, I'll yell. When you hear me, grab that yellow rope in both hands and pull hard. That'll spill the air out and drop you neatly back on the beach. As soon as your feet touch, start running. I'll be right there with you. Now off you go, and don't you dare close your eyes. Enjoy every minute."

Laughing, he patted her behind and jumped out of the way of the billowing 'chute. Dimly, Susan heard the motor roar, felt the 'chute pull her and started running. Seconds later a hard jerk yanked her off her feet, and she was floating free above the surf and out over the bay.

175

"Yow!" she screamed, in fear or delight, she wasn't sure. She caught her breath as the beach fell away behind her. The boat swung in a wide arc toward the headland, and, as it headed out into the bay, centrifugal force carried her over the rocky shore, and she looked down directly onto the sharp rocks and boiling surf.

"Oh, please," she whispered, "don't drop me on that." A quick glance at the headland told her that her fears were unfounded. She was higher than the top of the hill. She looked down, astonished to see a tiny cottage in the trees that was completely invisible from below. She smiled to herself - - *someone's private hideaway.*

She was heading out over the water again and deeper into the bay, toward the town. The whole town was laid out below her, and she could see the route they'd taken earlier on the bus. No longer afraid, as they rounded the bottom of the bay and started back to the beach, she tore her glance from the tiny harbor and looked out over the water. She gasped in delight. There was their ship, the Pacific Venturer, riding at anchor in the center of the bay. Its white superstructure gleamed in the midday sun. As she looked down at the ship, Susan realized for the first time how high up she was and wondered, with a tiny ripple of fear, how she was going to get low enough to land on the beach.

The tiny boat below turned lazily in a small circle, and, as the parachute above whipped around in a much larger circle, Susan screamed again, this time with delight. This was the most fun she'd had in years; she was so glad Adam talked her into it.

All too soon, the boat cruised in close to shore and Susan noticed she was rapidly losing height. The beach was rushing up fast, much too fast, she thought. For a moment she was worried, but Adam was standing there, hands on his hips and a big smile on his face, so she must be landing OK. She heard Adam yell and wave his hands. Momentarily puzzled, she realized she had forgotten all about the yellow cord. Yanking on it with both hands, she heard the parachute flapping above her, and then she was on the ground, running for her life, with Adam holding her arm and laughing exuberantly as he ran with her.

Then she was in his arms, laughing and crying at the same time, the harness still between them, the 'chute billowing around them.

"Thank you, Adam. That was wonderful, marvelous, and stupendous. That was...oh, Lord, why am I crying? That was an experience I'll never forget."

One of the men helped Adam free her from the harness, grinning broadly at her excitement. Before they walked back to the others, Adam pulled some folded bills from his pocket and handed then to the man, who was very effusive in his thanks.

"I thought you'd already paid them for the ride? At least that's what you told me when I didn't want to go."

"I did," said Adam absently. "That was just a little bonus."

"That was a pretty big tip."

"Actually," he said sheepishly, "I promised them a bonus if they gave you a good ride and landed you back down on the beach and safely."

"Adam Joffrey! Do you mean there was a chance something could have happened?"

"A very slim chance. They seemed to know what they were doing, and I went first just to make certain. But accidents do happen. Nothing really worthwhile is ever risk-free."

Susan was prevented from dwelling on that by Grace and Charles who were waving excitedly and brandishing a small digital camera.

"We got it all." said Grace, smiling delightedly. "Was it as much fun as it looked?"

"Better," said Susan as she hugged Grace enthusiastically. "But after all that excitement, I'm starved. Let's go see about lunch."

Later, the bus dropped them off in the town's main shopping area for an hour. Susan tried on a floaty sea-blue gauze jumpsuit that Adam said matched her eyes. She bought it, not because she liked it so much but because Adam did.

She scolded herself bemusedly as she walked back to the dock. Tonight was her last night with Adam; she might not ever see him again. This jumpsuit wasn't something she would ever wear in Buffalo.

"Wear it tonight," whispered Adam in her ear, as they stepped down into the ship's tender at the dock. For a moment Susan wondered if he could read her mind, and, with his next words, she was sure he could. "I want to have the fun of taking it off you." Her legs suddenly went weak and Susan collapsed onto the seat. Adam gave a wicked laugh and squeezed in next to her, playfully bumping her with his hip to make more room for himself. Wedged tightly between Adam and another passenger, she felt his hair-roughened leg pressed against hers, touching from thigh to ankle. The heat from his skin seeped into her until she was aware of nothing else but his feel and his scent.

So lost was Susan in the feel and awareness of Adam next to her that she was surprised when the tender touched the ship, and everyone started to stand. She was horrified to realize that she hadn't made sure that all her charges were back on the boat when it left the dock. She shook her head in disgust. She shouldn't let her personal life overshadow her responsibilities.

Correctly interpreting the look on her face, Adam stepped to one side on the gangway and pulled her with him.

"I think they all got on, but we'll count them as they come off just to make sure."

Susan sighed with relief when the last one stepped off the tender and she knew they were all back on board. She was angry with herself for forgetting her job. Her group still had one more evening left on board, and it was up to her to see that they had the best time possible.

When the evening was over, however, she promised herself, Adam and she would have the rest of the night together. She didn't plan to get much sleep.

178

CHAPTER 10

They hurried along the companionway and down the stairs to their cabin deck, Adam holding Susan's hand firmly in his larger one. On his mind was one thing, gaining the privacy of their cabin. Once there, he intended to waste no time in shucking their clothes and getting both of them into the shower. He could almost taste her sweet-scented skin as he washed the day's accumulation of salt, sand, and sweat from every delectable inch of her. He groaned inwardly at the anticipation of her doing the same to him. His body tightened as he remembered their last shower together.

Pushing the cabin door open, his foot caught a white envelope that had been pushed under the door. Thinking it was for Susan, he picked it up and gave it to her, but, after glancing at the name printed on the front, she gave it back. He frowned as he opened it. His father was the only person who knew where he was, and he wouldn't contact him unless it was an emergency.

"It's a message to call my father as soon as possible on an urgent matter."

"Oh, no," said Susan in dismay. "I hope there's nothing wrong in your family." She put her hand on his arm and looked into his eyes with such a depth of caring in her own blue eyes that Adam felt weak in the knees.

"Me too," he said grimly, with a touch of regret for his plans of a few moments ago. "But I'd better go find a ship's satellite phone and make the call; I don't think my cell phone will work out here. The sooner I find out what's going on...." His words trailed off as he went out the door again.

Susan showered and washed her hair. As she worked the suds through her hair she remembered how Adam had washed it for her the second day on board ship. Had that really been only a week ago? It seemed a lifetime. In a dreamy, sensual haze, she finished rinsing the soap out of her hair and stepped out of the shower. She scrubbed herself dry, her skin pink and tingling and her nipples erect. Ruefully, she glanced down at herself; just thinking about Adam was enough to get her aroused. How was she going to manage when she was back in Buffalo and he was in Honolulu?

She was thankful they still had tonight and part of tomorrow together. Her group was scheduled to leave on a flight at 2 p.m., and Susan was planning to take them to see the Acapulco cliff-divers in the morning. Adam was going with them and taking a late-afternoon flight back to Los Angeles.

She hummed to herself as she put on the blue jumpsuit she had bought that afternoon, smiling as she remembered Adam's comments. Looking at herself in the mirror, she frowned. The outfit alone was fine for daytime wear, but for evening it needed a little dressing up. She reached for the silver belt that Adam bought for her in Mazatlan, blushing as she remembered what the woman who sold it to them said to Adam. "She wished us many bambinos," Adam had said, "and gave me a discount on the belt because she was sure it wouldn't fit for very long."

She sighed as she clasped the belt around her waist. The only way it wouldn't fit is if she ate too much at the midnight buffet. She and Adam weren't going to be together long enough to do anything else. Still, the thought of having Adam's child, of watching it grow and pushing out the silver belt, gave her a funny feeling inside. Adam would make a good father, she thought. He loved Jenny Sue, and he hadn't even met her.

Adam had been gone an hour, and Susan was dressed and ready for dinner when he finally returned. She looked at him with a question in her eyes as he came in the door.

"My family is all fine," he said, running his fingers through his hair wearily. "But there's trouble at the hotel. The head chef was in an accident earlier in the week. His leg was badly broken, so he's going to be off work for several weeks. The next in order of seniority is the pastry chef, so my assistant manager put him in charge of the kitchens. That's when the trouble started. Phillippe is a fantastic chef, but a little lacking in diplomacy. And that's a diplomatic way of putting it." He smiled thinly. "Most of the kitchen staff hates his guts, but it doesn't usually matter, because they don't work too closely with him. With Phillippe in charge, the kitchen is in an uproar, and the staff is threatening to strike or quit *en masse*. Bob, my assistant, tried to backtrack a bit by putting Phillippe in charge of menus and ordering and then looking after the staff himself. But Phillippe won't budge an inch; he's in charge of the kitchen, and he won't give up one scrap of his authority. So I have a revolt on my hands."

"What are you going to do? What can you do from here?"

"I've been on the phone for the past hour. After I called my father and got the news, I talked first to Bob and then to Phillippe. I think I bought a little time, but I have to be back in Honolulu by tomorrow night."

"But how can you...?"

"The ship docks at 6 a.m. in Acapulco, and I have a flight to Los Angeles booked for eight and a connecting flight to Honolulu." He gathered her in his arms, burying his face in her fragrant hair. "I'm sorry, my sweet. I'd hoped to spend tomorrow morning with you. But I can't take a chance on losing my kitchen staff, and I can't jeopardize the reputation of my dining room."

Susan sighed. One thing she understood was job responsibilities. Giving him a quick hug, she told him so.

"But we still have tonight," she said. "The shower's all yours. I'll meet you in the dining room."

Hattie Bromsgrove was not at dinner and, when Susan questioned Lily, her roommate, Lily said she was "not feeling well." Mindful of how quickly seniors can fall ill, Susan thought momentarily of sending the doctor to her cabin. Then, remembering that Hattie had been at the beach all day, she dismissed the idea as being overprotective. The older woman probably just had a little too much sun.

She was conscious of Adam beside her all through the meal. He seemed to look for excuses to touch her, patting her arm, squeezing her knee, holding hands under the table between courses. She wore the blue jumpsuit, and Adam kept making outrageous comments in her ear about how the suit fit her and outlining the various ways he was considering removing it.

"Adam, be quiet," she hissed. "Someone will hear."

"They're not interested is us, my dear," he whispered back. "They're too interested in their own conversation." Indeed, when she tuned into the general table conversation, they were all recounting the sights they had seen, the food they had eaten, and the bargains they had made in the past nine days. Everyone was talking at once, and no one was interested in the talk and meaningful glances between Adam and Susan. As they left the dining room after dinner, Adam steered her toward the door and out on deck.

"It's our last night together for a while," he murmured. "Let's make the most of it."

Susan's breath caught in her throat. She was afraid it was the last night they would ever be together, so she had even more reason to savor it.

They reached the bow of the ship and, turning to lean back on the railing, looked at the ghostly superstructure of the ship, shining with a silvery-white glow in the moonlight. Susan shivered, and Adam pulled her back against him, wrapping his arms around her to protect her.

Protect her from what?

The cold, her responsibilities, the future, himself?

He didn't know.

Susan sighed as she leaned back against Adam, snuggling into his arms.

"I can't believe this is our last night out. It's been such an eventful cruise, and with so few problems...."

"Problems which you've handled admirably, I may add. But I guess you become good at troubleshooting on these escorted tours."

"Actually, considering the size of this group and their ages, this trip has been very good. Sometimes I get inundated with small problems; just annoying things like two people who don't get along and refuse to sit at the same table, or maybe the air-conditioning doesn't work and they want to move to another cabin, or misplaced eyeglasses. But the members of this group all know each other from the Senior Citizen's Center back in Buffalo, and they seem to get along quite well, and

182

they're quite independent types who don't need a lot of coddling." She hugged the arms that were wound around her waist. "And my worst problem on this trip was taken care of by you, when Tom Mayberry had that cardiac arrest."

She smiled up at him and half turned in his arms. "You saved his life, you know."

Adam opened his mouth to say something, but Susan turned the rest of the way around and flattened herself against him so all that came out was a groan as his body tightened.

She slipped her arms around his neck and whispered against his open mouth, "You're a very special man, Adam Joffrey." He dipped his head and claimed her lips, warming her to her toes and dispelling the cool ocean air as it slipped across the open deck.

"I think it's time we stopped solving the problems of the world and went back to our cabin and solved a little problem of our own."

She laughed and wriggled suggestively against his arousal, which was fast becoming evident between them. "Not so little, if I remember correctly."

"Oh, you remember, all right. If not, I'd be very happy to refresh your memory."

Tucking her hand in his she said, "Let's take one more walk around the deck. I want to store up some memories. This night has to last me for a while," she added wistfully.

They walked toward the stern of the ship, the wind blowing her fine hair across her face and making her shiver in the thin blue cotton. They reached the aft deck and stepped into a corner of the pool bar, out of the wind. Adam leaned against the wall and pulled her back against him, opening his jacket and wrapping it around both of them. The moon hung large and bright, just beyond the stern of the ship. Moonbeams danced crazily in the churning wash of the ship's wake, leading to a more serene track that stretched to the horizon.

"A lovers' moon," whispered Adam. "Perfect for our last night onboard ship."

And perfect for our last night together, thought Susan with a tremor. She leaned back, letting his warmth seep through her.

They weren't the only couple enjoying the romantic ambience of a full moon onboard ship. Another couple, from the glint of moonlight on their silver hair obviously much older, leaned on the railing, arms entwined, staring out at the moonlit ocean. Another, much younger couple, were closely entwined on a single lounge chair, oblivious to the moon and to anyone else on the deck.

Adam tightened his arms around her, and his lips found the soft skin and throbbing pulse on her temple. Susan sighed and turned her head, lips seeking his. Adam groaned and was about to suggest returning to their cabin when he heard a voice calling Susan's name.

Reluctantly they pulled out of their embrace. Lily was threading her way between the lounge chairs, arms pumping, limping badly but moving faster than Susan had ever seen her move.

"I'm so glad I found you. I've been looking all over," puffed Lily, trying to get her breath back.

"What happened? Is something wrong?" Susan straightened up in alarm, remembering with a guilty twinge that she hadn't given much thought to her charges that evening.

"It's Hattie. She's awful sick." Lily was obviously upset. "When I went back to the cabin after dinner, she was much worse than when I left her."

Susan looked stricken, remembering how she thought of sending a doctor to see her, and then decided not to.

Leaving a puffing Lily lumbering along their wake, Susan and Adam ran along the deck and through the doorway that gave the quickest access to the stairwell leading to their cabins. They found Hattie curled into a ball of misery on her bunk, her knees bent and her hands pressing against her stomach. Susan felt her forehead which was hot and dry with fever, then glanced at Adam who nodded. He picked up the phone and quickly dialed the doctor's number.

The ship's doctor arrived within minutes, asked Hattie a couple of quick questions, and sent for a stretcher. Susan went with the stretcher bearing Hattie to the ship's hospital and, at the older woman's request, stayed with her while the doctor did a more thorough examination and ran a couple of blood tests. Within a few minutes it was obvious where the questions were leading, and the diagnosis was soon confirmed.

"Appendicitis," said the doctor, drawing Susan into his office after giving his nurse a few instructions, "and a bad one. We'll be lucky to get this one before it ruptures."

"How soon can we get her to a hospital?"

"No time. We'll have to operate here, and the sooner the better. Time is of the essence now."

Susan looked at him with alarm. "But...but, do you have the equipment, the people...."

The doctor nodded. "We have a fully equipped operating room here. I'm a board-certified surgeon, and one of my nurses is a nurse-anestheologist. The other is quite capable of assisting in surgery."

Susan stayed with Hattie while the operating room was being readied. The older woman, although sedated, was obviously frightened and clung to Susan's hand.

"Thank you for staying with me, Susan, especially as I know you don't like me." Then seeing the stricken look on Susan's face she went on. "I know I'm an irascible old lady and I've given you a hard time. I'm trying to change, but it's difficult."

When Susan protested that her job was to look after her charges and see that they had a good time, not to like or dislike them, Hattie shook her head and smiled. As the sedation took hold, Hattie relaxed and started rambling on about her earlier life. She told of a deprived childhood and later being in an abusive marriage. She told of her husband turning her children against her, so when she finally left him she was left with no one who cared about her. Then her voice softened as she told Susan about the wonderful man she married late in life, and about how he died so soon after that she never had time to get used to the joys of a happy marriage.

"And I've been angry ever since," she mumbled, on the edge of sleep. "And taking it out on everybody else," she said with a clarity that belied her sedated state.

Susan sat in the waiting room while Hattie was in surgery, going over in her mind the reasons for her animosity toward Hattie. She chided herself for forming an opinion without learning the facts.

How many other people have I treated unfairly simply because they rubbed me the wrong way the first time? She wondered.

Adam came in while she was sitting there and tried to get her to go back to their room.

"I can't. I promised Hattie I'd be here when she woke up."

"But it's our last night onboard ship," he said. "How long do you think you'll be?"

"I...I don't know. It depends," said Susan guiltily, knowing she couldn't leave until she had talked to Hattie and assured her that she didn't dislike her. One look at Adam's face, however, and she knew by the closed look that he had misinterpreted her reasons. She sighed and shook her head. She was too tired and too close to tears from her own disappointment at their spoiled evening to go into involved explanations. It would just have to wait.

"Well, I'm going to bed," he said abruptly. "I have an early flight in the morning."

With a heavy heart, Susan watched him leave, wishing she could explain, but it was too complex. Tears were close to the surface. She had really looked forward to her last night with Adam, knowing in her heart that she would never see him again.

After the surgery, Susan sat with Hattie until she was fully awake; reassuring her that the operation had been a success and that she was fine.

It was only a couple of hours till dawn when Susan wearily let herself into the cabin. Adam was sound asleep, the

186

covers bunched around his shoulders and his feet bare, as they had been the first morning she awakened onboard ship. She pulled the top blanket down and tucked it around his feet, wondering wryly if she was going to spend the rest of her life covering his cold feet. Then reality swept over her like a cold blanket, as she realized this would be the last time. Someone else would be keeping him warm in the future.

Knowing that their bags would have to be packed and put outside the door by eight a.m., she wearily set the alarm for six, only two hours away. Giving Adam a regretful look for their lost last night onboard ship, she fell onto the bunk and went instantly to sleep.

The sun was streaming through the cabin window when Susan awoke. She lay there for a moment, knowing something was wrong, then sat bolt upright as she realized what it was. The sun was shining! At six o'clock it was supposed to be barely light. She looked over at her bedside clock and saw that it was seven-thirty. Then her glance took in the rest of the room. There was no sign of Adam. His bags were gone, and the closet stood open and empty. Her luggage lay on Adam's bunk, completely packed and ready to be closed. A note was perched on top.

My goodbye present to you...an extra hour's sleep. Wear something warm; it's only 10 degrees in Buffalo. Love Adam

"Oh, Adam," she whispered as a sob pushed its way to the surface, "if only you did love me. But I'm afraid this really is my good bye present."

She would have liked to give in to the tears that hovered on the surface, but she knew she really didn't have time. There were arrangements to be made. Tom Mayberry was well enough to fly home with the group, but Hattie would have to stay in a hospital in Acapulco for a few days. Actually, Susan thought, she was amazed at the speed of Tom Mayberry's recovery. A week earlier when his heart stopped twice, she wouldn't have thought it was the same person as the smiling, cheerful man she spoke to last night. He would be staying onboard ship until just before flight time and would be taken to the airport in an ambulance, but he would be flying home with the rest of his friends.

As there were several hours between disembarkation and their flight home, Susan arranged for the group to go on a guided tour of the city of Acapulco and to see the famed cliff divers. She got through the day on automatic. She supposed she was polite, friendly, and helpful to the group; at least no one complained. When the busload of seniors arrived at the airport just before flight time, she couldn't remember anything that she'd seen.

It was a six-hour flight back to Buffalo, including a short stop to change planes in Dallas/Ft. Worth. It was very late when Susan arrived back at her house on Grand Island. The house was cold, and it had never looked so empty. Something was missing.

As she drifted into sleep, curled up in a ball in the cold bed, she knew. There was nothing missing in the house, only in her heart. Adam had become so much a part of her in the past ten days, a very special part of her, that his leaving left a gaping hole in her soul that she knew would never be filled.

Driving to work the next morning was almost a repeat of the day over two years earlier when she spoke to Adam for the first time on the phone.

"March is coming in like a lion," she muttered to herself as her car was buffeted by a strong gust of wind on the bridge. "I hope that means it will go out like a lamb, and we'll have an early spring." The ice-choked river below looked gray and uninviting, and Susan was envious of Adam, back in Honolulu, gazing at warm blue water and gently rolling surf on a sun-washed beach. She shook her head. Adam was over and done with. *Finis*! The sooner she stopped thinking about him the better. Somehow, she knew that wasn't going to be easy.

Terri greeted her with a whoop and a hug. "You look fabulous! What a tan! How was the cruise? Any problems?" She was about to add "How was the mysterious Adam?" when a glance at her friend's face and the pain deep in her eyes, forestalled the flippant question.

Instead, she listened as Susan described the places she had been and the problems encountered; about Tom Mayberry and Hattie Bromsgrove. Adam was dismissed in one sentence as Susan simply said that he had been a great help to her, especially on the shore excursions.

When Susan asked how she'd managed at the agency during her absence, Terri launched into the story she had been bursting to talk about ever since Susan walked in the door.

"Guess what!" she said. "Clifton Skye came by while you were away." Susan sighed. Terri had had a crush on the radio weatherman for three years.

"I suppose you were glad I was away so you could have him all to yourself."

"Well," she said with a self-satisfied look, "actually Nancy was here when he came in, but he asked for me. He said he'd never forgotten my name or my big brown eyes."

Susan's eyebrows shot up. "After more than three years?" The radio station was only two blocks from her office, and she thought the man could have come in any time, if he wanted. She would not, however, say that to Terri. They say misery loves company, but just because she, herself, was miserable over a failed love affair, was no reason to sow doubts and make her friend miserable.

"And we have a date on Saturday night," said Terri, ducking her head and suddenly having to rummage through a drawer. "After he gets back from his trip to Albany." Susan smiled at Terri's discomfiture, knowing from her friend's behavior that the date was an important one. She changed the subject; asking a question about business. Terri, relieved to be off the subject of Clifton Skye, launched into a recounting of her week.

Susan had lunch with Jacey, who was not as diplomatic as Terri. Jacey prodded and probed until she extracted most of the story of the week's events. Not even to Jacey would Susan admit just how hard she had fallen for Adam. Since she wouldn't be seeing him again, she had to keep one small part of her pride intact.

That evening she wandered around the house aimlessly, straightening cushions, unpacking, starting a load of laundry, too restless to settle in one place. Brutus followed her around as if afraid she would disappear again.

She even stayed up to watch the Late Show, something she rarely did. When she finally got ready for bed, she glanced at the clock and found herself calculating what time it was in Honolulu. That's when she admitted to herself what she'd been waiting for all night, the phone to ring and Adam to be on the other end of the line.

She shook her head in disbelief. "You've got it bad, my friend," she muttered.

The next evening she went to a movie with Jacey, determined not to spend another night waiting for the phone to ring.

Susan had planned to spend Sunday with Trish and her family but made an excuse to come home early before she made a fool of herself by crying in front of the children. While the boys were exclaiming over the Mexican blankets and castanets she brought them, her eyes blurred with tears as she thought of the fun she and Adam had choosing them. When Jenny Sue excitedly grabbed at the tails of the colorful windsock that Adam picked out, she ran for the bathroom and bathed her eyes to tamp down the tears. Trish noticed her distress and asked some questions, but Susan was too upset to talk about it.

The next two weeks passed in a blur of misery. She lost weight, her hair lost its luster, and her eyes took on a haunted look. One night, when she was trying to decide between a can of soup and a can of tuna for dinner, she answered the door to find Trish standing there with a bag of take-out Chinese food. Surprised to find how hungry she was, Susan dug in while Trish reminisced about the last time they shared take-out Chinese; the night Jenny Sue was born. When they'd cleared away the plates and put the leftovers in the fridge, Trish stated the real reason for her visit. She wanted to know what really happened on the cruise ship, and she wasn't leaving until she found out.

Susan started by telling the bare facts, then, realizing she had told more than she intended to, poured out the whole story. By the time she finished, tears were streaming, and she was soaking handfuls of Kleenex as fast as Trish passed them to her. By that time Trish's eyes were wet too as she considered her sister's misery and the no-win situation she was in.

"If it was just us," said Trish hesitantly, "I'd say go to him. I'd miss you, of course. We all would. But," she smiled through her tears, "I'd love an excuse to visit Hawaii in the middle of a Buffalo winter."

"As much as I love you and the boys and Jenny Sue, if you were the only consideration, I would go. I could always come visit if I got too lonely. But," she sighed, "I have other obligations. I've spent four years building my business. I can't just chuck it, even if I could get out of my lease. There's Terri to consider, and Nancy and Odel; and I've just contracted to take on another student from the community college."

"I know you don't want to sell the agency, but have you ever considered taking in a partner, a working partner who could run the business in your absence? You could always come back a couple of times a year and check on things."

Susan was thoughtful for a few moments. "That's an idea," she said slowly, liking the idea more as she thought about it. A tiny ray of hope started to blossom then was dashed in the next instant. "But who could I trust to run *my* business? If I brought in a new manager Terri would probably quit, and she's the only other one I could trust. Maybe if I got a silent partner and made Terri manager...."

The two sat companionably watching a game show on TV, neither really watching it, both deep in thought. When Trish got up to leave, Susan followed her to the door and gave her sister a hug.

"Thanks for coming tonight. I'll think about what you said."

While driving to work the next morning, she made the decision to discuss the possibility of a new partner with Terri. Terri would, of course, have to work with the new partner, and it might make her feel better about it if she were in on the process from the beginning.

Terri, however, had a surprise of her own for Susan. She was jumpy and nervous during the early morning rush of ticket printing and faxing or e-mailing and evaded Susan's questions by grabbing the phone every time it rang. When things slowed down a bit, she took a deep breath to bolster her courage and asked Susan if she could speak to her in private. Anxious to find out what was bothering her friend, Susan got up and led the way to her small private office at the back.

Terri sat wringing her hands for a minute then blurted out, "Susan, we've been friends for a long time, and I'd never want to hurt you in any way."

"For heaven's sake Terri, from the way you're behaving I know something's wrong. But it can't be that bad. What is it? Does it have something to do with Clifton Skye?"

"Er...yes, it does. In a way." Terri looked at her friend imploringly. "I've never told you this, but I've always dreamed of owning my own travel agency. I've been saving for the past couple of years, but sometimes I think it's futile. I'll never have enough for start-up costs and to cover costs for the first year or so until it starts to make money. I know how long it took you to break even."

Susan's heart sank. She hadn't realized until now how much she was counting on Terri's cooperation in her new venture. Terri was a good travel agent, and she would rather have her on her side than a competitor.

"I don't know what to say, Terri. I just never realized...I guess I thought I'd have you with me forever." Then she looked at her friend penetratingly. "But you just said that you don't have enough saved, so why are you doing this? Is there something else you haven't told me?"

Terri nodded. "It's Clifton. He wrote a book *The Layman's Guide to Weather Patterns*, and made a lot of money on it. He's looking for an investment and has offered to back me. We'd set up an office in the suburbs," Terri rushed on, as reluctant to stop now as she had been to talk earlier. "I don't want to compete against you even if I could afford downtown rents. And Susan, I promise I won't take any of your customers, except for the radio station of course," she added as an afterthought.

Susan took all this in while a glimmer of an idea spiraled around in her mind.

"Is this a done deal?" she asked bluntly.

"No..., no it isn't," Terri answered. "We've talked about it for a couple of weeks, but I didn't want to do anything definite until I discussed it with you. You've been good to me, Susan," she said earnestly, "and I told Clifton that if my going out on my own upset you too much, I might have to rethink it. I know you're going through a bad time yourself right now."

"Just how committed are you to Clifton?" Susan persisted, thinking that if Terri even considered rethinking the deal on her behalf, she wasn't all that committed.

"To tell you the truth, I'm not a hundred percent certain that I want to be in a business partnership with him, but," she said longingly, "it's my one chance to own my own agency."

Susan felt as if a heavy weight had been lifted from her. "Forget Clifton," she said, her smile widening into a delighted grin. "I have the perfect partner for you."

"So Terri's my new partner," she told Trish on the phone that evening. "We're both so happy about it. She was a little iffy about Clifton but was willing to risk it to own her own business. And even if I'd brought in a new partner, I really wanted Terri to run the agency, because she's done it before when I've been away. She and I think alike, we have the same business philosophy, and I trust her."

Trish listened indulgently as Susan rattled on about lawyers and partnership agreements, happy that her sister had pulled herself out of her depression and was getting her life back on track.

"And I'm going to start looking for a new staff member to replace me, and then I'll be free." Her voice caught, "Free to go to Adam. Do you think he still wants me?" she asked, her voice dropping to a whisper. "I just realized that I haven't heard from him since I left the ship, and it's been almost a month. Trish," she wailed, "have I been a fool or what? Now that he's back with his family and his hotel and his rich Hawaiian friends, what does he want with a travel agent from Buffalo?"

Trish tried to comfort her but had to admit to herself that she had some misgivings. Finally she suggested, "Why don't you call him, just to say `hello' and sort of sound him out. If he sounds off-putting, you can always hang up."

Instead Susan reverted to their old means of communication and e-mailed him. For two days she checked her messages every hour but there was no message from Adam.

On the news that night there was a story about Hawaii, the volcano on the Big Island was acting up again. Susan looked at the stock shots of surf and beach and decided to give it one more try.

Half an hour later, after screwing up her courage, she dialed the number she had never forgotten.

"Honolulu Bay Hotel. May I help you?" asked a lilting voice. Through the long-distance hum, Susan imagined she heard the wind in the palm trees and the surf crashing on the beach. *No wonder the desk clerk sounds so upbeat,* she thought, *living with that just outside her door.*

"May I speak to Adam Joffery, please?"

"He isn't available right now. May I take a message?"

"Could you tell me when he will be available? It's important."

The voice on the other end of the line hesitated. "I'm sorry, I can't tell you that, but if you'll give me your name and number I'll see that he gets it."

Susan almost hung up, but thought that if she'd got this far, she might as well finish. If he didn't return her call, she would know it was the end, and she wouldn't embarrass herself by chasing after him.

"It's Susan Jeffrey from Harbor Square Travel in Buffalo, and my num....."

"Susan? THAT Susan? Wow!" Then, as if realizing how unprofessional she sounded, the voice sobered a bit, but was still conversational; not the formal telephone-answering voice from before.

"Adam's been in San Francisco for the past two weeks. His father is sick. I'm surprised he hasn't called you, but maybe he found things worse than he thought and hasn't had time. Nobody here has spoken to him all week. We just pass on his messages to the switchboard at the San Francisco Bay. Are you really Susan?" The lilting voice sounded excited again, and Susan could picture a young girl in a Hawaiian muumuu behind the hotel desk. "Adam hasn't talked about you, of course," she added hastily, "except one night after work. We were all in the bar, and we asked him about his trip and about you. He said you were beautiful and a good travel agent and that he had a great time on the cruise. But we knew you were someone special. He's had a smile on his face ever since he got back, even with all the trouble in the kitchen." The voice abruptly stopped as the girl on the other end answered a question for someone. She came back on the line with a laugh. "I hope I haven't talked too much. I've been told I tend to do that. I hope to meet you sometime, Susan. 'Bye."

The connection was abruptly cut off, and Susan sat staring at the phone with a bemused expression. Only one fact in all that really stood out; Adam thought she was beautiful. She went over to the hall mirror and looked at herself critically: big eyes in a thin face, thinner now than it was even a month ago; shoulder-length blonde hair, caught up in a ponytail; baggy sweats, her favorite evening-at-home wear, at least they covered up the weight she'd lost in the past month.

"If he could see me now," she said aloud to Brutus, "he'd turn tail and run." She brushed back from her face some strands of hair that had come loose from the ponytail. "I'm going to have to do some major repair work before I face Adam Joffrey again." She turned away from the mirror and frowned as she heard a car door slam outside. She wasn't expecting anyone that evening, and it couldn't be Trish because she'd just spoken to her on the phone less than half an hour earlier.

CHAPTER 11

When Adam returned to Honolulu, the situation in his kitchen was worse than ever. Guests were starting to complain, and Adam, for once, was indecisive. Short of firing Phillippe and the whole kitchen staff, and starting with a whole new crew, he didn't know what to do. He shuddered at the thought of that, knowing how long it took to build up a kitchen's reputation. Then he had an inspiration.

Ten minutes later he was on the phone to Tiny in Mazatlan. Less than 24 hours later Tiny arrived. He stopped in his room long enough to change into his whites, picked up the largest cleaver he could find in his suitcase (he couldn't cook with anyone else's knives but his own, he explained to Adam), clapped his tall chef's hat on his head, and headed for the kitchen.

No one in that kitchen ever forgot Tiny's entrance. He stormed into the kitchen, the cleaver held high above his head. "Like King Kamehameha must have looked when he invaded Oahu 200 years ago," said one awed apprentice cook to his wife later than night.

Thwack! The cleaver descended on the nearest chopping board with a ringing crack that silenced everyone in the room. Tiny stood for a full minute without making a sound, glaring around until he had made eye contact with everyone in the room. Then with an economy of words that made Adam smile as he stood watching from the doorway, Tiny told the kitchen crew what he thought of them and what he expected of them. Within an hour, order was restored, squabbles settled, Phillippe had returned, sulking, to his baking corner, and Tiny stationed himself by the kitchen door, critically checking every plate before it went through that door.

With the kitchen crisis settled and things returning to normal, Adam started a long e-mail to Susan. Then came the phone call from his mother, and the e-mail stayed in his outbox, forgotten and never sent.

As Adam buckled himself into a first-class seat on the 787, it seemed like more than just a week ago that he'd flown the same route in the opposite direction. When his mother called earlier that day telling him about the mild stroke his father suffered, it capped one of the busiest and stressful weeks of his life. His father was doing well, his mother assured him, and expected to recover, but he wouldn't be working for a while. Meanwhile the largest convention of the year was booked into the hotel starting in three days, and the assistant manager, who was already working around the clock, simply couldn't handle it. Since the Honolulu hotel was heading into its less busy "shoulder" season, could Adam, she wondered, come home for a couple of weeks and take over for his father?

At the end of the couple of weeks, when it became obvious that it would be a long time, if ever, before the elder Joffrey would be ready to go back to the physically demanding and stressful job of running the hotel, a meeting was called of the board of directors.

The result of that meeting gave Adam new hope that maybe he had found a solution to his and Susan's problem. That was when he remembered that he hadn't finished the e-mail to Susan and that he hadn't contacted her or heard from her since they left the ship in Los Angeles almost a month earlier. Alarmed, he dialed the number of Harbor Square Travel in Buffalo, only to be told that Susan was out. Later that evening he called her at home and got no answer. Suddenly afraid that he was about to lose something very precious, he called the airline and booked a flight to Buffalo for the next day.

At the Buffalo airport he dialed her number three times, getting a busy signal every time. Frustrated, he picked up his bag and went outside to the waiting line of cabs. If her phone was busy, he reasoned, at least she was home.

Adam was enchanted by the drive across Grand Island. A fresh snowfall had covered everything with a dusting of pure white. The trees and rooftops glistened with frost in the moonlight. After years of living in the tropics he had forgotten how beautiful a snowfall could be. Whispering Wood Lane, a short residential street, had not yet been plowed, and snow crunched beneath the tires. When the cab pulled up in front of

Susan's house, he noticed with relief that there were lights on and that her car was parked out front.

The snow gave a satisfying crunch under his feet as he walked up to the door. He noticed Susan's footprints on the walkway and steps, and the thought passed through his mind that this is how it would be if they were married and he was coming home after a hard day's work. The light in the window and the footprints made his heart feel warm with anticipation. Then a sudden fear hit him as he wondered what his welcome would be. He hesitated a moment, then resolutely punched the bell.

Susan opened the door, and then reeled backward in shock. That couldn't be Adam standing there! Her knees went weak, and she clutched the door.

"Think you could invite me in?" he asked wryly. "It's awfully cold out here for a California boy."

Stepping inside and shucking his coat, he glanced around at the homey comfortable living room and at Brutus who was eyeing him warily from the kitchen doorway. Then his eyes settled on Susan, who still hadn't said a word. God, she was beautiful. Standing there in her tattered sweats with her hair falling softly around her face where it had come loose from the ponytail, she looked about fifteen, but so desirable that he thanked heaven she wasn't.

Susan finally found her voice. "Adam," she croaked, "where did you come from? I haven't heard...I mean, I was just...."

"Thinking about me?" he finished hopefully. She nodded, and then smiled in delight.

"You're really here? I'm not dreaming it?"

"Not unless I'm dreaming too." He reached for her, and she launched herself into his arms, not sure whether she wanted to laugh or cry.

Later, they were curled up on the sofa before the fireplace with mugs of foamy hot chocolate liberally laced with Amaretto.

"Guaranteed to warm you to your toes," said Susan as she handed Adam his. "Now, what's this about your father

198

being sick? How come you've been in San Francisco? And did you get your kitchen problem solved?" The burning question she really wanted to ask was left unsaid for the moment.

Adam shifted his shoulders and settled more comfortably into the sofa. "I really don't know where to begin. So much has happened in the past few weeks. But first things first. Yes, I did get my kitchen straightened out...."

He told her about Tiny using his huge bulk, exaggerated by the tall chef's hat, as an intimidation factor in bringing order into the kitchen. When he got to the part about the cleaver, Susan laughed so hard she had to put down her cup for fear of spilling it. Her eyes clouded with sympathy as Adam told her about his father.

"When mother first called, she said it was a mild stroke, and I guess maybe it was. But he's not recovering as fast as they thought. He was left with a weakness in his leg and arm on one side, and he'll probably be months in therapy before he regains the full use. Apparently, he hasn't been well for a while and mother has been trying to talk him into retiring for the past year. Now, with the doctor urging him to take it easy, and mother on his case as well, he's agreed to take a less-active role in the company. He still retains the chairmanship, but I'm the new president of the company, and," he looked at her with trepidation, "the new manager of the San Francisco Bay Hotel."

Susan gasped. "You've given up the Honolulu hotel? I thought you loved it there."

"Yes," he said with a wistful note, "I did enjoy Hawaii. It was a great place for a young single fellow to sow his wild oats, but I think I've outgrown it. Chris is coming back from Hong Kong to take over in Hawaii. His wife, Ann, is pregnant, and they're anxious to get back on good old American soil before the baby comes. How about that?" he said with a smile. "I'm going to be an uncle again."

He sighed and rubbed the back of his neck as if trying to relieve the tension. She wanted to get up and rub it for him, but she sensed what was coming next was important, so she forced herself to sit still.

"So now that we've solved everyone else's problem we're back to us. I know you can't just give up your business, and I also know that you can't run the kind of agency you have now if you were in Hawaii. Hawaii is a destination not a departure point. But," he hesitated for a moment, then reached out and touched her hand where it lay on the sofa back, idly playing with her fingers, "now that I'm back on the mainland, in San Francisco, how would you feel about taking in a partner to run things here in Buffalo and establishing a branch office of Harbor Square Travel in San Francisco? The hotel has a large shopping concourse on the lower floor, and right now there's an empty store right down at the end with its own street-level entrance and view of the bay." He smiled at her. "You could call it Harbor View Travel."

The smile that started at the mention of a partner blossomed until she was beaming with delight. She was tempted to tell him about Terri and her new partnership deal, but that would take too long. Right now, with the fire dying down and the room getting chilly, there were other priorities.

"Come," she said, getting to her feet and holding out her hand to pull him up. "Let's go to bed. There'll be time enough in the morning to talk business."

EPILOGUE

Six months later

On a hot, sticky day in late September, Susan stood on the balcony of the penthouse suite atop the Honolulu Bay Hotel. A mid-afternoon shower had just swept through, sending the casual beach walkers scurrying for shelter. The *kama'ainas*, or regulars, stayed where they were. They knew it wouldn't last long, and when you've been swimming in the ocean all day, a little rain isn't going to make you any wetter.

As the rain clouds swept out to sea and the sun broke through again, a rainbow danced across the headland and arced over Diamond Head. Susan stood there entranced, unable to tear her eyes away, though she knew it was time she went inside to get dressed. Tonight they were doing something "touristy;" they were going on a sunset dinner cruise on a windjammer sailing ship. She had been watching the ships sailing up and down the bay, silhouetted against the sunset, each night since they'd arrived a week earlier. Tonight they were going to sail in one themselves.

She watched the waves crashing on Waikiki Beach as it curved around and met the headland beneath the imposing rock that was the extinct volcano, Diamond Head. The balcony where she was standing had, undoubtedly, the best view on Waikiki.

Three years earlier when Adam had first laughingly invited her to Honolulu, he'd promised her "the best room in the house." When they arrived there a week earlier on the first leg of their honeymoon trip, it was to this suite overlooking the beach that he brought her. The manager's suite was no place for a honeymoon, he said, even though Chris and Ann, who now lived there, were in San Francisco for a visit, and said they could use it.

"Besides," he laughed as he carried her over the threshold, "I always keep my promises."

Her thoughts wandered back over the wedding, just a week earlier, in the little church on Grand Island. She smiled as the memories came crowding back.

Trish arrived early in the morning to help with last-minute details. She brought Jenny Sue with her, but that little one, used to being the center of attention when her Aunt Sue was around, was soon screaming her frustration at being ignored. Adam, arriving in the midst of this hubbub, scooped up Jenny Sue and took her for a walk along the lakeshore. Two hours later he brought back a tired and sleepy, but happy, little girl, and announced that they had come to an understanding. Later Susan found out that he had spent at least part of that time teaching her to say his name.

It came in that most solemn part of the marriage ceremony where the groom says, "I Adam, take thee Susan...." Jenny Sue, who until then had been sitting quietly on her father's lap, heard Adam's voice and began chanting in her high baby voice, "Aa-dam, Aa-dam, Aa-dam...."

The church full of wedding guests broke up, and laughter rang through the rafters. Adam laughed so hard tears came, and he had to wipe his eyes before he could continue. Trish was scandalized and, from her position at the front as Matron of Honor, pinioned her husband with a glare. Jenny Sue, confused by the uproar her outburst caused, subsided in her father's arms and sucked her thumb through the rest of the ceremony.

Susan laughed again when she thought of it. She was going to miss Jenny Sue.

A door slammed inside, and Adam came swiftly across the room and out onto the balcony. Her heart leaped as she looked at this wonderful man who was her husband of one week. She might miss her old home a bit, but she knew that from now on, home was wherever Adam was.

Helen Kaulbach is a travel writer and retired newspaper
reporter. She lives with her husband in British Columbia,
Canada. They love to cruise and travel often to Hawaii.

Made in the USA
Lexington, KY
28 August 2017